Secrets in the Dales

Diane Allen was born in Leeds, but raised at her family's farm deep in the Yorkshire Dales. After working as a glass engraver, raising a family and looking after an ill father, she found her true niche in life, joining a large-print publishing firm in 1990. She now concentrates on her writing full time, and is Honorary Vice-President of the Romantic Novelists' Association. Diane's novels include *Wartime in the Dales*, *The Yorkshire Farm Girl* and *A Child of the Dales*.

Diane and her husband Ronnie live in the Dales market town of Settle, and have two children and four beautiful grandchildren.

By Diane Allen

DIANE ALLEN

Secrets in the Dales

PAN BOOKS

First published 2025 by Macmillan

This paperback edition first published 2025 by Pan Books
an imprint of Pan Macmillan
The Smithson, 6 Briset Street, London EC1M 5NR
EU representative: Macmillan Publishers Ireland Ltd, 1st Floor,
The Liffey Trust Centre, 117–126 Sheriff Street Upper,
Dublin 1 D01 YC43
Associated companies throughout the world

ISBN 978-1-0350-5026-0

Copyright © Diane Allen 2025

1 3 5 7 9 8 6 4 2

A CIP catalogue record for this book is available from the British Library.

Typeset by Palimpsest Book Production Ltd, Falkirk, Stirlingshire
Printed and bound by CPI Group (UK) Ltd, Croydon, CR0 4YY

MIX
Paper | Supporting
responsible forestry
FSC
www.fsc.org
FSC® C116313

Visit **www.panmacmillan.com** to read more about
all our books and to buy them.

For Robert J. Pitcher
A brilliant musician, and a dear friend

Chapter 1

31 May 1940

Edward Riley buried himself deeper in the shelter of the sand dunes, the sound of aircraft flying low with the rat-tat of their guns making him duck his head and hold onto his British Army edition helmet. The whole of the British Expeditionary Forces were caught like rats in a barrel. He turned onto his back, reloaded his trusty rifle and aimed at the oncoming soldiers who were after his hide.

In front of him were the burning ruins of Dunkirk, bombed and in flames, riddled with Germans. Either side of him were dead and dying men, their moans heard over the attack of enemy machine-gun fire. Behind him was the sea, his only escape – but on the beaches, tanks and armoured vehicles lay ablaze, with hundreds of soldiers lying forsaken as the tide lapped against their motionless bodies. The only way out was to make a run for it down to one of the many jetties, which looked alive with a crawl of green-uniformed soldier-like caterpillars desperate to get into one of the small boats for home. The Germans were playing games with them as Messerschmitts flew low and precise over the undefended troops. They were trapped, and they'd be lucky if any of them survived the onslaught.

'Shit!' Edward swore as he aimed his gun and fired at an oncoming German who had found him hiding in the dunes. He pulled the trigger back, but it was locked and wouldn't move as the tall, blond man stood above him, eyes filled with hatred.

The German hesitated for just a moment before lifting his gun with the bayonet attached and thrusting it down, hard, into Edward. Then he moved on to seek more prey, certain that his enemy would not survive, even though his eyes were still open and he was still breathing.

Edward was numb with pain. Blood soaked his uniform and he could feel that his battle with life was nearly over. Slowly he reached into his inside pocket and pulled out a picture of the girl he loved, Sally Fothergill. She was fading in front of his eyes as he kissed the picture and whispered, 'I'm sorry, Sal. I'll be coming home in a box, if I'm lucky enough to be found at all. But I love you. I always will.'

He closed his eyes and thought about the times they'd walked together on summer days next to the river Dee, down Dentdale. How they had kissed while lying together in the sweet green grass. He thought of his mother and father back home. His mother would be cooking at the stove in the stone-flagged kitchen, as she always was, and his father would be striding out across the rough pastureland and home fields to check on the new spring lambs. Edward could smell the clear Dales air and hear the birds singing in the orchard's apple trees. He closed his eyes and felt his lifeblood seeping away as he slipped into sleep. He was going home, home to his Sally, back to the dale that he loved.

'Father, Father, come here – look, look, it's our Edward! He's home, I swear he's home! I've just seen him standing down there by the field gate in his uniform and he's looking up here. I swear he is, Burt.'

It was a quiet Sunday morning in the dale, and Maggie Riley had just stood up after putting a pie in the side oven. As she took off her pinny and gazed down the farm track, she thought for a moment that she must be going mad. 'He was there . . . I was sure he was there,' she murmured. Burt, her husband, came to her side, and together they peered out of the doorway of Rayside farmhouse.

'There's no one there, Mother, you're imagining things. I can't hear or see anything, only the sheep bleating.' Burt put his arm round his wife's waist. 'He'd have written to tell us if he were coming home. You're only seeing what you want to see, my owd lass.'

'He was there, I tell you. Something bad has happened and he's come home. I saw him with my own eyes . . .' Maggie felt tears coming and dropped into her chair beside the fire, sobbing into her pinny.

'Now, Mother, don't take on. It would be a shadow, that's all. There's low cloud today and you've seen what you wanted to see. Our Edward is in France and he'll be just grand. He's kept his head down, and if I know

3

him, the bloody Jerries will be taking a pasting. He knows how to handle himself. He'll be right as rain.'

Burt got back to his chair and his newspaper, shaking his head in dismay. For just a moment he had hoped Maggie might be right, and disappointment was written all over his face as he watched her dry her tears.

'I did see him, Burt. He was there, as large as life,' Maggie said. She could feel herself trembling. 'He's in danger, or worse still. You know I have the gift – I sense things, always have.'

'And you know what I think of that. Superstitious rubbish. How long's dinner? My stomach thinks my throat's been cut,' Burt said. He didn't want to show his concern, although in the back of his mind he knew his wife's sightings and feelings were often right. 'He'll be all right, lass. He'll be all right.'

Later, they heard a knock at the door, Maggie knew what was waiting for them. She opened it in her apron, saw the post lad with a telegram in his hand and tried to smile at him. Young Norman Thwaite was only doing his job, but lately he had delivered far too much bad news to the households of the dale.

'Thank you, lad. Here's a threepence for your bother. It's not the best of jobs you have, and you'll not be made welcome at many a door with this news,' Maggie said as she took the envelope from his hand.

'That's kind, but you haven't read it, and really I shouldn't take any money,' Norman replied as they exchanged money and telegram.

4

'I don't need to read it, lad. I know what it says. Now, God bless you, and don't you get involved in this war. Keep safe and work for your father on that farm of his, whether you want to or not.' Looking at the young lad of thirteen reminded Maggie of her Edward at that age, innocent and full of life.

She turned back into the low-ceilinged farmhouse and passed the envelope across for Burt to open. 'Here. I told you,' she said, lifting her apron to her eyes as she began to sob again.

Burt pulled strongly on his pipe as he opened the telegram, concentrating on the words that no parent ever wants to read.

'It says here that he's missing in action. It doesn't mention he's dead, Mother. He might still be alive. You saw in the headlines of the paper that the evacuation of Dunkirk was chaotic. We don't even know he was there. He could be anywhere over there, and hopefully safe, no matter what this telegram says!' Burt put his arm round his wife as she wept.

'No, Burt, he's left us. I know he has. The newspapers and radio aren't telling us how bad it really is. They're making a lot of how they got the soldiers out of Dunkirk, but they aren't saying how many casualties there are. We've lost our lad and there's nothing we can do about it.'

'You don't know that, Mother,' Burt said. He looked out of the farmhouse window.

'The lass he was courting will need to be told,' Maggie said after a moment. 'It's no good her loving a ghost like I will. She's young. She'll find another if she has sense.'

She looked hard at Burt. He could take on the task of breaking the lass's heart.

'I'll go and see 'em at Daleside in the morning. I suppose they'll have to know he's missing; I won't have it he's dead, though, Maggie. I'll show them this letter and then it's up to the lass what she does.'

Burt sat back down in his chair, knowing full well that he was grasping at straws. He'd heard the broadcasts and seen the papers. It had been chaos on the beaches of Dunkirk. Their lad could be lying dead on the beach, or floating in the sea. Or could it be that he was injured and hadn't been recognized? Or was Burt only fooling himself?

The Fothergill family sat around their kitchen table. Bob and Sally had just returned from checking on their lambing sheep, and Ivy had just put two cups of tea down in front of them when there was a knock on the kitchen door.

'Anybody home?' Burt Riley called. He'd hoped they wouldn't be, but the door was slightly ajar, and he peered in to see Bob Fothergill with his feet under the table. A glance at the kitchen showed that this was a true Dales home: the kitchen table and chairs stood in the centre of a flagged floor, and there was a dresser adorned with china and baking implements. It was a little spartan, but spotless.

'Aye, come on in, Burt,' Bob greeted him as the tall, ageing man stepped into the kitchen. 'You'll have a brew with us and a piece of bannock?' He pushed a plate

6

loaded with rounds of shortcrust pastry filled with currants across to Burt and nodded at Ivy to make their visitor a drink.

'Nay, I'll not stop. It's not good news I bring, and I'll have to get back to my Maggie.' Burt looked at Sally, who sat quietly with her head bowed. The families didn't know each other well and he'd only met her a time or two, but he could see why his lad had thought a lot of her. 'Now, I know, lass, that you were courting my lad.'

The words cut into Sally's heart. *Were – what did he mean by that?* she thought, looking up to meet Burt's eyes. Edward had always talked about his father with respect and love. Sally felt her mother come and stand behind her, placing both hands on her shoulders.

'We had a bit of bad news yesterday. There was a telegram to say that our lad Edward is missing in action. He must have been somewhere in France, and now they don't know where he's at.' Burt lowered his head for a moment, then went on, 'At least they don't say dead, lass. There's hope he's just lost.' Then he looked at Ivy and Bob. 'My wife is broken-hearted. She swore she saw him coming up home just before the telegram arrived, but it wasn't him. I don't know what to make of it all.' He turned his gaze back to Sally and saw that tears were rolling down her cheeks. 'I'm sorry, lass. I know he thought – thinks a lot of you. There's so much confusion, from what I can gather. He could be fine, so don't despair.'

'I'm sorry. I can't help it – I thought a great deal of him, too, and I know that's the news you get when the soldiers are usually dead. Truth is, I love him, and I don't know how to feel.' Sally looked up at her mother before rising from the table, pushing her chair back and heading for the open kitchen door. 'I'm sorry. I need to be on my own.'

'Nay, stay here, Sally – stay, and we'll be here for you,' Bob said, trying to take her by the arm.

'Let her be, Father. She'll need to be on her own. She always needs time to herself to sort her feelings and her head out,' Ivy said as she watched their tearful daughter turn and flee. Ivy knew that Sally was fearing the worst. She turned back to Burt. 'Aye, I'm sorry, Burt, for you and Maggie. Is that all the news that they gave you? Our lass loved your lad. I could have seen them getting wed if he'd returned.'

'Yes, that's all. We don't know if he's alive or dead, or where he's at. Neither will your lass. It would happen have been better if we'd heard he was killed, in some ways. At least we could mourn and put him to rest. No doubt we'll get to know one way or another before long.' Burt sighed. 'It's the not knowing. I'll have to get back to my Maggie, and you'll need to see that your lass is all right. I know my lad wouldn't want her upset if he could help it.'

Bob stood up and, unusually for him, patted Burt's shoulder and then embraced him.

'He was a good lad, was Edward. We would have been proud to have him in the family. There's too many been lost in this war already.' Bob stood back. 'He might turn up like a bad penny yet, so don't give up hope.'

'Nay, I can't help but think the worst, just like your

8

lass does.' Burt straightened his shoulders. 'What I wouldn't do for him if he turned up on our doorstep. I should never have made him go and work at the coalyard – he should have stopped and farmed at home. He would never have been called up then. It's my fault that he's dead, or missing.'

'Don't be hard on yourself, Burt. It's this bloody Hitler's fault – aye, and our government for getting involved. You don't see them standing on the front line with guns in their hands, do you?'

They made their way outside to where Burt's old farm horse stood waiting for him. 'I'll let you know if I hear anything more,' he said as he mounted. 'You take care of yourselves. And tell that lass of yours she's welcome at Rayside any time she's up the top end of the dale. Edward would have wanted it that way.' He nudged the horse's sides to urge it towards home. He had broken the bad news to the Fothergill family; now they would have to support their daughter and hope for any bit of news of Edward that they could get.

Sally curled up at the back of the hayloft, weeping. Her heart ached. Where was her precious Edward? She didn't think she could face a future without him. They had made so many plans for his return from the war – a farm of their own, and hopefully a family.

She closed her eyes, seeing his face, and whispered his name. The scattered hay around her reminded her of the harvest that had been under way when he was last here, when they'd walked so happily together, hand in hand.

Now she felt there was no purpose in her life. *Please let Edward be found. Don't let him be dead. Please, God, don't let him be dead . . .* As she dissolved into tears again, she heard her mother's voice calling up to her from the barn.

'Sally, come on, my love,' Ivy shouted up to the hayloft. She knew this was one of the places Sally always went when she wanted to be alone. 'Don't take on so. He might be all right; he might come back to you yet without a scratch on that bonny face of his.'

'He won't, Mam. I know he won't. He's dead, lying somewhere on that beach, forgotten and all on his own.' Sally could hardly get the words out through her sobs.

'He might not be. You've got to have faith, Sally. He could just as well walk up the farm track tomorrow, God willing.' Ivy took hold of the loft ladder, wondering whether she could manage to climb up and comfort her daughter. She was afraid of heights.

'Just leave me, Mam. No amount of words will bring him back. I know I've lost him, no matter how I try to look on the bright side. I've not had a letter from him for weeks, so I know that he's gone.' Sally took a deep breath. 'I'll come back in soon. I need to have a cry and be on my own.'

'All right, Sal, but we're here for you. You know that we love you, don't you?' After a moment, Ivy let go of the ladder and turned away. Above her, in the hayloft, there was silence.

Chapter 2

26 May 1944

Bob Fothergill stood at the gate of his main hay meadow. It had been a wet, cold spring and the grass had only just started growing, but now, as he leaned on the wooden panels, he knew that the summer sun would soon be warming the earth and haytime would be with them before long. This year he would still be using his horse and cart. By next year he hoped to own a tractor – unless, of course, he decided to move house and home.

Bob's one desire, all through his adult life, had been to own his own farm, but no matter how much he saved it had always been out of his reach. He lifted his cap up from his head slightly and sighed. Perhaps he should take the War Ag up on their offer of free labour this summer, take one of the Italian prisoners of war to help with the harvest. They were based at Sedbergh, and early each morning an army wagon dropped them off at various farms up the dale. It was a way for them to help out and earn their keep while being imprisoned in the country. Bob certainly had enough work on, and as long as the Italian was decent enough, he would treat him right.

Brian Harper, the Fothergills' next-door neighbour, had had one working for him these last six months and talked highly of him. The Italians were only like their own lads, after all – drawn into a war they didn't want to fight. They had been used by their ruling dictator, just like Hitler. Benito Mussolini had led his people towards disaster and war with his empty promises of a better life, only to lose half of them on the battlefield. Bob had decided a long time ago that war was for fools who followed like sheep; however, he was not complaining, as he'd benefited financially despite the hard times and many heartbreaking moments.

'Did you not hear me, Father? I've been calling out the front door at you for a good five minutes.' Ivy came to her husband's side and put a hand on his arm. 'Dinner's out, going cold if you don't hurry up. Just a fried egg sandwich, but it's better than many are having to eat nowadays.'

'Nowt wrong with that. I'm glad the hens are laying well. They bring in a good income now. I was just thinking, we're not doing so badly, my lass.' Bob turned to look at his hard-working wife and decided he'd put his suggestion to her. 'I was wondering whether we should happen to take advantage of free help with one of those Italians this summer. Our Ben will be about, but he's more interested in helping down at the garage when he's

12

not at school, and it's hard work for Sally and yourself. They might as well earn their keep and make our lives a bit easier.'

'Oh, Father, I don't know. Can we trust them? Will he speak English? And what would I feed him? I'm not buying in anything special for him – he'd have to make do with what we eat.' Ivy tugged on his arm as she spoke, trying to get him to come in.

'He'd not be a guest. He'd be like a farm man, and he'd get fed whatever we give him, no need to make owt special. They're all low-risk prisoners at Sedbergh, Brian says, and all they want is to eventually go home. But they're good workers. And all talk good English because they've been here a while now. I'll have a think about it,' Bob said as they crossed the dry farmyard, the scent of chickweed filling the air as it was crushed beneath their boots. 'Is our Sally home yet?'

'No, she said she'd be late back from work at Middleton's shop. She's going to call in on Mrs Mounsey, give her condolences after seeing her Harry was lost in Belgium last week.' Ivy made for the kettle as they entered the low-beamed farmhouse, and Bob sat down at the table.

'Aye, another lad lost. At least it sounds as if we're winning now. Them Nazis are having a taste of their own medicine, the Russians are holding their own, and although a lot of lives have been lost both there and at Monte Cassino, I can see that there's some hope this war will be won at last. I bloody well hope so – I don't want our lad being enlisted. Thank heavens he's still too young,'

Bob said as he looked at the cold fried egg sandwich that was his dinner. They seemed to live on eggs and bacon nowadays. Better than nowt, he thought as he lifted it up to his mouth.

'Well, I'm just glad we don't live in London or any other big city,' Ivy said as she sat down opposite him. 'I don't know how they can sleep of a night, the poor devils – being bombed to within an inch of their lives, and their homes and loved ones destroyed. I know we've had our fair share, but nothing like them.' She looked at her husband. 'Sally never talks about Edward any more, have you noticed? I doubt he's going to come back, although they never did find his body.'

'Aye, I think we'll never know what's happened to him. Sally needs to move on and live her life, although I dislike saying it. She's too bonny to be an old maid.' Bob sat back in his chair and looked out at the sunshine falling across the dale.

'She still cries of a night for him. I hear her,' Ivy sighed. 'That young Mason lad keeps asking about her. I wish he'd pluck up courage and ask her out to a dance or something.'

'Aye, well – someone will turn up and hopefully replace Edward. You can only love a ghost for so long. Stop worrying about her, Mother, she's all right. I'd have been lost without her this lambing time. She's better than any fella, but don't tell her that. She knows every sheep we have just by looking at them. It's a skill, is that.'

'Not so long ago, you were wanting Ben to be the farmer. I'm glad you can see now that he's clever enough

14

with his hands to make a living that way. Bill Morphet says there's a job waiting for him at his garage in Sedbergh when he leaves school this summer. At least it's only two miles down the road, and he'll pay him well, I bet. More than he would earn being a farmer any day.' Ivy smiled. Her husband had mellowed of late; he was making good money, and the long-held hope of a farm of his own was nearly within his grasp. Another few years and hopefully, with a bit of luck, they would make their dream come true. They had scraped and saved every last penny, but now, when they visited Martin's Bank in Sedbergh, they could hold their heads up high as the clerk took their paying-in book and checked their balance.

'I'd still like him to work at home, but he's making money hand over fist, tinkering and mending things for folk. That pile of old pushbikes keeps growing, and he keeps doing them up and selling them to the soldiers in the army camps and the guards at the prisoner-of-war camp. Two or three of those sold and he's got brass in his pocket. I'll give him his due, he's a canny devil.'

'Takes after his father, then, doesn't he? You like your money a bit too much sometimes. I often wonder how you get away with some of the things you get up to,' Ivy laughed.

'That's because I keep them in authority looked after. A salmon lifted out of the beck and a joint of lamb keeps Sergeant Taylor more than happy, and long may it remain so. Best to keep 'em close.' Bob winked.

'You are an old rogue, Bob Fothergill. Lord knows why I married you,' Ivy said fondly. She glanced up as

Sally passed by the window. 'Aye up, Sally's back. I'll make her some dinner.'

'Well, that's the eggs delivered,' Sally said as she came in. 'Mrs Middleton will take another two dozen for the shop if you've got them next week. And if Ben has shot any rabbits, she'll take two or three of them – only for customers she trusts,' she added, taking her place at the table with a glance at her father.

'She'll be lucky with the rabbits. Ben must have shot every one for miles around, although they breed fast. He's been making a small fortune with taking them up to Dent station and hanging them up for the train drivers to pay for and sell in Leeds. Takes after his father, does that lad.' Bob grinned as Ivy gave him a dark look. She could remember a time when he'd despaired at his son's lack of interest in farming.

'How's Dora Mounsey? Did you call and see her?' Ivy said, placing a cup of tea in front of Sally along with some bread and cheese.

'Broken-hearted. He was only eighteen, Mam. I really can't understand why anyone would want to fight in this war. But I never said that to Mrs Mounsey, because I know he chose to join up.' Sally bit into her cheese and bread. The four-mile walk into Dent and back had sharpened her appetite, and she'd hoped her mother would bring some cake out from the pantry – or, even better, a piece of apple pasty. But she was to be disappointed, as Ivy sat down at the table without offering her anything else. Sugar was in short supply these days. So Sally ate every mouthful of her dinner and was grateful for it.

16

'Are you coming with me to check the sheep when you've finished your drink? That old ewe we've been waiting for has finally lambed this morning. She's only gone and had triplets. I might have to take one off her and mother it onto a mother with a single lamb.' Bob stood up, reaching for his walking stick.

'Last one to lamb, thank heavens. The next thing will be clipping and haytime,' Sally smiled. 'The grass is growing fast now it's warmed up. It was a pleasure to walk back from Dent – all the hedges are in full blossom and the cow parsley is really shooting up. You'd not know there was a war raging if you forgot about it for a moment.' She picked up her mug and quickly finished her tea. They'd been waiting a long time for that old ewe to lamb; she was long in the tooth. Neither of them had really expected her to survive the harsh Dales winter, let alone lamb again.

'Your father's just said the same. I had to go and get him from leaning over the meadow gate, his dinner was going cold. He's talking of taking on a prisoner of war to help this summer. What do you think?' Ivy asked as she cleared the table.

'No, Father, you can't do that!' Sally looked shocked. 'They're the ones that have killed our men. Why should we have them on our farm? Please don't even think of it, for my sake.' She felt her stomach churn at the thought of someone she classed as an enemy sitting opposite her at the kitchen table or working alongside her. 'You wouldn't. He could be the one who killed my Edward!'

'They're mostly all Italians that are held in Sedbergh, and most of them have been vetted by the authorities,'

Bob explained. 'They were just in the wrong place at the wrong time, and they're no danger to any of us. Brian Harper next door says he's never had workers like them. I thought we might as well take advantage, especially as I'm still working part-time for Jim Mattinson. He'd help you a lot, Sally. And he would've had nowt at all to do with Edward losing his life,' he added more sharply. Even if it was only an idea for now, he wouldn't be told what to do by the women of his house.

'Oh, I should have known it had something to do with Brian Harper. I saw you two talking at the bottom of the lane this morning.' Ivy looked between her husband and daughter, hands on her hips. 'I think I might be with Sally on this one. You don't know anything about them, Father. They could have done anything and we wouldn't know.'

'I don't care how much he'd help, Father. I wouldn't want anything to do with him. We'll manage without anybody. Ben leaves school this summer – he'll be about part of the time and he can help.' Sally pushed back her chair and went to the doorway, stopping there to wait for her father. The warmth of the May sunshine was welcome. It had been a long, dreary spring, and they were all glad that summer was on its way. But to think she might have to spend it working with the enemy . . . that would weigh heavily on her mind. Still, she knew that no matter how she felt about it, her father would have his way.

Bob strode out across the yard with his stick, heading towards the fields that joined to the fellside, which was kept from encroaching on the pastureland by age-old drystone walls. Sally walked beside him. They hadn't exchanged a word since leaving the house.

Sally liked being with her father, but when his head was set on something she disagreed with, she couldn't be bothered to talk. Both she and her mother knew that if Bob had decided on a plan, he would not be deterred from putting it into action. Bloody Brian Harper – he was always coming up with ideas and flaunting new contraptions to all the neighbours. He'd been the first up the dale with a tractor and now he was taking on prisoners of war. He always had to be first with everything and influence her father with his ideas.

'Tha's quiet, lass,' Bob said eventually. 'I only mentioned an Italian because it makes sense. We may as well use the foreign buggers as have them lazing about, being looked after for nothing. If we just got the one, he could help rake and scale the hay and do a bit of walling, as well as help with shearing. The jobs that you're not strong enough for, and the ones I keep saying I'll turn my hand to when I have the time. Working for Jim Mattinson three days a week doesn't give me much time for home, and you help in the shop nowadays. So he would come in handy.'

'You must do what you want, but I'll not make him welcome. They're all the same if they have gone to war. They are all responsible for Edward being missing, or perhaps dead.' Sally felt a stab of pain as she spoke the words.

'Aye, but they're all probably just like Edward was – not wanting to fight, but being made to by their leaders. Everybody's in the same boat, Sal. Anyway, I haven't made up my mind yet. I'd have to look into it. It was only a thought.' Bob stopped at the gate leading into the pasture where the newly lambed sheep were. 'See there? She's over there, the old devil. Look at her, proud as punch with her triplets.' He pointed his walking stick at a sheep with three lambs, their coats still yellow with afterbirth. 'They all look to be feeding all right, and their tails are wagging. Perhaps she'll manage them all. We'll keep an eye on her and see how she fares.'

'I hope she does manage. It would be a shame to have to take one from her.'

They watched the three lambs go underneath their mother for milk. As if knowing what Bob was thinking, the ewe raised her head to look at her audience and stamped her foot defiantly: a warning that her babies were not to be interfered with.

'There you go; she's made her feelings known to you,' Sally said, smiling at her father.

'It seems all my women are stubborn and are always telling me that I'm wrong. But we will see. Time always comes out on top, no matter what. Now, are you off back to help your mother? I'm going to put a top-stone back on the wall in the bottom meadow. I noticed one off when I was down there earlier, while your mother said I was wasting my time looking over the gate. Then I'm going to muck the pig hulls out. You can give me a hand with that if you want?' Bob turned to leave his daughter watching the sheep and lambs.

'I'll come and help you with the pig hulls, but first I'm going for a walk up the fellside. It looks so bonny, it's absolutely covered with bluebells and is such a beautiful hue. I'll pick Mam a bunch and just have five minutes to myself, Father, if that's all right?'

'Aye, you do that, my lass. It's always good to be up a fellside to make peace with yourself. Better than going to any church. Or so I tell your mother, when she's lecturing me to attend because she's decided we need a bit of religion.' Bob took a firmer hold of his walking stick and started to head towards the gap in the wall that needed attention. He'd leave his daughter to her own thoughts. Perhaps she would come around to his way of thinking about taking on a POW after all; it would benefit them all.

Sally gazed up into the blue sky. Far above, she could see the trail of fumes left by an aeroplane. Unlike further down the country, the Dales very rarely saw aircraft of any sort. There were no factories or industrial sites to bomb; the only times they'd been spotted had been during return bombing raids over on the west coast, or when a squadron from York or Leeds had been put into action. Otherwise it was relatively quiet and all in Dentdale were thankful for that, as was she.

She made her way up the side of the fell to sit on her favourite large stone, where she did most of her thinking. Earlier, she had sat and tried to comfort Mrs Mounsey, who had found it hard to put into words the pain Sally knew she was feeling. There had been fewer local men killed in this war, unlike the Great War, but their losses were still enough to envelop the dale with sadness.

She looked down and across to Brian Harper's farm.

21

His daughter Marjorie, Sally's best friend, had lived there until just before the war broke out, before she fell pregnant. These days Sally hardly heard from her, bar a letter now and then. Marjorie was living in Liverpool and for a while she had been working in a nightclub. Brian had washed his hands of her and her unfaithful mother when both had left him, and now he put all his time into farming and the land. Of course, it had to have been Brian who'd given her father the idea of taking on a POW. He was always having these ideas!

How could her father even think of it, when Edward was missing and other local lads had given their lives to fight the enemy? Had he no idea how Sally would feel about someone like that working on the farm? There wasn't a day went by that she didn't think of Edward. Her heart still hurt, and she still wondered whether he was alive and lost somewhere in Europe; or, like so many, dead and unburied.

Sally exhaled and closed her eyes, concentrating on the warmth of the sun. She leaned back on her hands and breathed in the fell's aroma of peat and wild thyme mixed with moss: the smell of home and contentment. Her head was filled with thoughts, of Edward, of her family, and the coming months when she would be busy in the shop and on the farm. Her mother kept encouraging her to join this group or that organization, to find a friend her own age, but Sally wasn't bothered. She was quite content with farm life.

She looked at the verdant green of the new bracken on the fellside and the patches of vivid blue where the bluebells were growing. That was what she had come for – a bunch of bluebells for the kitchen table. Nothing nicer to make her mother smile and to feel that summer was on its way. No doubt, whatever her father decided about the POW, she would have to go along with; but not without letting him know exactly how she felt. She climbed down from the rock and made her way to the brightest patch of blue along the fellside.

Chapter 3

'Oak Bob Day, the 29th of May, if we don't get a holiday, we'll all run away,' Ben chanted as he left the house and made his way across the yard to his workshop, which was in an old hen hut behind the barn.

The May bank holiday had arrived – Ben would soon have two days off school, and he couldn't wait. Two days where he was free to do whatever he wanted, and that was to fix and mend bicycles. Many people in the dale had need of them, especially now that petrol rationing had hit home. Ben had found a quick way to bring welcome funds into the family coffers and it was something he enjoyed doing. He sold the bicycles to local folk, soldiers and the guards of the POW camp who cycled back and forth up the dale, to and from work and to the pubs. It was a much-needed service and it was everything he had dreamed of, bringing in money as well as showing his father that there were other ways to make a living besides farming.

Come summer he would be free of school, and then he had a job already promised at Morphet's garage down in Sedbergh. Bill Morphet had been quick to realize that Ben was a canny lad with a spanner and would be a boon to his ever-growing garage once the war had ended – and end it would, eventually.

Ben whistled as he sized up his latest acquisition, an old sit-up-and-beg bicycle. It had no gears but it was a good basic model. Once he'd oiled the chain, given it a lick of black paint and put new brake blocks onto it, it should sell. He looked around the hut at the shelves full of paint, oil, jam jars filled with nuts and screws, spare tyres, wheel spokes and puncture repair kits – which everyone had started to ask him for, now they knew that he would fix their punctures for a minimum fee. He was in his element. Farming was not for him; he would leave that to Sally. She was the one who looked after the stock and discussed the farm with their father. Ben would never be like her. His heart wasn't in the seasons like hers was – he was more excited about an oily rag than the first spring lamb. In that way, he was aware that he was a disappointment to both of his parents. It ought to be a lad who was the farmer of the family, and well he knew it, he thought, as he started to unscrew the front wheel. He would strip the cycle down to its basic frame, ready to be painted and then dried outside in the spring sunshine.

'Eh up, Ben. Is this your latest? It's a bit of a wreck,' George Mason said as he put his head round the shed door to see his best friend at work. 'I've just been delivering

25

some milk to Pratt's. D'you fancy going fishing this evening? I hear there's a right big trout in the pool at Ibby Peril. Just needs catching, and we're the ones to do it.' He grinned. 'We'll have to keep out the way of the beck-watcher, else he'll have our guts for garters.'

'My father will kill me if we get collared by the beck-watcher. But yes, I might join you. Mam would like a nice fish or two, and I need to get into her good books. I need to borrow her big dish to fill with water to test for any holes in this bike's inner tube. She always plays hell with me because she knows when it goes missing it's here with me, but it is better than a bucket.'

'Lord, Ben, you don't half know how to live life danger-ously. Your mam never has a bad word for anyone, from what I've seen of her.' George pulled his cap down over his head.

Ben grinned. 'You've not seen her in a bad mood. She is lethal with a wet tea-towel. One quick flick and you don't half yelp, if she catches you in the right place.'

'She'll still not be as bad as my father. He's always taking his belt off to me. He's nobody to stop him, that's the problem, since my mam died. And my brother being a prisoner in Burma isn't helping, as he's always worrying about him.'

'Have you heard from him lately? Is he still building that railway? It must be hell working in a steaming hot jungle. At least them Italians down in Sedbergh are better looked after than your poor brother.'

'Anybody's better looked after than the soldiers being held in Burma – the conditions are terrible. Scotchergill

Farm have just taken on an Italian. He's been helping with the lambing. He seems all right. Can only just talk English, though.' George leaned against the shed, in no hurry to get home to an abusive father.

'My father's talking of taking an Italian on but our Sally isn't for letting him. She's a stubborn one, but so's he. She'll not win.'

'I can't blame her for not wanting one of them on the farm. My father won't have one. But then again, he doesn't need one; he's got me as his slave. Is Sally all right? Didn't see her when I came into the yard,' George added casually. He tried not to show his feelings for his best friend's sister, especially as she was far too old for him. But she was so beautiful in his eyes.

'She's all right. Always moaning about something and playing hell with me when more bikes come to be mended. I can never do anything right in her eyes. Nobody can, since Edward went missing. He's more than bloody missing – I'd say he's dead now, and she needs to look for another fella,' Ben said callously. He was beginning to wish George would get himself home so that he could get on with mending the bike. 'I'll see you tonight, George. Meet you at Nelly Bridge when it's just falling dusk. I need to crack on now so I've got this finished before we go back to school on Wednesday. With a bit of luck I'll have it sold by next weekend, if I put it down the bottom of the lane.'

'Aye, all right, I can see you're busy. See you about nine, then. Fetch a lamp and a net and I'll bring the rest.' George turned and headed back down the lane to where his horse was grazing in the hedgerow with the cart still attached. He and Ben would catch the big trout that nobody else had been able to, if he had his way tonight.

Ben shook his head as he watched his friend depart. George was a good lad, and Ben felt sorry for him. His father had always been a bully but he'd become even worse since George's mother was found dead in their bed. She had taken her own life by drinking rat poison; she'd been that fed up of life with her lazy, cruel husband, who never did a day's work even though they had their own farm. George always looked as if he'd just fallen out of bed. His shoes had holes in, and he wore other folks' cast-offs. He got fed where he could whenever folk took pity on him. But he was a true, good-hearted friend, and that was what mattered to Ben. Bending over the bicycle, he swore at a nut that had rusted tight on the back wheel. It would take all his strength to loosen it.

'And where do you think you're off to at this time of night?' Bob looked up from his newspaper as he sat beside the fire Ivy had just lit for the evening.

'I promised George Mason I'd do a spot of fishing with him. I know it's late, but they bite better when it's going dark,' Ben said, hoping this explanation would satisfy his father.

'You must think I was born yesterday, lad. You're going in darkness so that Duckie Wildman the beck-watcher doesn't catch you. If he does, don't think I'll be coming to bail you out.' Bob puffed on his pipe and looked sternly at his son. He knew exactly where Ben was going: there had been plenty of talk among local lads, and even grown men, about the big trout in Ibby Peril pool further up the dale. So far it had evaded capture, and anyone who managed to get hold of it would have reason to be proud. 'You'll not get that big bugger in Ibby. He's too clever for the likes of you two,' Bob added, watching as Ben took the torch from under the sink and picked up his fishing rod.

'We'll see. Somebody'll have to catch him. George is a good hand at fishing – if anybody can do it, he can. I'll not be long,' Ben said, heading for the door. He wanted to get out of the house before his mother came downstairs and Sally returned from taking a last look in at the lambs.

'Aye, well, mind what you're doing. It's a full moon – Duckie will be able to see what you're getting up to. Stay low and out of sight. He knows everything that goes on up there. Take care.'

Bob folded his newspaper as the door closed behind Ben. It didn't seem five minutes since he was Ben's age himself, and the lure of a big fish in the deepest dub up Cowgill would have had him sneaking out of the house at night. Nowadays, he just caught the odd fish when he had time – at least, until the salmon started jumping in autumn. Then there was added income to be made, providing he avoided the dreaded Duckie Wildman. Duckie patrolled that particular part of the beck for the landowner; it was private fishing only in that part of the

Dee and he guarded it with his life. Salmon was a delicacy, used by many a poacher to barter with the local coppers and judges when it came to petty crime.

Ben cycled up the dale, his fishing rod balanced on his bike and the torch in his pocket. Not that he'd be wanting that, he thought, glancing up at the dimming sky. As his father had said, there was a full moon just starting to appear over the dark mountain of Whernside. It was a perfect night for a bit of poaching or fishing, just as long as he and George didn't get caught.

Dent was quiet as he cycled through the cobbled streets. Lights were just going on in the houses and the pub sounded full of men, enjoying a pint ahead of the bank holiday and discussing their lambing season. The sooner he was out of the village – or town, as the locals called it – the better. He'd put the local copper behind him and there'd be no one about on the road up to Cowgill. He put his head down and cycled faster, the church clock chiming nine as he crossed the church bridge and made his way up towards Nelly Bridge. He would leave his bicycle there and join George down in the river at Ibby Peril, the deep pool where locals claimed a witch lived within the depths. Ben wasn't bothered about the witch; his mind was on the trout waiting there for them to catch. And catch it they would, even if they had to sit on the bank until dawn.

'Where've you been? I've been waiting,' George greeted him in a low voice. 'Hide your bike in the trees, don't leave it by the bridge. Billy Haygarth sometimes crosses

30

here of a night and he'll know what we're about if he spots it. You don't want word getting back to Duckie.' He watched as Ben hid the bike in thick foliage before joining him on the bridge. 'Leave your rods there and all. You'll not be needing them, not the way I'm going to catch that big bugger. It doesn't take bait.'

George pushed his way through the hazel bushes that grew along the riverside. Ben followed closely, wondering how on earth George intended to catch the fish without a rod. They both held onto the bushes for balance as they stumbled down the sharp banks of the Dee towards the river bottom. The river itself was not that deep; most of the water ran underground, through the limestone pavement that made up the dale. But the stones were green and slippy as they stumbled towards the deep pool known as Ibby Peril. The moon was beginning to rise as they stood at its edge and looked into the murky depths.

'Right, this is what we're going to do. Easiest way to catch a fish yet,' George said with a grin. 'I pinched a bag of quicklime from out of my father's shed. If we block the pool off and spread it on top of the water, it stops oxygen getting into the pool, and the fish float to the top gasping for air. It's the best idea I've had for a long time. I remember my dad saying one of his mates used to fish that way when they were going hungry.' George looked satisfied with himself as he turned to pick up a boulder from above the trickling stream to block it off. 'Go on, then. You dam up the bottom and I'll do the top. Another two hours and we'll have caught the monster of Ibby Peril.' George's feet slipped and slid on the bedrock boulders as he began to dam the top of the pool.

Ben looked at the bag of lime sitting on the bank beside the dim lantern that George had brought along. He shook his head.

'That's no way to catch fish. There's no skill to it – you're just poisoning them. I don't know if I'm right happy with that.' He picked up a stone and set it in place to start blocking the flow of water.

'Nobody will know how we've caught it, unless you open your gob. We can brag about it for months to come.' George straightened up and looked at Ben. 'Come on, then – get a move on. This dam isn't going to build itself.'

Ben hesitated, then said, 'No. It isn't right. Fishing is a sport. There's no sport in suffocating them with lime in the water.' He threw aside the stone he was holding and looked at his mate. 'I'm off home,' he said after a moment. He didn't want to fall out with George, but the fish had no chance if they went through with this plan. It didn't seem fair.

'Suit yourself. I'm doing it anyway. There'll just be me bragging that I caught the big bugger. Don't you be opening your mouth, though,' George warned. He should have known this would happen. Ben had always been squeaky clean in everything he did – and frightened to death of what his father would say.

'Right, I'll be away then. You're on your own with this one. Mind what you're doing, and I'll not say owt

32

to anyone.' Ben climbed out of the river bottom and stood on the bank for a few moments with the smell of the river filling his nostrils. The wild garlic was nearly overflowing, and its pungent odour filled the air as he trampled over it on the way back to his bike.

George didn't even lift his head to say goodbye. Ben was cross with him. This idea of 'fishing' with lime was all wrong and he wanted no part of it. He put his leg over the crossbar, balanced his fishing rods and torch, and headed home under cover of darkness.

On Wednesday, after Ben's first day back at school following the holiday, his father came in with news that explained why George had been absent.

'That mate of yours is in bother. I hope you weren't with him when he limed the dub up the dale,' Bob said as he arrived back from work at Jim Mattinson's. 'He's the talk of Dent, him and his father.' He sat down at the kitchen table, took off his cap and looked at his son, whose cheeks had turned bright red.

'No, I'd nowt to do with whatever he's done. You know I was only gone a short while. I got just past Dent, and then I decided not to bother with fishing. The full moon was so bright, I thought Duckie Wildman would spot us as clearly as in daytime. It didn't feel worth it.' Ben kept his head down, hoping his excuse sounded plausible.

'Aye, well, he'll not be in school for a while. The silly bugger took a bag of lime, dammed the beck and killed all the fish. He might have caught that big trout, but

Duckie Wildman caught him. When that rain came the next day, his dam burst and all the dead fish he'd left floated downstream. He'd left the bag of lime with his home address at the side of the pool, and it led Duckie Wildman straight to him.'

Ben gaped at his father. 'Is he in bother?'

'You could say that, and some. More than any beck-watcher or copper could give him. His father's brayed him to within an inch of his life, from what I've heard. Duckie Wildman had gone up to their farm and tackled the lad, said he'd be getting fined. But his father set into him and then threw him out of the house. He's broken his ribs, given him two black eyes – the poor lad can hardly walk. He dragged himself down to the doctor's, he was in such a bad way. But he wouldn't let the doctor call the police to see his father.' Bob shook his head, swearing under his breath. 'That Dick Mason is a bad lot. He always did have a temper when I was at school with him. The lad would do well to leave home as soon as he can. He'll have had it hard since his mother died, but he shouldn't have limed the beck. That was no way for that big trout to die.'

'He caught it, then?' In spite of everything, Ben had to hide a smile.

'Aye, he caught it,' Bob confirmed. 'They were about to sit down and tuck into it for their dinner when Duckie Wildman called on them. They couldn't hide the evidence. I think Duckie felt so sorry for the lad after the beating he got that he's going to drop the charges. It'll learn your mate the hard way, but it wasn't the best of endings for a grand big fish like that. It should have been caught by a line or let to live. I'm just glad you weren't involved, else you would have got a belting and all. But not as bad as George.'

'No, Father, I'd never do anything like that. And I knew nothing about it.' Ben felt his father's gaze raking over him, as if he had an idea of what had really gone on that night.

'Aye, well, George won't be doing it again himself for a while. You stick to mending bikes – you're better at that anyway. Has your mother given you the money from that fella who bought the last old boneshaker you worked on? He never argued once about the price. He worked at Dawson's coalyard and needed it to get to work.' Bob tousled Ben's hair. 'Tha'll be a millionaire yet, lad. Happen you can help me buy that farm I've got my eye on.'

'No, she's not said anything,' Ben beamed, knowing his mother would have put the money in the old copper kettle where he kept his savings. He'd open a bank account soon and then start to save for his own garage. It wasn't only his father who had plans for the future.

Chapter 4

Sally sat on the edge of her bed. She was tired and, if she was honest, a little bit lonely as she pulled her jumper from over her head, yawning. The days were long and she rarely had a minute to herself. Which was a good thing, as whenever she did, she only started thinking too deeply about her problems.

She looked at herself in the wardrobe mirror that faced her. Twenty-one, with no boyfriend; a love lost for ever; and stuck on her father's rented farm. Her prospects weren't good, she thought as she pulled her nightdress on. And she had only herself to blame. It wasn't as if there had been no other lads interested in her since Edward – it had been her choice to remain faithful to his memory, in the slender hope that one day he might return. Her father had encouraged her to court many a lad up the dale, especially the ones whose fathers owned their own farms, in a bid to make her life secure; but so far there hadn't been a single one who could compete with Edward.

She climbed into bed and pulled the eiderdown up over herself. It had been a long day on the farm, but tomorrow and Friday were her days to go and help in Middleton's shop. She had jumped at the chance to work there when Phyllis Richmond had decided to marry a soldier from Catterick and move out of the area – it had come like a gift from above not long after her kindly former employer, Annie Mackreth, had died. It meant Sally had money to spend on the few things she needed as well as something to contribute to the family pot, to go towards the farm her father was working so hard to find and buy. More than that, it got her away from the farm for two days a week and gave her a chance to hear from the customers about everything that was going on in the dale.

Sally sighed and lay back. It was lambing time, so she had been up at first light and hadn't finished until all the lambs and their dams had been checked for the night. Her father was still working for Jim Mattinson as his farm man; most days, he came home just as tired as she was. Meanwhile, her mother fed any pet lambs that needed bottle feeding, looked after the hens, and kept everyone fed and dressed decently and the farm accounts in order. It was a pity Ben wasn't interested in farming, but he hated it – and now he had been promised a job at Morphet's garage, his father had given over trying to make him into a farmer. Sally hoped he had also given up on the idea of taking on a POW to help around the farm.

She turned to reach for her book. Just a few more pages and she'd have finished the story that had helped her drop off to sleep most nights lately. Tomorrow in

Middleton's shop she would look for another. The shop stocked absolutely everything – candles, toys, baked goods, lamp oil – and it even had a little room of books that Sally was working her way through under the guidance of Sarah Middleton, the owner's daughter. She'd enjoyed every page of *Keep the Home Guard Turning* by the Scottish author Compton Mackenzie – she could just see her father and his fellow farmers and neighbours getting up to the same exploits in the Sedgwick reading rooms, where they practised keeping the dale safe in case of invasion. Ben had earned a smack on the head when he'd burst out laughing at his father dressed in his Home Guard uniform, with a pitchfork in one hand and his small rifle for shooting rabbits in the other. It was a serious job, her father had insisted, and marched off down the road to do his duty by attacking any invading Germans with his pitchfork.

She finished the last page as her eyelids began to close. Tomorrow was another day, she thought, as she turned off her bedside lamp and dozed off to sleep.

Bob had already been out to check on the lambs, and had then left for Jim Mattinson's on his motorbike, by the time Sally rose the following morning. It was the sound of his bike pulling out of the yard that woke her up. Her bedside clock told her it was six-thirty, and the sunshine dancing through the uncurtained bedroom window told her it was a glorious spring day. She lay still for a minute and watched tiny specks of dust floating like fairies in the stream of light, then urged herself to move. She had to be at Middleton's for eight, and it took her a good half hour to walk there.

Usually she walked into Dent with Ben, although he was embarrassed to have his older sister by his side. He wouldn't have to put up with her presence for much longer, though, not when he started work in Sedbergh. He couldn't wait to work in the small market town at the bottom of the dale. It was always busy and had more shops than the village of Dent.

'Come on, Ben, rise and shine! It's nearly time for school and you've got the hens and dog to feed. Move your shanks!' Sally knocked on her brother's door as she made her way downstairs to where she could hear her mother already busy in the kitchen.

'I've knocked for him once. He always leaves it to the last minute to do everything! He's going to have to organize himself a bit better when he goes to work,' Ivy said as she kneaded the bread for the day. 'The kettle's boiled, if you fancy pouring some boiling water on that bucket of Euveka for the dog. At least it will have gone cool for the poor thing when Ben gets round to feeding it.'

Sally took the kettle from the stove and poured boiling water over the golden maize flakes and household scraps, mixing them with the wooden stick that was always used to stir the morning's feed for Spot. Then she picked up an empty bucket and made her way out to the shippon, where the cow was waiting to be milked. She breathed in deeply. The sun had only just started to warm up the air around her but it was going to be a glorious day, she thought as she watched the newly arrived swallows and swifts doing aerobatics in the sky above her head. They were catching the early-morning flies and midges before going about their business of building nests and rearing their young under the eaves of the barns and houses down the dale.

She pushed the shippon door open and was met with the familiar smell of cows, hay and manure, which she knew a lot of people would not appreciate but to her, it was a comforting smell. She walked up the concreted walkway and put her hand out to pat the roan shorthorn cow that her father had already brought in from the field, ready for milking.

'Morning, Rosie, how are we today? No kicking or putting up a fuss, please. My father has already fothered you, so let's get on with milking and then you can get back into the bottom pasture and enjoy your day.'

Sally pulled up the small, worm-eaten milking stool, rubbed her hands together to warm them and then squatted down beside the cow, resting her head on its flanks as she pulled on each teat, expressing the warm milk that frothed into the bucket until the cow's bag was empty and the bucket was full. She put the full bucket aside, went to the cow's head and undid the rope that had secured her by the neck during milking. She passed a wooden toggle through a loop to unfasten it before patting Rosie and guiding her back onto the path that led back outside. Rosie needed little prompting; she knew the morning procedure well. Now that she was out in the spring fields, she was all too happy to lead the way back to her life of greenery and buttercups as she went across the yard and through the already open farm gate.

'Hey, you wait your turn! I'll fill your saucer,' Sally yelled at the farm's tortoiseshell cat as she made her way back into the shippon to find it standing on its hind legs, lapping at the bucket of milk. She shooed the thief away and then filled its saucer, as she did every morning, before carrying the bucket out of the shippon and back to the kitchen for the house's use.

'Oh, you are up then, you've decided to show your face,' she said as Ben crossed her path on his way to feed the dog, collect the eggs and let the hens out as well as give them a scoop full of corn.

'It's too bloody early. And what's the point of me going to school these last few weeks? I've learned what I've learned, and I might as well leave school now. I'm sure the teachers are as fed up with me as I am with them.' Ben emptied the bucket of food into Spot's bowl outside her kennel, watching her gulp down her breakfast before disappearing around the corner of the barn to the hen hut. He hated school. He wanted to start working as a mechanic, making money, as soon as he possibly could.

Sally shook her head; she had loved school and been loath to leave it. Ben would soon find out that being an adult was a lot more difficult. He knew nothing yet, she thought as she re-entered the kitchen. She poured the bucket of milk through a muslin cloth to remove any impurities before sitting down to her breakfast. Ben re-appeared and joined her at the table.

'That's the jobs done, and now you'll be off to Dent,'

41

Ivy said. 'I've a shopping list, if you can get me a few things? There's nothing heavy, and the ration books are on the dresser – you'll need them, as we're out of tea.' She placed her bread dough into two loaf tins and covered them over with a tea-towel to let them rise. 'I'll churn what cream I've been saving in the pantry this morning; we're nearly out of butter. You can tell Middleton's I'll have some spare to sell them in the morning. It brings a bit more income in.'

'All right, Mam. I think I'll be working with Sarah today, so I've got good help. Ben, are you nearly ready? You can walk with me on the way to school.' Sally looked at her brother, who was standing up now and eating his porridge as fast as possible, dribbling it down his chin.

'Yes, but I'm calling for John Oversby on the way. He's got some bike wheels to give me. I want to look at them before I pick them up tonight.' Ben wiped his chin. He didn't want to walk with his sister; she would only lecture him over something or other. She'd become obsessed with her work and the farm since losing Edward, and she thought he should be the same.

'Go on, then, you go your own way and I'll follow on. I can see those wheels are really important,' Sally said with a smirk. She knew full well that John Oversby's bike wheels were not the real reason Ben was calling by. John had an older sister called Maureen, and even though Ben was not quite fifteen, he had his eye on her.

'I'll get off, then. See you tonight, Mam.' Ben gave his chin a final swipe with his jacket sleeve and nearly ran out of the house.

Ivy smiled. 'He's sweet on that Oversby lass, but he thinks we don't know. He's far too young – she'll not look twice at him. I hear she's going out with the Booth lad, anyway.'

'Yes, she is. She knows our Ben's sweet on her and she's always kind to him, but I think his heart is going to be broken. I should tell him not to give it away so easily. It's better not to get attached to anyone. It only gets you hurt.' Sally pushed her chair back, putting her breakfast pots in the sink. 'I'll be on my way now, Mam. I'll be back just after five.' She picked up her basket with the list Ivy had put inside it and left her mother washing up, and wishing that her daughter wasn't so cynical when it came to love.

Sally walked down the farm lane and onto the main road to Dent. It was still relatively quiet as she wandered up towards the village. On dry days like this one, the walk was a pleasure with the morning sun warming her through her coat and the smell of bluebells and star of Bethlehem growing in the hedges along the roadside. The bleating of newly born lambs filled the air, and a distant cuckoo could be heard calling somewhere in the woods near Gawthorpe. Spring and summer mornings were a delight, but the days when rain or snow blew down usually outnumbered them by far. Sally relished every step as she made her way across Bath Bridge, over the Dee, and into the village of Dent. The streets were still covered with their original cobbles, and the carts and the few cars that were used in Dent and the dale rattled noisily over them. Passing the school, she looked for her brother, but there was no sign yet of him or any other pupils; only Miss Bentham, opening the school's large oak door in readiness for the hordes to descend. Most of them would sit at their desks and try to concentrate instead of staring out the windows and wishing they were home and helping on the farm. Despite Sally's love of school, she had done that herself on numerous occasions, and now she spent two days a week working in a shop and doing exactly the same thing. On wet days the shop was the best place to be, but when the sun shone, the outdoors called to her.

Sally said hello to Miss Bentham and walked on through the village, past the Penny Bank, the baker's, the doctor's and the Sun Inn, which was taking a delivery of beer barrels. They were being loaded into the cellars from a dray cart pulled by two large Shire horses, which stood placid and biting their bits despite the barrels rumbling noisily down behind them.

'Morning, Sally,' called Matt Robinson from the George and Dragon, Dent's second pub. She lifted a hand in greeting as she carried on towards the village's main shop, where she would spend her working day. Middleton's was always busy from the second its doors opened. Sally heard wheels coming over the cobbles and hopped up onto the George and Dragon's steps to let a green-covered army wagon pass along the narrow, winding street.

Not so long ago, Dent had had neither electricity nor decent roads. It was a quiet backwater of North Yorkshire that took great pride in its most famous son, the world-famous Victorian geologist Adam Sedgwick; a granite fountain on the main street marked his importance, next to the church gates and across from the George and Dragon. It was here, as Sally stood on the steps, that the army wagon pulled up. A man dressed in a guard's uniform jumped down from the cab with a gun across his shoulder. Walking to the rear of the wagon, he pulled the tarpaulin partly back and let the backboard down for some of his cargo to alight. The publican, standing near Sally, muttered under his breath.

'Bloody POWs! The vicar must've got them in to clear the churchyard. I don't know how he can, with some of our lads buried in that same churchyard after fighting that lot and their mates, the Germans.' Matt spat a mouthful of chewed Kendal Twist onto the cobbles as he stared at the two prisoners of war who had climbed down from the back of the wagon. The guard escorted them up the main path of the church.

Sally, watching them, noticed the younger one turn his head and look at her before he was told to get a move on. He was olive-skinned and quite handsome, but she didn't bother returning the gaze. He was the enemy, dressed in grey overalls with a red spot of material sewn to them to denote he was an Italian prisoner of war. She shared Matt's views, and frowned as the men disappeared into the church.

'At least they aren't Jerries. They mostly seem to do farm work; I bet there are some in the back of that wagon for work further up the dale. If you ask me, it's a tinder pot mixing them and the Italians together in the old workhouse at Loftus Hill. They say they're no threat, but they're our enemies, the bastards!' Matt looked at Sally. 'I'll bet you feel the same, what with your fella still missing. It must be hard not knowing if he's alive or dead.'

Sally felt a lump come to her throat but managed to swallow it back down. 'It is, Matt. I think of him every day and pray that he'll return – or at least that his body will be found. Then I could move on.'

'He's got a true'en in you, lass. But perhaps he would understand if you decided to move on anyway. Life's too short, so think on, Sal.' Matt glanced at her, saw the pain on her face and decided that he had said enough. 'Right – this pub won't run itself, and no doubt the Middletons will be waiting on you.' As he spoke, the green army truck started up and wound its way through the narrow streets of Dent, heading further up the dale towards Cowgill.

'Aye, I'd better get a move on, they will be waiting for me.' Sally tucked her basket under her arm and looked across at the church entrance, where the vicar stood with his two enforced labourers. She glanced again at the younger of the two and then decided to get a move on.

The whitewashed shop stood just on the roadside, and outside it were already displayed brushes, coal scuttles, shovels and empty petrol cans. Somebody had already started the day, Sally thought, as she pushed open the door and the shop's bell gave a welcoming ring. The wooden floors were well trodden and the walls laden with shelves filled with everyday items, anything that the local shoppers could possibly wish for. From the beams hung unopened clotheslines, boards of sewing needles, pins, fuses – just about anything you might need in a small community. The air was filled with a mixture of paraffin, Kendal mint cake and Mrs Middleton's good, homely baking. It was a welcoming shop, much used by the people of Dent – especially at Christmas, when the windows were filled with items to delight any child and an upstairs room was opened for parents to reserve presents for the big day.

'Good morning,' Sally called as she made her way towards the counter, taking off her coat. She stepped into the storeroom to hang it up on her peg and donned the white apron that she wore while working.

'Morning, Sally. It's a grand day. We should be busy. Can you finish putting some of the hardware out as soon as you're ready?' Mrs Middleton asked, coming through with a basket of fresh bread that the baker had just dropped off.

'Yes, of course. Mam says she'll send you what butter she has spare tomorrow morning. Will that be all right?' Sally picked up six coal shovels tied together by a piece of string and the same amount of hearth brushes, all of which she carried through the shop to be put on display outside, seeing the weather was being kind.

'Yes, that will be fine, lass. Have you any spare eggs as well? Your hens should be laying in the good weather here, or at least I'm hoping so. I know that farms always have plenty, but some folk in Dent are not that lucky and still have to put them on their ration card – unless they have caring neighbours who can supply them.'

'Yes, I'm sure we will have. Remind me before I go

home. And I've also a list of what Mam wants, and our ration books to give you, when we have five minutes spare. Is Sarah in today? I need her advice on what book to read next. I've brought some money to buy it with.' Sally took her place behind the counter and watched as Mrs Middleton arranged the bread for sale and put some thin paper next to it for wrapping.

'She should have been here by now. She'll have slept in – she's taking advantage of being our daughter. She knows her father's gone over to Hawes in his van to pick up some Wensleydale cheese, so the house is empty and no one's there to chase her.' Mrs Middleton shook her head.

'It doesn't matter to me, so don't worry,' Sally smiled. She didn't blame Sarah for having a sneaky lie in; she usually worked very hard for her family firm.

'All I can say, it's a good job you never let us down, else we'd get nothing done. I know now that my husband will take all day picking the cheese up, because he will sit and natter with Kit Calvert at the dairy, and then there will be someone else he has to have a brew with and catch up on gossip with, leaving us women to run the shop. I hope he remembers to pick up some bacon from the piggeries down Widdle. We're nearly out of it, and we have an understanding with them at the piggeries. I hate to see our locals going short because of this rationing. It must be terrible if you live in a town or city; they can't get their hands on anything, poor things.'

'I was telling Dad we should have more than the one pig we have for home use. If we reared a piglet or two, would you be interested in buying them once fattened

48

up? He'll be going for our piglet in the next week or two, so I'll mention it.' Sally looked wistful. Another way to make a bit of income, especially if they could sell the bacon on the black market and not through a government scheme.

'I don't know – I'd have to ask Mr Middleton. He's set in his ways, and we have always bought our bacon from the piggeries in Widdle . . .' Mrs Middleton went quiet as the first customer of the day came in. It was elderly Iain Baxter, who always listened to everything that was said within the shop and then went and told whoever would listen to him. 'Serve Mr Baxter, would you, Sally love? I'm just going to pack some butter and hope that we have enough until your mother can supply us tomorrow. Because, knowing my fella, he'll not think of bringing any back from Hawes Dairy. Even though I did remind him we were running low.'

'Oh, so your mother supplies butter to here, does she? I didn't know that,' Iain Baxter said to Sally as he approached the long wooden counter.

'Only when there's a shortage in the shop, Mr Baxter. We don't have the cows to supply on a regular basis. Now, what can I do for you today?' Sally smiled.

'Just a tin of these Black Imps. They're about the only sweets you can buy at the moment. Not that I'd call them sweet. They're terribly strong in taste, and hot little devils; no wonder they're called Imps.' Iain picked up the small tin and shook it, rattling the small, extra-strong liquorice cuttings that smelt of menthol. 'I have one of these every morning and every night. They keep my chest

49

clear, and they're just the right amount for putting on my ration card.' He fumbled in his pocket for his money and his ration card and then placed his treat into his pocket. 'I see the vicar is making use of them POWs this morning. They need to be given some work, else they'll only turn to doing no good if they have time on their hands. We might as well get some work out of them as keep them for nothing.' He shook his head and added disapprovingly, 'I heard they even have Mrs Lawson from up Firbank going in and mending their clothes, and making sure they can write home and keep in touch with their families. I bet the Jerries aren't looking after our lads that well.'

'I don't know, Mr Baxter. I just wish this war was over for all of us, and that life could get back to normal,' Sally said. Glancing over his shoulder, she noticed Sarah approaching the shop door from outside and then hesitating as she saw Iain Baxter standing at the counter. Sarah changed course towards the shop window and stood there, pretending to look at the display, until he finally went on his way.

'I thought he was never going to leave!' she said when she finally entered the shop. 'He's a nice enough man, but he never shuts up and he's always moaning. Have you seen my mother? I bet she's playing heck with me for being late.' She dropped her voice to a whisper. 'I had to have a lie in – I read my book until the early hours, I just had to finish it.'

'I can hear you, Sarah Middleton, and yes, you are late. Now come through here and help me unpack these tins that arrived yesterday from Kendal. You can stack them and price them up,' Enid Middleton called through to her daughter, without showing her face.

Sarah shrugged her shoulders and grinned. 'I'll catch up with you when you-know-who decides we deserve a break.' She called back, 'Coming, Mother – I was just about to tell Sally about my book.'

'You can tell her later, when we haven't got so much to do. There are some orders to put together for delivery, and they've to be checked next to their ration books. This war makes work for everyone; I wish to heaven it was over.' Enid stood next to the storeroom doorway and watched as her daughter pushed past her. 'And don't you be so cheeky, madam. You have a life of luxury compared to some . . .'

Sally smiled and kept herself busy as she listened to the mother and daughter bickering. It happened in every family, especially if you all worked together.

A little later, hearing the shop bell tinkle, she raised her head from tidying beneath the counter to see her latest customer – and felt her stomach churn as she recognized one of the Italian prisoners of war. He was the one who had looked at her earlier, as she stood on the George and Dragon's steps. She couldn't help noticing again how handsome he was, even though she hated herself for the thought.

'*Buongiorno*. You sell tobacco, no?' he asked in a rich Italian accent. 'I can pay, and I am allowed.' He pulled a little money out of his pocket, along with papers that confirmed he was allowed either a packet of cigarettes or an ounce of tobacco.

'Cigarettes or tobacco?' Sally said, without showing any warmth.

'Cigarette, *grazie*. Woodbines?'

She passed him a packet of twenty.

'*Grazie*, but –' he put up his hands and showed his fingers – 'I only have money and are allowed that many.' He smiled, revealing the whitest teeth Sally had ever seen.

'Sorry.' She replaced the twenty pack with ten and took his money without saying anything else.

The POW stood for a moment, regarding her intensely. 'My name is Luca. I – how do you say – I love your country.' The way he was looking at Sally made her blush.

'Good. I'm glad that you do. Sorry, I have work to do. Thank you,' she said, noting the look of slight dejection that crossed his face.

'I too have work today, across at the church. The priest is a good man.' Luca had hoped this pretty local girl would be willing to talk with him a little, but it was becoming clear that she had no intention of doing so and had found a task that was more important. He sighed to himself as he turned to leave. Nobody made him welcome in this cold, miserable country.

'*Arrivederci* – I will go on my way now,' he said as he reached the door. This didn't get a reply from Sally, and he stepped outside and then paused to light one of his precious cigarettes before returning to the churchyard.

Sally watched him discreetly through the window. If he had been a local Dales lad, she would have passed the time of day with him. But in her mind, he was the enemy, and she didn't want to give him any attention.

She saw him take a long draw on his cigarette and then start across the road to the churchyard. He was handsome, but she hadn't understood half the words he'd said. And besides, he was a dirty Italian. She hadn't even wanted to serve him.

'Did I hear one of those Italian POWs in here?' Sarah came out of the storeroom carrying a box full of tinned peas and started to place them on a shelf.

'Yes. His name is Luca, and he bought ten fags. I don't think he should be allowed them. He shouldn't be allowed anything that brings him pleasure,' Sally said harshly as she started dusting shelves.

'Wouldn't you want your Edward to find comfort in a quick smoke, if he's still alive and a POW?' Sarah said, to Sally's surprise. 'That one's not done anything wrong – he's just got conscripted, like our lads have. Besides, all those that are held at Loftus Hill in Sedbergh are supposed to be of no danger to anyone. They're here because they can be trusted.' She continued placing the tins of peas in a neat row on the shelf.

'But my Edward isn't alive. And that's because of the likes of him, and the Jerries. I try to tell myself that he might be . . . but he isn't, is he, Sarah? Four years without a sighting or a word. I sometimes think I'm in love with a ghost.' Sally sat down on a stool behind the counter and sniffed and wiped her eyes.

'Oh, Sally. You never know. Don't give up hope.' Sarah rushed to her friend's side and gave her a big hug. 'My cousin thought her young man had died in the trenches in the Great War. She'd even had a letter saying he had.

So she got on with her life and married another lad, only to find when the war was over that her original boyfriend had been in a hospital in Germany and then held as a POW. I think it broke his heart when he returned to find her married. Worse than anything the war had thrown at him.' She looked at Sally with sympathy, then smiled. 'I know what will cheer you up. I'm about to unpack a box of new books for the corner over there, and you can have the first pick. They've just come in from Titus Wilson's in Kendal. I believe there's a copy of *The Hound of the Baskervilles*, if you dare read it. It is a bit grisly, I'm told.'

'I'm sorry,' Sally said, blowing her nose. 'I thought I was doing so well after losing Edward . . . but it was just the POW coming in. He looked the same age as him, and – oh, this war has just been such a waste of life.'

'I know. Listen, I'll tell Mother to put the kettle on, and we'll have a brew and look at these new books before the rush begins. Wherever Edward is, let's hope that he's safe and not in pain, and that one day you'll be with him again.'

'Bless you, Sarah – you're always so kind. I'll not lose hope. Dreams do come true.' Sally managed a smile as she stood up. She was lucky to have some good friends; it made a hard life more bearable, she thought, as she followed Sarah into the back to view the new box of books.

Chapter 5

Bob Fothergill picked up a heavy lump of limestone and looked at it closely, weighing up which way to place it into the gap of the intricate stone wall he was repairing. He was doing the job he loved best, away from everybody, out in the countryside with only the skylarks and lapwings in the blue sky above to keep him company.

It was the first day of June, and the small pink flowers called after the month of May nodded their heads in the fellside breeze. He bent down to open the knapsack that held his sandwiches and a pop bottle filled with cold tea for him to drink when he got the time. It was a thirsty job, walling, and a hungry one too. He noticed the ham-and-pickle sandwiches that Ivy had packed for him waiting for his dinner break and tried to resist having one early. Bye, it was a grand day, he thought as he leaned back against the limestone wall and looked around him. All the sheep had now lambed, and the voices of the young creatures bleating for their mothers could be heard from the valley below. Looking around him, he could nearly see down into Dent town one way and the rising fell of Whernside in front of him, with the next valley of Garsdale behind him. There was nowhere else grander, he thought to himself as he took a sip of his tea and surveyed his hands, roughened from the morning's walling.

He was taken aback when he heard a sudden scrambling noise close by, and a black-and-white border collie with a piece of twine around its neck jumped up onto the wall at his side. Its tongue dripped with saliva as it looked at him in the hope of something to eat, trying to keep its balance. Bob patted its head.

'Now then, where did you come from? Not lost, I hope? You'll not be chasing my sheep, I hope, because you only look a young'en.' He put his hand around the string and looked for a name tag but found none.

'Lassie, you devil! You're going to have to learn to come to a command,' an out-of-breath Arthur Metcalfe shouted, rushing up behind Bob. He stopped when he reached the wall and put his young whelp of a dog onto a length of string. 'I only got her last week,' he explained. 'Her mother's a right good worker, but this 'en must take after her father. Either that or she's deaf. She'll not chase anything, though. There's no harm in her.' Arthur, a rugged Dales farmer who was nearing seventy but still relatively fit, leaned against the other side of the wall to catch his breath as he held Lassie tight under his arm. 'Doing a spot of walling, Bob? I've some gaps where the wall has weakened and fallen to be put up before I ask Richard Turner to come and value our place. We've decided to move. The

Mrs wants to be nearer our lass – she moved up into Lanarkshire last year when she got wed, and now they have a family on the way. We've just bought a two-hundred-acre farm next door to them, hence the new dog.'

'You can't be leaving, Arthur? You're Garsdale born and bred, and two hundred acres is a big concern. Will you be able to manage it all? I never thought you'd leave Deep Well. That farm's been in your family for years,' Bob replied with surprise in his voice. He had always admired the Deep Well farmhouse. It was a cleanly whitewashed, low-set longhouse; the small cottage garden was filled with flowers in summer, while the holly tree outside was laden with red berries in winter. Ivy had always said when they'd called that she would love to live there. He had to agree – not only was it a good family home but it also had some of the best meadowland in Garsdale, along with good grazing.

'Aye, but our lass wants us near her, and land is cheap up there at the moment. So we're off, before we get any longer in the tooth and while we can still enjoy our grandbairns.' Arthur cosseted the dog.

'Well, you'll be missed. We've always popped in to yours at Christmas – you'll not be wanting a turkey delivered now. Or if you do, I'm not bringing it up to Scotland for you,' Bob joked. He looked down at his feet for a moment and then said, 'I'd be interested in knowing how much your place gets valued for, Arthur. I daresay it'll be a bit out of my price range, but would you let me know when Richard Turner has been round, and before you put it up for sale?'

'I can do that with pleasure, Bob. It would be grand

if you could afford it, but I'll have to ask a fair price. I'm going to need every penny to stock this new place up. But we could see what he says, and I'll let you know.' Arthur straightened up and pulled Lassie from off the wall top. 'Your lass would like living there. She's said many a time to Mary that she loves the view and gardens. You'll have to tell Jim Mattinson you need more brass for the work you do for him.'

'Chance would be a fine thing. And Jim's been good to me, anyway. He pays me fair enough, and look at the view I get when I'm in my office on a good day.' Bob opened his arms to indicate the vista around them.

'Aye, you can't beat it, can you? I'll keep in touch, and you'll be the first to hear what Deep Well is worth. It would save me brass by not putting it up for sale if you could afford it.' Arthur let Lassie loose from the piece of string and watched as she sniffed through the tufts of moorland grass. 'Now, let's see if she knows where home is, and if I can keep up with her,' he called back as he followed the dog over the rough grass and sphagnum moss. 'I'll be in touch, don't you worry.' His head went out of sight down the fellside.

Bob took a deep swig from the bottle of tea and breathed out. Arthur Metcalfe's farm would be ideal for his family, but Metcalfe would want too much for it. They had saved and saved of late and the bank balance was looking good, but he'd still need to borrow some from the bank if they were to move. Then he and Ivy would be back to square one, trying to make ends meet and dreading letters from the bank, just like when they were first wed.

The idea was fanciful, he thought, as he picked up another stone and got on with his work. Still! He'd mention it to Ivy tonight when he got home. If she dared to think about it, then they would try to make a go of it.

Bob lay in bed and watched as Ivy let down her long, greying hair and brushed it. She plumped her pillow before climbing into bed beside him. Their bedroom was still warm after the evening sun had shone through its ageing windows, unlike in winter, when everyone hurried to get into bed. Ivy took a sip of water from the tumbler she always kept on her small bedside table. The room was basic, furnished with hand-me-downs, but everything in it was cared for with love.

'I saw Arthur Metcalfe today when I was walling a gap above the station,' Bob said casually. 'He says he and Mary are soon to be leaving. They're packing up and going farming up in Scotland.'

'Mary will want to be near her lass. She's having twins, they think, so I don't blame her,' Ivy said, pulling the covers over her.

'He's selling Deep Well. I told him we might be interested. I know you've always liked that house, and it has some good land with it. Richard Turner is going to be valuing it. I asked Arthur to let us know how much it's going for.'

'You did what! Sometimes, Bob Fothergill, I think you lose touch with your senses. How on earth could we afford Deep Well?' Ivy looked at her husband with disbelief.

'Well, we'll not know if we don't ask or try. All the sheep have now lambed, and I'm not working for Jim tomorrow. First thing in the morning, we'll have a ride up Garsdale on the bike and just drive past it. It'll jog your memory on how bonny set it is. You know you like the place.' Bob put his arm around Ivy.

'There will be none of that. Nothing you do will talk me round, Bob Fothergill. You know we can't afford Deep Well, so don't even think about it,' Ivy protested as he kissed her on the cheek.

'Just a look. We'll go up on the bike and drive past. That costs nowt,' Bob murmured.

'I know what it looks like. And you know all too well that it's one of my favourite houses up Garsdale. Mary has one of the homeliest kitchens, and a big pantry – she's got everything I haven't. But that's because we can't afford it!' Ivy said, and turned her back on Bob.

'Make breakfast early. We'll go for a ride out past it when Ben has gone to school. There's no need for Sally to know anything just yet,' Bob whispered.

'Bob Fothergill, you'll be the death of me with your ideas above your station. But I do like the place,' Ivy said, thinking about her friend's kitchen and garden, which she had always admired.

'Then a quick look won't hurt. They will never know we've driven past. Now, how about a kiss to seal it?' Bob said, wrapping his arms around her.

'Night, Bob. You can't always get what you want,' Ivy said. She gave him a quick peck and then snuggled down in bed, thinking of Deep Well and what wallpaper she would put on the walls and where the big dresser would fit, if their dreams did come true.

Chapter 6

Sally, back early from work that day, looked at her father as he sat back in his chair after enjoying his lunch. For some reason, he seemed more relaxed than usual.

'It's grand that we've finished lambing, isn't it, Father? And it's been a good spring, weather-wise. Let's hope the grass starts growing a bit faster, and then we should get a good crop.'

Bob puffed on his pipe and nodded amicably.

'I was talking to Mrs Middleton at work,' Sally went on. 'She's happy with the butter and eggs Mam's been sending. But then she mentioned bacon, and how they buy it from the piggeries down Widdle. It got me thinking, as you're going to be buying a pig up for our own use come this autumn – could we not have two or three pigs? And then we could supply the shop, if they're willing to take them?' She looked hopefully at her father. She knew it would mean taking money out of his savings to buy the pigs, but the income from selling them would make it worthwhile.

'I've been thinking along similar lines myself,' Bob said. 'But I didn't think of selling the bacon through Middleton's shop. I thought we could take on a few extra and ask the neighbours to help contribute to their upkeep in exchange for a guaranteed share when butchered. So I've gone ahead and ordered them from Dick Harrison. We'll have to keep it quiet and only ask our true friends, because the War Ag will want us to give them to the effort – but we'll make a quiet bob or two doing it my way.' He nodded at his daughter. 'The Middletons won't change from buying their bacon from the piggeries. They'll be tied into a contract there. But it was worth a thought, lass.'

'So you'd already decided on getting an extra pig or two? Is that why you were cleaning both pig hulls out?' Sally asked. She felt a little left out of the plan.

'Aye. And I thought if we put a slop bucket halfway up the lane for folk to put their potato peelings and leftovers in, that'll be a way for them not to cost so much to everybody concerned. They don't have to walk up to the house every day then, just once a week while they're passing our lane end – that will be enough. We'll need every penny in the next month if me and your mother are going to do what we've decided on.'

Sally wondered what he meant by that. 'Why would we need extra money, Father? Ben starts work in summer, he'll start to bring a wage in; and I'm pulling my weight working at Middleton's. We're all paying our way already.'

'Aye, well . . . we weren't going to say anything, but your mother and I had a quick look at a farm up Garsdale

62

this morning. Arthur Metcalfe said he was putting Deep Well up for sale, and we both agreed we wouldn't mind having a stab at buying it if we could afford to. He's having it valued but it won't be up for sale until the autumn, when his stock is low and there's less work to be done outside.' Seeing Sally's expression, Bob thought perhaps he shouldn't have said anything.

'Deep Well – but that would mean leaving Dentdale!' Sally was taken aback. She had lived in Dentdale all her life; her friends and family, everything she knew and all of her memories were there. She couldn't imagine how it would feel to leave the dale of her birth, even if Garsdale was only the other side of the fell.

'I know, but it's the ideal farm for us all. It hasn't happened yet, lass, but the pigs will. And I tell you another thing – I'll be going down Sedbergh this afternoon to see about getting an Italian to work for us for nothing. He can do a bit of walling, clear the meadows of any rubbish on the land and be here for haymaking. He can be in charge of the pigs and all. That'll give me more time to help Jim Mattinson and happen to get odd jobs here and there over the summer. As I say, we'll need every penny if we're to get that farm your mother and I have set our hearts on.'

'Oh, Father, no. We can manage without. I'll give over working at Middleton's if I'm needed more on the farm. I don't mind not having money for myself. There's nothing I want anyway.' Sally shook her head urgently. It was what she had dreaded hearing: an Italian working next to her! She wished she had never said anything. It had been such a peaceful morning, and now her day was spoiled. And the rest of her life too, it would seem, if they were really going to move.

'No, we're going to take one on. I was talking to Jake Winn at Scotchergill and he said his lad is a real help. Good with horses, and he speaks good English. Seemingly there are German POWs and Italians. The Germans are going up Cautley and Howgill onto farms, and Garsdale and Dent have the Italians. I'd rather have an Italian than a Jerry any day.' Bob knocked what tobacco was left out of his pipe into the fire grate and tucked the still-warm pipe into his jacket's top pocket. 'You can come with me to Loftus Hill if you like, where they're all held in the old workhouse. But you'll not like it there; it's a grey, dismal spot. It's where everybody round here used to dread ending up when they got to an age that they were no longer able to work and had no family to look after them. My father used to say he'd rather shoot himself than end up in a place like that.'

'I'm not coming with you,' Sally snapped. 'I'm not having anything to do with Loftus Hill or an Italian. We had one in the shop – he came in for some cigarettes. The fact that they're allowed cigarettes at all is bad enough, without us making them welcome. Besides, I thought Brian Harper would be coming and mowing the meadows? Won't he be doing most of the mowing down the Dales, with his tractor that he uses for the War Ag?'

'He might be able to mow the meadows, but he's not going to come every day to rake and scale the grass to get it dry and then put it in our barn. No, Sally, we'll get a POW. Let's make life a bit easier for ourselves while we have the chance, and make a bit of brass.'

Sally stared at her father. He ought to understand why she didn't want a POW on their farm, no matter how much easier it might make things. She pushed her chair back and went out into the sun-filled yard, leaving Bob shaking his head at her. He swore under his breath just as Ivy came downstairs and into the kitchen.

'Bob Fothergill, I heard that. I thought we were having a quiet day, and there's me hearing you and our Sally arguing. What's going on, for heaven's sake?' Ivy stood in front of Bob with her arms crossed.

'I told her we might be interested in Deep Well. And then I told her that I'm about to get a POW to help around this farm. Neither went down well, and on top of that, she had an idea about selling bacon and pork to Middleton's shop in Dent, and I hadn't told her I was ordering extra piglets to rear and butcher for locals.' Bob rubbed his forehead. 'I sometimes wonder who's running this farm, me or her.'

'Aye, Bob, you never were one for tact. She loves this place, you should know that. And even though she knows we've wanted a farm of our own for so long, leaving here would be a big wrench for her. As for getting a POW – can't you see, she sees them as the enemy? She's still not sure what's happened to Edward, and she blames them for whatever it is.' Ivy sighed.

'Tears and moping about on this farm will not bring Edward back,' Bob said sharply. He watched Sally through the window. 'She's off up that fell again. She sits many an hour on that big stone just after the high pasture. Happen it will do her good if we move to Garsdale – there'll happen to be a lad there that'll take her eye.'

'I think it will take more than moving to Garsdale. Get your POW to work for us, but tread gently with our Sally. She'll get used to him eventually. I must admit, I'm not over keen myself.' Ivy shook her head, her gaze following Bob's out the kitchen window. 'Sally's lonely. She lost Marjorie from next door as well. I know she puts on a brave face most of the time, but she can't fool me. I know that lass of ours like the back of my hand.'

'Well, she needn't take it out on me. I can't do anything to help her with that. It's a pity Marjorie Harper got herself in the family way, else she'd still have her as a friend. Even if she was a bit fond of her menfolk,' Bob muttered.

'You never did like Marjorie. Sally will be all right, just give her time. Somebody will come along. I'll have a word with her tonight when you're tending the sheep – I'll put her mind at rest with this POW, and the move. Not that I think we'll ever be able to afford Deep Well anyway, no matter how many flitches of bacon we might sell.'

'Well, I'll leave her to you. As usual, I can't do right for doing wrong with the lass.' Bob picked up his cap and decided he'd better check on the potatoes in the paddock he'd ploughed for the War Ag before heading across to Sedbergh. His world was on its head; he was trying to do right by everybody and anybody, make his smallholding as profitable as it could be and supply what

66

others needed as far as he was able. If only he could, though, he would turn down any money he was making just to see his daughter smile and be happy again. That was something he'd never have expected to feel when it came to making money.

Later in the afternoon, Ivy sat knitting while Sally read the latest book that she and Sarah had decided upon from the newest batch in the shop.

'I don't blame you for not wanting to go with your father to Loftus Hill,' Ivy said. 'Why he thought you'd want to go with him I do not know. The last people you want to see are German and Italian soldiers, even if they're not the dangerous kind.' She put down her knitting and looked at her daughter, who remained silent. 'You know, a lot of those men have only been fighting in the war because they were conscripted – just like our lads. It must be a real hardship to be away from their families, not able to see the ones they love. They're cooped up like rats because nobody knows what to do with them.'

'At least they're alive, Mam. And their families know they are,' Sally retorted. 'I can't let go of Edward, not yet. Not while there's a glimmer of hope that he's still alive. So don't ask me to.'

'I'm not asking you to, love. But enjoy your life. Edward wouldn't want to see you getting so low. Make the most of each day, and when this POW comes, be kind to him. He's perhaps got a girlfriend or wife that he's missing.' Ivy saw Sally's eyes fill with tears. She set her knitting aside and got up to give her daughter a hug. 'As for your father's idea of moving us into Garsdale, it will all come to nowt. You know him and his ideas. But it would be lovely living there; I've always admired that farm. So nicely set, has a view right down the dale and plenty of bedrooms.' She kissed Sally's head. 'Now, I'll make us some tea, and you try and be right with your father when he comes back in.'

Sally didn't reply. She picked up her book again and tried hard to concentrate on reading. She hated feeling the way she did, but some days she just couldn't stop thinking about Edward. Her mother was right; she was in love with a ghost. But maybe, just maybe, he would still return – and until she knew otherwise, Sally would be faithful to him.

Bob made his way down the road to Sedbergh on his treasured Royal Enfield. There had been hell on at home when he'd first bought it, but the motorbike had easily paid for itself by now.

As he crossed the bridge spanning the river Rawthey, the outskirts of Sedbergh came into view. With the rounded fells of Windsor as their backdrop, the ancient buildings of Sedbergh Private School stood dignified, as they had for centuries. Bob rode up the sloping hill towards Loftus Hill workhouse, then up the path to the building, and found a place to park his bike. He took off his goggles and pulled the bike onto its stand.

The workhouse was a long, grey building, two storeys high, with several rows of windows on each side. Bob had never been near it before, and he had always vowed that nobody in his family would ever have to enter such a place. However, this afternoon was different. He made his way to the back entrance, noticing that the old workhouse signage had been removed. In its place, the Ministry of Defence had erected new signs giving various instructions to callers. Behind the building, in what had once been the inmates' exercise yard, stood three tarpaulin-covered army wagons, empty of both drivers and men. The place seemed quiet, although Bob could hear the clatter of a typewriter in a downstairs room as he approached the green-painted back door and rang the bell. After a few moments, he heard footsteps. He stood to attention, expecting a military man to open the door.

It swung open, and a face he recognized looked up at him.

'Now, what are you doing here, Bob Fothergill? Let me guess: you need the help of one of my soldiers? Half the dale has been asking for them this last day or two, with the summer months coming and haytime not far from starting.' Amy Lawson opened the door wide for him to step inside.

'Your soldiers? What are you talking about, Amy? Surely you're not in charge of them?' Bob replied, smiling at the middle-aged woman. He had known Amy all his life. She and her husband farmed a small strip of land near Firbank, and Amy was known for her homeliness and for making people welcome when they visited the farmhouse.

'No, not as such, you daft ha'peth. But I look after them. I do their mending and cook their meals and help them write home to their loved ones. All most of them want is to go home and live in peace, you know, and forget all about this war. Now, am I right? Are you after a farm man? If so, you need the second door down on the right-hand side of the corridor.'

Bob nodded. 'Aye. We could do with a bit of help, and it seems everybody else is making use of them. Tell me, Amy – are they to be trusted? My Ivy's not so keen on me signing one up. And as for Sally, she's right against one helping on the land.'

'They are just the same as anybody else – there's good'ens and bad'ens. On the whole, none are really bad. If the captain thinks they're going to cause any bother he soon sends them back to where they've come from, the more secure POW camps. Most of them speak English, some more than others. They'll be a great help to you this summer if you are allocated one.' Amy smoothed down her apron. 'Now, it's Captain Bennett you'll be wanting to speak to. He's busy in his office on the type-writer, doing more swearing than my ears can hardly stand because his secretary is off ill. Follow me – I'll show you to his door. I've just given him a cup of tea, so he'll be easier to talk to at the moment. Sometimes he can be a real stickler.'

Amy walked ahead of Bob and then stopped a quarter of the way down the long, dark corridor, in front of a door with Captain Bennett's name on it. 'Just knock. He'll call you in.' She watched as Bob plucked up his courage. It was a little daunting to knock and disturb a military man.

'Enter,' a gruff voice shouted from within. Bob glanced at Amy, as if for permission.

'Go on, he doesn't bite. At least, he hasn't done yet.' Amy grinned and then made her way down the corridor. She had socks to darn and clothes to mend. With fifty men to care for, her work was never done.

'Good afternoon, sir.' Bob removed his cap as he stood in front of the army officer's desk. Captain Bennett, dressed in his khaki uniform and looking very important, threw a piece of screwed-up paper into his overflowing wastepaper bin before looking up.

'Confounded typewriter, I can't get used to the machine. I wish to heavens my secretary was back,' he growled, and then sat back in his chair. 'Now, what can I do for you? In need of one of our POWs, I'd say, by the looks of you?'

'Yes, sir, that's what I'm here for. It'll be haytime shortly and another pair of hands is always welcome. Although there's plenty of work to be done now, if we can have one start as soon as possible,' Bob added, feeling awkward.

'You need to fill out a form. Now let me find it in one of these drawers.' Captain Bennett rummaged in one of his desk's side drawers and passed Bob a crumpled form to fill in. 'You can either take it home or fill it in here, it doesn't take long. I only need your name, address and the nature of the work our man will be given to do. Oh, and your preference as to German or Italian.'

'I'll fill it in here, thank you, sir.' Bob took the form and the captain passed him a pen, motioning for him to sit down. He sat in the chair facing the desk and began filling in the form, hesitating as he reached the end without finding any mention of preference. 'Preference, sir . . . there's no mention of it on the form.'

'No, you won't find it there. I only ask it because I know some farms don't want Jerries. Never forgiven 'em for the last time round, what! It doesn't make much difference to us. All the men here can be trusted, else we wouldn't be letting them out of their rooms. There's a list here of how we expect them to be treated and a few other general instructions.' He passed Bob a pamphlet and took the completed form in return. 'Now – Jerry or Italian?'

Bob thought for a moment before replying, 'An Italian. They didn't start this war, and my lass's fella is still missing from when he first joined up and went with the Expedition force. So perhaps an Italian would be easier for her to accept.'

'Bloody Germans. Good men went missing – some may return, others may not. She has my sympathies. An Italian it is. You'll have a letter from us soon, giving you a date for him to start on a trial basis and a few other details. Is that everything?' Captain Bennett rose from his chair and extended his hand for Bob to shake.

'Yes, thank you, sir. I think so.' Bob hesitated, and the captain saw his uncertain expression.

'Rest easy, man – he'll be a boon to you this summer. I know just the right man for the job. I'll look at his details now and I'll see that he's sent your way once all the information has been processed.'

The captain watched Bob leave his office before going to his filing cabinet, where all the POWs' details were kept. He opened a drawer and flicked through files, eventually pulling one out.

Luca Bugatti, a private in the army, was a farmer's son hailing from Tuscany who had enlisted against his will. He would fit in well to his new employment, the captain thought as he glanced over Bob's application; Luca probably wasn't so very different from that missing boyfriend of the farmer's daughter. He ought to feel quite at home at Daleside, if they could place him there.

Bob dismounted and parked his motorbike outside the kitchen door. He could hear the murmur of Ivy and Sally's voices as he made his way into the house. Both looked up as he entered the kitchen; Ivy, who was peeling potatoes, paused and looked at him expectantly. Sally, washing up the tea things, took a few moments to finish the job before giving her attention to Bob.

'Have you done it, then?' Ivy asked, unsmiling.

'I have. The captain at Loftus Hill was a grand man. There'll be no problems, or shouldn't be, with us having a POW. He's given us this leaflet to read and I've had a quick look at it. It sets out the guidelines. Says they'll remove him at the first sign of any problem.' Bob saw Sally's face cloud over and added, 'He'll not be a Jerry that comes. I've asked for an Italian.'

Sally's expression grew furious. 'It'll make no difference what he is. They're all murderers! I don't know how you could, Father.'

'Because it's free help, lass, and will benefit all of us. Now, hold your whisht and make the best of a bad job,' Bob said firmly.

He watched as Sally turned back towards the sink. 'He'll bring nothing but worry and bad luck, I know it,' she said. Ivy shook her head, but didn't add to the argument.

'Well, he'll be joining us shortly, so you're just going to have to lump it.' Bob's tone was sharper now. What with everything else on his mind, he was not going to be answerable to his daughter's mood.

Chapter 7

Brian Harper leaned over his farm gate and looked at Bob, his next-door neighbour. Although nowhere near as wealthy as Brian himself, Bob was rich in other ways. He had a good wife and a loving family, even if he didn't always fully appreciate that. Brian had recently received a letter from his own daughter, Marjorie, to say she was coming to visit with some news. He was dreading her imminent arrival.

'It's going to be bloody hard, Bob, being right with my lass. I can't help but think she's after something; otherwise, why would she show up after so long? She takes after her mother, you know. Loose with her morals and always wanting something I can't afford,' Brian said glumly.

'Marjorie might have changed in all this time,' Bob reminded him. 'She wasn't that bad, Brian. She was young and daft, and she got herself into bother. That baby of hers must be nearly school age now. Do you never think of trying to find him? I'm sure I'd have to if he were my grandson. It wasn't his fault he was born.'

'No; it was that bloody Birbeck lad's fault, although she never named him.' Brian shook his head. 'The baby will have a good home in Ireland – it needn't know about us. After all, what would I do with a bairn? I've no wife and not enough hours in the day, now I own the farm over the dale and all. Happen Marjorie has heard I've bought that and decided to come and claim what's rightly hers. But I'll not be parting with a penny, Bob. She caused me embarrassment, along with her mother running away with that smarmy cattle-feed dealer. I never want to see either of them again.'

'Aye, Brian, it's not always about brass. Sometimes the call of home can get the better of you. She might just want to make up and clear the air. Give her a chance. I know on the quiet you regretted sending her away – after all, she's your lass, your only lass. Welcome her back and see how she stands with you.' Bob spoke quietly. He couldn't even imagine disowning his lass, Sally, or sending her away pregnant; and he would never turn his back on Ben, his lad.

'You're lucky with your two. They never give you any bother. Sally's always had a sensible head on her shoulders,' Brian said.

'Ta. But our Sally, by God, she's a stubborn one. I'm in her bad books because I've gone and taken on an Italian from down the workhouse. I thought he could help out this summer because our Ben is starting work at Morphet's garage once he's left school. But she's dead set against him coming.' Bob shook his head.

'You can't blame her, Bob. She'll be thinking about her

fella. I don't suppose there's been any news of him? It's a shame it wasn't the Birbeck lad. I hear he's started writing home. He's in France, and he's been saying our lads are starting to get the better of Jerry in some places. He'll land home. Bad pennies always turn up, it seems,' Brian growled.

'Well, if we are allocated one of the Italians, Sally will have to like it or lump it. I'm busy and I need a hand on with the home. I've plenty of work on with Jim Mattinson – I'm drystone walling for him at the moment. There are more gaps than wall around some of his fields. Besides, we need any extra money I can make. Don't say anything to anybody, but Ivy and me, we fancy trying to buy Deep Well up Garsdale. It's going to be up for sale this autumn, and I'm going to have a stab at buying it.'

'That'll cost you a bob or two,' Brian observed. 'There's a good bit of land with it, and the house is a lot larger than Daleside. I wouldn't mind a look at it myself. How much is Arthur Metcalfe wanting for it?' He saw Bob's face cloud over and immediately regretted asking.

'I don't know, Brian. He's getting it valued and he's going to let me know. Haven't you got enough on your plate without buying one up Garsdale? You'd be better off buying ours if Franklin, our landlord, would let you have it once we leave.' Bob sighed. 'Your pockets must be a hell of a lot deeper than mine.'

'Aye, that would be better, as you say. Let me know how you go on. I'll see how the land lies with old Franklin before you leave.' Brian knew not to push his luck. His best friend had a temper when riled. Bob would struggle to buy Deep Well, but Brian could afford to bide his time. 'I'd better get a move on. Too much to do and not enough time. Tell your lass I'll send Marjorie over to see her – she's coming later on today and staying a night or two. That is, if we don't fall out straight away.'

'Nay, don't do that. Make her welcome with open arms – you know that you've missed her. I'd be lost without my Sally, but I'd never dare tell her that. I'll need to get a move on as well, I've some piglets being delivered and the pig hulls aren't quite ready for them yet. I'll take myself back home. But you think on, Brian. Make your Marjorie welcome, no matter what she has to say.' Bob nodded a goodbye as he started back across the fields. He knew that if Brian decided his daughter hadn't changed, he'd have nothing to do with her. It was his loss more than hers, Bob thought as he walked towards home; Brian had been lonely ever since his wife and daughter had left him. Perhaps now it was time to win one of them back.

On reaching home he glanced in at the farmhouse before he went to muck out the pig hulls. 'Marjorie's coming home, Sally. Hopefully she'll visit you if she has the time. I'm glad she's coming back to see her father. Brian's missed her, although he'd never admit to it.'

'Marjorie coming home! When? How long for?' Sally's excitement swept away her earlier bad mood.

'Brian says she'll be here later today, staying a night or two. He's convinced himself she wants to make some kind of claim on his brass. It's all that man thinks about nowadays.'

'Today! Oh, it'll be lovely to see her again – it's been

so long. I wish she'd told me, but she hardly ever writes. She used to, but I've not heard from her in a good six months now.' Sally shook her head, smiling. If Marjorie didn't come to her, she would go across and drop in at the Harpers' tomorrow morning. Although their friendship had always been turbulent, she still classed Marjorie as a close friend. There had been nobody else to fill that role since she'd left. She liked Sarah a lot, but didn't see her at all outside of work.

'Aye, well, no doubt she's coming for a reason. I only hope it isn't what Brian thinks. She was always wanting something out of him, just like her mother.' Bob glowered. 'I'm going to start on those pig hulls before tea. Dick Harrison's delivering me three piglets on Monday, so that'll be a job for the Italian when he starts with us. That'll suit you, putting him in charge of the pigs,' he said with a half smile as he walked away.

Sally's voice floated out after him as he crossed the yard. 'A pig in with pigs! No matter what he does, I'll not like him.'

'You don't have to like him, just put up with him,' Bob yelled back, still with a smile on his face. Sally would come round in her own time, and meanwhile, Marjorie's return had given her something else to think about. Besides, the Italian wasn't coming to enter a popularity competition. He was coming to work, and that's what he would be doing.

Sunday was a day of rest in the Fothergill family, with only the essential jobs getting done. The previous day's post had brought a letter from Captain Bennett's office confirming that a prisoner of war had been made available to them, along with a list of what to do and what not to do while he was working on their property. He would be starting straight away on Monday.

'Luca Bugatti – what sort of a name is that?' Sally put the letter down on the table.

'It's a good one. He might own the Bugatti racing-car factory. I'll ask him when he comes,' Ben said, tilting back in his chair.

'You keep away from him, Ben, just until we get used to him,' Ivy said. 'And you and all, our Sally. He's only twenty-two, it says here – I hoped he would be a bit older, but never mind.' She looked across at Bob.

'He's been in the army, Mother. He's not going to be an old man, now, is he? We'll take him as we find him,' Bob said. 'If we're right with him, then he should be right with us. He couldn't be coming on a better day – I'm not working for Jim tomorrow and the piglets are arriving, so I'll be here to see how he shapes up. I'll set him on cleaning those two calf pens out now that the cattle are all in the fields. That will tell me if he's worth anything.' He lit his pipe and nodded at Sally. 'There's been no sign of Marjorie from next door. Are you not going to see her? I saw a posh car in the yard when I went up to the fell bottom earlier to put a straggling lamb back with its mother. So she must be here, and it looks like she's learned to drive.'

'I thought I might go before Sunday dinner. Is that all right, Mam? I hoped she would come and see me, but she and Brian must be making up for lost time.'

'Aye, you go and see her. You don't have to rush back.

80

It's only meat-and-potato pie for dinner, nowt fancy. It'll keep warm for you.' Ivy smiled. It would do Sally good to see her old friend and catch up on her news.

'Then I'll go rabbiting, Mam. There's tons of them in the wood, and I can sell them up at the railway station if it's Jack Sedgwick in the signal box. He sells them to the train drivers to take to Leeds. Good money that I put back into mending my bikes.' Ben grinned.

'All right – it'll be your own fault if your dinner isn't fit to eat when you come back. I'm not cooking all day; it is, after all, Sunday, not that any of us go to church until we need to.' Ivy shook her head fondly at her son. He was always planning something. Sunday dinner wasn't important in his eyes, and yet Ivy knew that plenty of city folk would have readily begged for her home-made pie.

'You'll not take all day, do you hear?' Bob said. 'And let's get this clear: when you start working at Morphet's for proper money, you put your share into the family pot. We'll need every penny if and when we move.' He watched as his children prepared to leave the house, looking as if they couldn't get away fast enough. 'You're too soft with them, Mother. I'd have made them both come back for one o'clock.'

'Aye, leave them be, Bob. Just let them enjoy their day.' Ivy looked at her husband. 'That Marjorie must have done all right for herself if there's a car in next door's yard.'

Bob didn't reply. Glancing at the Sunday newspaper, his eye had been caught by a headline: TROOPS ABOUT TO BEGIN A BIG PUSH. He thought about the young lads he knew who were fighting against the evil that had spread over Europe. What a bloody waste, and all for nothing, he said to himself as he lit his pipe.

Sally walked across the fell bottom, following the wall towards the stile she had climbed all her life in order to visit her friend next door. Memories of all the happy times they had shared flooded her mind as she went down the steep incline and then entered the Harpers' yard.

She secretly hoped that Marjorie was back for good. Sally had missed her so much as a friend, but she knew that after Marjorie had been made to give up her baby, things had changed in her life. Her old friend was no longer simply a farm lass from out of Dent. That was clear in the infrequent letters Marjorie sent, filled with details of her new life in Liverpool. Those salad days without a care between them had well and truly gone since the war had come along, she thought as she opened the garden gate, stood on the porch and knocked on the door. It was closed despite the warmth of the early June day.

Sally glanced across at the gleaming black Ford that stood in the yard and smiled. Trust Marjorie to do it in style, coming home in a car like that – it was just like her. She turned back to the door as she heard footsteps approaching inside and Marjorie's voice saying, 'I'll get it.' The ancient door handle moved and the door opened.

There was a second or two of hesitation as the two friends looked at one another, and then they both smiled and embraced. Sally could smell expensive perfume on her friend's elegant clothing as she held her close and whispered, 'It's so good to see you.'

'Oh, Sal, it is so good to see you! You have no idea how much I've missed you,' Marjorie gushed, holding her at arm's length. 'Look at you – hasn't life changed us? You would never think we were the same people from all those years ago.'

Sally smiled and looked down at her feet. She wasn't used to being called Sal and she certainly had not changed as much as Marjorie, who stood before her looking like a movie star. She now had the brassy peroxide hair she'd always wanted, and her face was made up; her bright cherry-red lipstick must have taken an age to apply so perfectly. Sally suddenly remembered that she'd always felt like the underdog compared to Marjorie. It looked as if, despite her fall from grace, her old friend had still managed to get everything she wanted from life.

'You look so glamorous! Are you here to stay? Your father must be so glad to see you,' Sally said. She could hear voices coming from the kitchen – Brian was talking to another man.

'Oh, Lord, no. It's only a flying visit to say goodbye to my father and give him the news that I am now married. Hank is with him in the kitchen. Would you like to come in and meet him?' Marjorie opened the door and let Sally walk down the hallway to the kitchen, where Brian stood with a tall, dark-haired man in an American uniform.

'Hank is a GI, and we got married in Liverpool last week. I'm to sail out to America next week – Kansas, where his family own a ranch.' Marjorie stood next to her handsome GI, slipping her arm into his. 'Isn't he cute and dishy?' She smiled and stood on her toes to kiss the six-foot soldier on his cheek.

Brian Harper said nothing. He looked down, fixing his gaze on the kitchen hearth, as Marjorie showed off her new husband to her oldest friend.

'You must be Miss Sally? I've heard a lot about you,' Hank said, offering her his hand to shake. 'I couldn't believe Marjorie said yes to my proposal, so we didn't hang about. My folks told me to send her over to them to keep herself safe. They think all of Britain is ablaze with the bombing – they don't realize that in the country you're relatively safe.' He smiled ruefully.

Sally returned the smile. Hank was the first GI she had ever seen in person, and he was certainly very handsome. His accent was different, too. She could see why Marjorie had decided to marry him – her friend had always been mad about American film stars.

'It's a pleasure to meet you, Hank. All this comes as a surprise! You should have written and told me, Marjorie – I could at least have sent you a card.' Sally looked at Marjorie, who was still holding onto Hank's arm with a determinedly bright expression.

'They've only known one another two months. Two months, I tell you! And she's daft enough to trail off to America. Nowt's changed.' Brian Harper sat down suddenly in his chair beside the cold fireplace. He looked up at his daughter, then at Sally. 'She's come for my blessing, but it's a bit late for that – she's already wed!'

'Father, don't spoil it. We love one another, and that's all that matters. I just wish you would give us your blessing before we leave. Why, you might never see me again.'

Sensing the growing tension in the kitchen, Sally thought she'd better not get involved. 'Marjorie, I'm afraid Mam will be putting dinner on the table; I'd better get back. I'm sorry I can't stay, but it's been lovely to see you.' She turned to leave.

'Thanks for coming to see me, Sally. I'm sorry I haven't been keeping in touch. I'll send you my address when I'm settled in Kansas. You never know – perhaps you could come and visit me sometime,' Marjorie said as they walked back out of the farmhouse. 'Have you not got another fella yet? Surely somebody's taken your eye by now? It's no good living in the past, you know. You've got to move on.'

Sally met Marjorie's gaze and realized for the first time how shallow she actually was. 'No; I'll be faithful to Edward until I know what has become of him. There's nobody else in my life. But I'm happy for you, Marjorie. I wish you all the best in Kansas, and Hank seems a nice fella.' She put her arms around her oldest friend, knowing as she hugged her that this was the last time she would see Marjorie Harper. Dentdale never had been enough for her, unlike Sally, for whom it was where her heart lay in more than one way.

'Did you see Marjorie? You've not been long,' Ivy said, placing the meat-and-potato pie on the table as Sally slumped into her chair next to her father.

85

'Yes, I saw her; but I'll not be seeing her again in a hurry,' Sally said glumly.

'Why, whatever is up?' Ivy dished the dinner up, setting a plate aside for Ben in the cooling oven.

'She's got married to a GI and she's moving to America. She only came back to say goodbye to her father. But I don't think she should have bothered – she's only made things worse between them.' Sally tried to keep the concern out of her voice. 'You should see her, Mam. She's like a blinking film star, done up to high heaven with permed blonde hair. She made me feel like a poor little farm girl.'

'She always was a bit of a tart. I bet the lad has money, else she wouldn't be looking at him.' Bob picked up his knife and fork. 'Going to America isn't going to solve her problems.'

Ivy looked at her daughter and guessed what she was thinking. 'You are the bonniest woman up the dale, our Sally. Hers will be all fake – it always was. Happiness will be yours one day, don't you worry. She can run away, but she can't hide from what she is.' She set her serving spoon down firmly and turned to the window, her eye caught by Ben crossing the farmyard. He had six rabbits in one hand and a bag of snares over his shoulder.

'Looks like you'll be calling in to see Jack Sedgwick in the signal box again soon, Father,' Ivy said. She went to the doorway, calling out, 'I hope you are going to gut and clean them? Once you've cleaned them, put them in my pantry, they'll keep fresh in there. But not until you have hung them in the outhouse for an hour or two – I don't want blood on my pantry floor.' She stood and watched her son, hands on her hips. If it wasn't one fella treading muck into her spotless, well-loved house, it was another, she thought. Ben pulled a face at her but did as he was told and changed course towards the outhouse.

Ivy returned to the table and sat down with a sigh. 'Aye, poor Brian,' she said. 'It'll have broken his heart to see Marjorie leave again.'

'He's not had much luck with his womenfolk,' Bob agreed. 'Now, I have luck there, but not with brass. But even that's beginning to look better nowadays, isn't it, my old lass? I have everything a man could wish for – a family that loves me, a roof over my head and food in my belly. So I'm saying nowt.'

'You soft old lump, Bob Fothergill,' Ivy said. She often found herself thinking how lucky they all were, despite the hardships they sometimes endured. Family love was everything, and even if they didn't always see eye to eye, there was plenty of it in the Fothergill home.

Chapter 8

'Now, whatever he is and whatever he looks like, you'll be right with him, Sally. It's me he's answerable to, after all,' Bob reminded his daughter. They were standing at the bottom of the farm lane, waiting for the army truck to offload the POW who was causing so much bad feeling between the Fothergills.

'I'll be civil, but that's all I'll be, Father. I still don't think we should have him here. He's the enemy as far as I'm concerned.' Sally tried to keep calm. She was determined not to make Luca Bugatti's life an easy one.

'Right, well, hold your whisht – I can hear the wagon coming. Now, you'll have to sign for him tomorrow morning when I'm not here, so I'll introduce you to the driver.'

'Good morning. Robert Fothergill, correct?' A guard emerged from the wagon and jumped down. He wore khaki and had a clipboard in his hand. 'You are taking delivery of Luca Bugatti for the day and are happy to take responsibility for him until we return this evening?'

His tone was brusque. Without waiting for an answer, he made his way to the back of the vehicle and began to pull back the tarpaulin that covered the POWs.

'Aye, that's me, and this is my daughter, Sally. She'll take over tomorrow morning and on any other days when I can't take charge of him myself,' Bob replied. He glanced at Sally, who stood silently at the side of the track and watched as her father signed the paperwork.

'As long as you're happy with that. Any problems, you must let us know as soon as possible and we'll come and collect him.' The guard called into the wagon, 'Bugatti! Out you get. You are signed over to Mr Fothergill. We will be back for you at five. Do as you are told and don't make any bother.'

Bob watched as a young man climbed out of the back of the wagon, dressed in the overalls issued by the Ministry and bearing the distinctive red spot to denote that he was a prisoner of war. He was tall and lean, clean shaven, with slicked-back black hair. He stood for a moment and looked around him before offering an extended hand to Bob.

'This'en, I'm sure, thinks he's here on holiday. He expects to be made welcome wherever he goes. But he's a good worker. You'll get used to him,' the guard said as he tied the tarpaulin back down and opened the door of his cab. Climbing in, he turned back one last time to add, 'Five o'clock sharp, remember.' With that, the wagon drove off.

Bob hesitated before shaking Luca's outstretched hand. 'Well, lad, at least you have manners if nowt else,' he

89

said, sizing the younger man up. 'Now, let's be about some work.'

'Work, yes – I am here for work,' Luca said agreeably, and then he spotted Sally. '*Ciao, come sta?*'

'We'll have none of that Italian rubbish, whatever you're saying to my lass. English, do you hear? Now come on, shift!' Bob urged Luca up the lane. Sally followed, saying nothing.

'I just say hello. I see her in the shop,' Luca explained. He glanced back towards Sally as if seeking confirmation. She avoided his gaze.

'Aye, well – think in English, then I'll know what you're saying.' Bob looked at Sally. 'She's called Sally, and "Mr Fothergill" will do me just fine. Let's get you to work mucking out a shed or two.'

'Mucking out?' Luca enquired, studying Bob's weather-beaten face.

'Aye. Fork and shovel, clean out?' Bob mimed moving muck.

'*Sì*, yes, I do it.' Luca glanced back once more at Sally. He couldn't believe his luck at having been placed on the farm where the girl who'd taken his eye lived.

Bob set Luca to work, showing him the calf sheds that needed cleaning out; dirt and bedding had built up over the winter from housing two calves that were now out in his fields. He watched for ten minutes to make sure Luca understood what to do – forking the nearly foot-deep bedding of straw and dirt into a wheelbarrow, and then taking it to the muck heap. The next stage would be for him to spread it on the land. Bob briefly wondered whether he should really have let the POW loose with a fork, but thought better of it as he saw how efficiently Luca went about the job.

'I'm going into the house now, and later I'll be over there,' Bob said. He hoped Luca would understand and not decide to run away while his back was turned.

'*Si*,' Luca acknowledged as he picked up a forkful of heavy dung and straw. His glance followed Bob's pointing finger in the direction of the pig hulls. He knew that he would be given all the worst jobs to do on the farm, but he didn't mind. Anything was better than being cooped up in the workhouse.

'Well, what's he like?' Ivy said as she made Bob a morning brew.

'Well, didn't Sally tell you she knows him from the shop? He knew her straight away. Where is she? She didn't follow us to the calf sheds.'

'She's hanging the clean sheets out in the orchard. It's too good a drying day to miss, so I changed our bed. She never said nowt, though, just said he was here.'

'He knew her as soon as he saw her,' Bob said again. He looked up from his brew as Sally came back in with the woven washing basket under her arm.

'He kens you, but you never said owt. Where's he seen you? Does he come into the shop?' Bob fired questions at his daughter.

'I've only seen him the once. He's the one who came in last week and bought cigarettes. I mentioned it, remember? He was helping the vicar in the churchyard,'

Sally replied. She put the basket away and went to the sink to finish washing her smalls through.

'Cigarettes, aye, I remember you saying.' Bob shook his head. 'Bloody hell – I have to think twice before I buy my ounce of Kendal Twist, and the POWs can have fags.'

'Mrs Middleton says they're allowed a packet a week, which they're given down at Loftus Hill. Anything else depends on what they're given when they help out. I asked her because I didn't think he should be getting them,' Sally replied evenly.

'Well, bugger me. They'll never want to go home if we look after them that well.' Bob drained his tea.

'I'm frightened he'll run away when you're not about,' Ivy said worriedly. 'Or what if he turns nasty, and Sally and I are on our own? And when she's at the shop, I'll be by myself.'

'We haven't got him every day, Mother. I only signed up to have him three days a week; I'm not having him here when you're on your own. And if he runs away, where the heck's he going to run to? It's a long way off, is Italy. There's a lot of water to swim before he'd get there, and that big red spot on his overalls tells you what he is.' Bob smiled. His women were rightly concerned, but from what he had seen so far of his farmhand, they needn't be. 'I'll take him a brew and see how he's doing. Then I'll set about whitewashing that last hull for the pigs coming tonight. It should be dry by this afternoon if I leave the door open.'

'Will he drink tea? I'll give him this old cracked mug. It can be his while working for us.' Ivy reached into the back of the cupboard and took out a mug she'd been planning to throw away. She put a scant spoonful of tea leaves into it without using the teapot before filling it up.

'Well, if he doesn't drink tea, he's going to go thirsty. He'll want his dinner and all, Mother. He's fed later on down at Loftus Hill, but he will need something to keep him going,' Bob said, heading for the door with the mug in his hand.

'I know. But he eats outside until we get to know him and trust him,' Ivy replied.

'That will be never, if I have anything to do with it,' Sally said, not lifting her eyes from the clothes she was scrubbing.

'Give him a chance, Sally. He may not be so bad, no matter who he is or where he comes from.' Despite her own doubts about Luca, Ivy was concerned about how bitter her daughter always sounded at the moment.

'We'll see.' Sally gave her mother a tight smile and got on with the job at hand.

'Now then, lad – you're doing a grand job for me, that's for sure.' Bob stood and looked at the work Luca had already done, and was impressed.

'*Mi scusi* – "grand"?'

'Good lad. Grand means good when you're in Yorkshire,' Bob said, passing him the mug of tea.

'You think? *Grazie*. It is like being back home. I am used to this work.' Luca drank deeply from the mug. 'My father is a farmer. I am used to hard work.'

'A farmer, you say? Well, I never. Sheep or cows?' Bob asked. This news made him see the lad in a different light.

93

'Wheat, cornfields and tomatoes. No animals,' Luca replied, and smiled. 'I try to speak in English, but it is not that good. But I know my animals.'

'It's better than my Italian, lad, that's for sure. In fact, I only just speak English, according to some. So why are you a soldier here?' Bob asked with interest.

'Mussolini, he is in bed with the Nazis. I was made to fight. I would rather be home with my family. My father and sisters.' A dark cloud came over Luca's face. 'He is, as you say, a traitor to his country. I spit on him and Hitler.' He spat a mouthful of saliva into the dust of the yard.

'So you hate them as much as we do, eh? I'll tell my lot; they will be glad to hear it. Now, I've work to do, I've some pigs to be delivered later today.' Bob started to walk away.

'Pigs – *porco?*' Luca said.

'Aye, *porco* for us to eat. But these will be for bacon.' Bob grinned.

'*La pancetta*, bacon. They will taste good. *Si?*'

'Aye, lad, that they will. And they will make us money, hopefully.' Bob smiled. His new farm lad might not be English, and he was difficult to understand. But he was a farmer, and that was what mattered – as well as being on the right side of the war.

Sally and her father looked over the pigsty's half-open door and watched the four young piglets curl up in their newly whitewashed hull, half hidden by the new straw and bracken that Bob had put down for their arrival.

'They're so bonny when they first come. Look at their little curly tails! So clean and pink.' Sally gazed down at the new arrivals. She was beginning to question whether she'd be able to eat them once they were slaughtered.

'You'll not give it a second thought when your mother's cooking you ham and eggs and the smell of it fills the kitchen. Nowt better than a good frying of bacon, some new potatoes and a fried egg. We want for nothing, when you think about it,' Bob said. He glanced sideways at his daughter as she leaned over the door next to him. 'Did you know *porco* is Italian for pig, and *pancetta* is Italian for bacon? Our POW told me. Seemingly he's a farmer's lad from Tuscany. Never wanted to get involved in this war. Hates the Nazis and Mussolini.'

'He's got you speaking Italian? Now that's a novelty! He's still an Italian, Father. I won't be trusting him, no matter what he tells you,' Sally protested.

But she couldn't ignore the nagging thought that her father might have a point. And Sarah had said something similar, too, in the shop last week – Luca was here in a foreign land without his family, just as her Edward might be. Perhaps she should give him a bit of slack.

Besides, she'd glimpsed him a time or two in the course of the day, and he'd seemed like a hard worker and pleasant enough. She was also finding it hard to ignore how good-looking he was, despite not wanting to admit that to herself. It had been a long time since she'd even noticed a man in that way, but Luca was exceptionally handsome.

It probably couldn't hurt to be more talkative with him in the morning, she thought, as she watched the new arrivals. *Porco* was not so far from *pork*; perhaps there wasn't such a lot of difference between Italians and English people after all.

Back in the kitchen, she picked up a letter that had been waiting for her since that morning. She recognized the writing as Marjorie's and the postmark confirmed it had been sent from Liverpool, but she was in no hurry to open it.

'Are you not going to read that, then? It looks like it's from Marjorie,' Ivy said.

Sally put the letter in her pocket. 'I'll read it later, Mam. It doesn't matter what she says in it; she's gone now. I'll not ever see her again, I don't think.'

'Now, you don't know that,' Ivy said. 'She might have changed her mind. Or she might come back to visit home a time or two once she's settled. I'll say this for her, she's braver than I'd be, going to live with a family she knows hardly anything about in a different country.'

Sally went upstairs, sat on the edge of her bed and opened the envelope to find a single sheet of notepaper with a hastily scribbled message in Marjorie's hand. There was no address.

Just thought I'd say goodbye, Sally. I'm sorry I hadn't more time to see you. I'm about to get onto a huge liner bound for America. A new life for me. Who knows, I might become a film star if I'm lucky!

Although I should just be happy being Hank's wife.
You look after yourself. Try and find the happiness
you deserve. Don't live in the past.

I'll write with my new address when I get settled.
Take care.

Love, Marjorie xx

Sally gazed down at the letter for a long time. She knew exactly what Marjorie was trying to tell her: forget Edward, and move on with her life. That would probably be easy for Marjorie to do, but not for her. Once she was true to someone, she would be true to them no matter what, or who, came into her life. She would always be Edward's until she knew exactly what had become of him.

Chapter 9

6 June 1944

Sally felt her hand tremble as she signed the workhouse guard's paperwork, taking direct responsibility for Luca.

'Thank you, Miss. We'll collect him at five. Any bother, let us know,' the guard said. He called to the men in the back of the wagon to keep quiet as Luca climbed down.

Luca jumped down the last step. His fellow inmates were gazing out of the back of the wagon, and they whooped and yelled as it drove away. He shouted back in a language unfamiliar to Sally and then said apologetically, 'Scusi, they are, how you say? Ignorante.'

Sally smiled. 'It's not your fault.'

They walked up the lane side by side. After a few moments' silence, she said, 'Today and tomorrow, if the rain stays off, my father wants you to spread the muck on our two meadows. To help the grass grow.' She pretended she had a fork in her hand and mimed moving the manure from the midden to the field.

'*Si*, Mr Fothergill gave me orders yesterday. He also says no hanky-panky, but I don't know what that means. Hanky-panky, what is that?' Luca asked. Sally blushed.

'It means you have to behave, that's all.' She went quiet as she thought about her father, keeping all in line even while he wasn't there.

'Ah, *si*, I behave, not like some of the Germans. I am glad that you have me, not them,' Luca replied.

As they walked into the yard, he headed straight for the muck midden next to the shippon and grabbed the fork. 'Mr Fothergill showed me the fields. I work now. I fill the cart and then you will get the horse?'

Sally watched him, noticing how his olive-toned skin set off his dark eyes and black hair. She felt her heart flutter but forced herself to concentrate on the task at hand. 'Can I trust you to get on with the work? I'll be in the shippon, sweeping it out, if you need me.' She pointed at herself and then at the shippon.

Luca started piling the first load of muck onto the cart that Bob had parked next to the muck heap. '*Si*, Luca good worker. No problemo.'

Sally turned away, and he dug into the strong-smelling pile of manure. It was going to be another morning of hard work, but at least he was alive, unlike some of his colleagues in the Italian army – and his mother.

Luca hated the Germans as much as anybody. Before Mussolini had been allied with Hitler, he had watched Germans come into his home village in Tuscany and plunder what they could from every family. His mother had run out of the house, hoping to hide some of their valuables, and he had watched helplessly as a soldier had lifted his gun and shot her dead without hesitation. The memory of that moment was on Luca's mind all the time, still as vivid as the day it had happened – he should have stopped her, he should have killed the soldier. Instead he had found himself caught in the fray of war, fighting a people with whom he had no grievance.

Luca spat on the ground and pressed on with his job. The manure smelt ten times sweeter than any dirty Nazi, he thought as he wielded the fork.

Sally took hold of the yard brush and started to clean where the two cows she milked had stood. It was at least easier now that they'd been let out into the pasture for spring. A few years ago they'd only had the one milk cow – a house cow, just for the milk they used at home. Now they had two, and her father had bought two calves earlier in the year. Money was getting a little bit easier, and he was ploughing it back into his dream of owning his own farm and having more stock.

She leaned for a moment against the old wood of the cow boose, looking around her. This, she thought, was the difference between herself and Marjorie. Marjorie liked the finer things in life, while Sally was happy sweeping out a whitewashed, cobbled shippon. There was a lot of difference between the sweetest-smelling perfume and the fragrance of cows and hay, but she knew which one she would miss the most if it was taken away.

Marjorie would be sailing her way to a new life in America now, and Sally would probably never hear from or see her again; meanwhile, she was content at home on the farm. Her father always said there was only land, sea and sky, wherever you went. Mind you, he had never been out of Yorkshire, so he didn't really know what he was missing, she mused as she pushed the yard brush forward with a large helping of cow muck. It would be added to the cart for Luca to spread later on. She swept it all into a heap and then pushed it onto the shovel and carried it out towards where he was working.

'No, no, *bella*, I do that for you.' Luca dropped his fork and took the shovel out of her hand. 'I do this for you. This is not a job for you.' He went into the shippon, scraped up the remaining manure, and added it to the cart.

'I like doing it. It's my job,' Sally said, with her hands on her hips.

'No, I am here for this. I help you where I can, *si*,' Luca replied, and then got back to his own work. 'No work for a lady.'

'I'm no lady.' Sally glanced up at the sky, then watched him for a few moments as he piled the manure into the cart. 'Do you want a drink? I'll go and get us both one, and then I'll finish washing down the shippon.' She was warming to the POW; he definitely was not what she had expected.

'Drink, *si* – a *caffè*?'

'No, not from a cafe. A mug of tea from my mum,' Sally said, and smiled. 'There's no cafes around here. I'll go and get us one.'

'Coffee? No?' Luca asked hopefully.

'Sorry, only tea here. No, coffee is too expensive, and you can't buy it for love nor money.' Sally shook her head. They never drank coffee, not even if they could afford it. Tea was the order of the day, and even that was on ration. The tea leaves had to be used at least twice.

'*Grazie*,' Luca replied, and watched as Sally made her way across the farmyard and into the house. He was indeed lucky to be working for the Fothergills. He filled his fork again and waited for her to return.

'Are you all right with that'en out there? He's not giving you any bother, is he?' Ivy said as she poured tea into the mug she had decided was good enough for an Italian. Sally handed her the biscuit tin, and Ivy begrudgingly gave her a shortbread biscuit each for herself and Luca.

'He's all right. He's a worker, I'll give him his due. He's never stopped, and he says he wants to clean the shippon of a morning. I told him that's my job when Dad isn't here.' Sally went to the sideboard, took down a tray and put the mugs of tea and biscuits on it. 'Come and talk to him. Some words I don't understand, but most I do.'

'I might at dinner time, but he's here to work, don't you forget that. Make sure he does. Don't spoil him. I thought you weren't going to talk to him, let alone serve him with tea and biscuits.' Ivy saw a flush come to her daughter's cheeks.

'He's a soldier who didn't want to fight, just as you

102

told me. Edward might be doing the same somewhere in Germany or France. Don't worry, he'll earn his tea and biscuits by the time today is out. We don't have any coffee, do we? He's used to coffee,' Sally added quickly.

'Coffee? Lass, we don't drink that foreign stuff. He can drink tea like the rest of us, and like it. He should be on water. Aye, I don't know – one minute you hate every bone of his body and the next you're asking for coffee for him,' Ivy said sharply. She watched as Sally left the kitchen. At least her daughter was being civil. Come dinner time, she would see what this POW looked like to make her change her mind so much.

'I, too, am a farmer. We have wheat and cornfields, and it is warm. Sunny skies, with those flying above.' Luca leaned against the limestone wall and pointed up at the swallows ducking and diving and screeching over the yard. There were dark clouds massing on the horizon, and he thought wistfully of the warmth of the Italian sun, the olive groves and the simple food that made it his home. He missed his family.

He sipped his tea, looked at Sally, and nodded and smiled as he took a bite of shortbread. 'Good.'

'It's my mam's shortbread. It's full of butter.' Sally set down her mug and pushed herself up to sit on the wall top. 'Have you got cows at home? Or sheep?'

'No. We farm corn and wheat. A goat for milk, and a horse; some *pollo*.' Luca pointed at the hens, scratching in the dust of the farmyard and pecking at the groundsel around the barn.

'Hens. Chickens,' Sally said, and smiled.

'*Si*, chicken. I learn better English with you? *Si?*'

'We'll see.' Sally found it hard to imagine a farm with just wheat and cornfields – and olives, whatever they were. No animals, apart from those that worked or kept the family in milk. It must be a boring place, she thought as she ate her shortbread. As they sat quietly, she found herself thinking about Edward and how he might feel about her fraternizing with the enemy. Although Luca didn't seem much like the enemy, now that she was getting to know him.

'Back to work.' Sally glanced up at the darkening sky. 'I'll finish cleaning the shippon and then I'll get the horse. You're a quick worker; the cart's nearly half full already.' She stood up and watched as Luca did as he was told. He was going to be a boon to the farm; her father had been right. Usually it would have been Bob loading the muck and spreading it when he came home from an already hard day at work, with the aid of Ben, who would complain every minute he was having to lift a loaded fork. Now, the job would already be done and life would be a bit easier – although, knowing her father, he'd think of another scheme to fill his hours and make him some money.

Chapter 10

Bob put his head down, almost lying flat over the fuel tank of his motorbike as he climbed slowly up the twisting, winding, steep road to Dent station. The clouds had burst and although the morning was still warm, torrential rain was sweeping down over the dale in sheets.

At last he reached the station-yard entrance. He climbed off his bike and stood in his oilskins with the bag of cleaned rabbits over his back. Looking up at the white station house, he waved to the stationmaster's wife as she stood in her bay window looking out over the dale. Margaret always liked to see who was coming for the train so that she could come down for a natter if she knew them, providing she had time and the weather was good. Today she just waved back and watched as Bob made his way through the maroon-painted gates and along the platform towards the signal box, passing and nodding at people he knew as they waited for the next train.

Jack Sedgwick would be in the box in charge of the line as far as Blea Moor tunnel. He would make Bob welcome with a cup of tea and a good line in local gossip, just until the weather subsided, and then Bob could go on to his walling job at Jim Mattinson's fell allotments. The walls had been somewhat neglected and would give him work well into summer if the weather played along. He was thankful for that, but not during a heavy shower like this, he thought as he walked up the steep steps into the signal box. He knocked on the small glass panes of the door to let Jack know he was there.

He could see that Jack had the small stove lit inside the box, the fire burning bright and the old iron kettle on one side of the top plate ready for his next brew. Jack was, like everybody else in the dale, a man of many jobs: he was a signalman, a farmer, and when days were quiet in the signal box he would occasionally give a good haircut to those in the know. That was in addition to selling anything and everything to the train drivers and passengers who pulled up when their steam trains took on water from the water tanks before attempting the long drag to Carlisle or going down to Leeds. Ben had made the most of this service and kept Jack well supplied with rabbits, earning himself and his family a nice bit of spending money.

'You're not up on the fell tops this morning walling, are you?' Jack said as he opened the door and let Bob into his refuge. 'It's piss wet through, man, although it gives out to get brighter again before long.'

'Aye, not the best of mornings, but our lad had these

rabbits to drop off with you.' Bob stepped into the cramped signal box, filled with levers to change the use of the lines and operate the signals. Bells and wires were everywhere to make Jack aware of oncoming trains. 'And I'm hoping you might give my hair a trim. It's getting long, and I've a bit of business to do down the dale in a while, so I'd better look respectable. Jim won't mind me camping here until the weather lifts. He knows I'll make up the time when he needs me.'

'That lad and his rabbits! Your place must be wick with them. The train drivers from Leeds can't get enough of them. There's not much meat up for grabs in the towns and cities, with the rationing. I always reckon rabbit tastes like a herby chicken, and it's good for you anyway, so they do right to buy it. Are they cleaned but not skinned, I hope, as usual? I'll hang them up outside the box. They can stop for a moment to pick them up and pay for them.'

Jack took the rabbits out of the bag and went outside with them into the pouring rain. He hung them up on a purpose-made hook between the track and signal box, just the right height for a train driver to reach across and do an exchange. He then came back in, pushed the kettle on to boil and gave Bob's hair an assessing glance.

'I'll wait until the next train comes through, then I'll give you a quick shearing. You've more hair on you than Irving's old Herdwicks, and it's the same colour,' he laughed as he passed his friend a strong brew of tea.

'Aye, I know, it's gone grey of late. You'd hardly know it used to be black as jet. That's what getting married and having responsibilities does for you. This bloody war hasn't helped.' Bob took a long sip from the enamel mug. He looked up as a bell rang inside the signal box.

'Aye up, the train's on its way, just leaving Blea Moor. Give us a minute to check my levers and make sure she's on the right track. She'll be pulling in before you know it. Your rabbits might be sold while you're here if it's the right driver, but the Leeds drivers are more likely to buy them.' Jack stood in the centre of the box and pulled on a cream-and-brass lever as he looked down the curve of the railway line towards Arten Gill's massive viaduct, where a cloud of steam was visible coming through the cutting. The approaching train was on time, and a crowd of people waited on the platform. The station master stood in front of them all, ensuring their safety as the train approached in its cloak of steam.

Bob looked at the passengers getting ready to board and recognized a lot of Dent locals. They would be visiting relations in Garsdale or going to the market day in Hawes, seeing it was Tuesday. Some would even be going as far as Carlisle for a larger shop, if they had the money and stamps in their ration books. All of them looked keen to get out of the wet as their train approached, passing the signal box and the rabbits before pulling up alongside the platform.

'No takers on this train, Bob, but there's plenty more to come.' Jack glanced down the platform. 'Hey up – I saw that bugger of a Birbeck lad heading off back to barracks yesterday. He'd not been home long, but I didn't think we'd ever see him again.'

'Oh, aye?'

'He'd been home to see his mother. He got off the Carlisle train on Saturday. Told Alf at the station he had a pass to come home before being mobilized for a big push. But you can't believe a word the devil says, so we took it with a pinch of salt. Although it must be right, else he wouldn't have gone back so soon. What surprised me was, he had sergeant's stripes on his arm. The army must have made something of him after all.' Jack shook his head and reached for the scissors he kept hanging on a nail in the signal box. 'I wonder if he went to see the Redman lass? He'd be in for a shock if he did. Alison has done well for herself, even with his baby to be taken in. Young Hartley married her. She deserved better than Birbeck, anyway.'

Bob nodded. Jonathan Birbeck had been the scandal of Dent for a good while, fathering two children at the same time to different young lasses, and then even after he went into the army he thought about absconding. Most felt the village had been well rid of him, but his time spent away at war had obviously changed things.

He decided not to mention this news at home. It would only upset Sally. She had told him that Jonathan and her Edward had always hated one another, and now the Birbeck lad was still alive while Edward was who knew where. It's always the good'ens that go first, Bob reflected as Jack combed his wiry locks and began to snip.

'You know, there's only one other fella round here with hair like yours, and that's Arthur Metcalfe. He has hair just like yours, and it was jet black when

109

he was younger. He takes a long time to make respectable an' all,' Jack said as he snipped away. Bob could see clippings of his peppered grey hair falling to the floor of the signal box.

'Looks like the day's going to get out after all,' Jack added after a moment. 'The cloud's clearing from over Coombe Scar. You'll be able to get some walling done after I've done this. I'll get you shorn just in time for the goods train on the downline. You'll look like a different man. Ivy won't be able to keep her hands off you,' he said with a twinkle in his eye.

'I think those days have gone. We're a bit steady nowadays.' Bob grinned.

'Well, I hear that you're thinking of moving. You know what they say: new house, new baby.' Jack smirked.

'By God, folk do talk. You can't take a pee round here without folk knowing about it. I'm interested in Deep Well, but there's a difference between being interested and being able to afford it.' Bob brushed his shoulders free of hair trimmings.

'Well, you never usually come here for your haircut – Ivy usually does it. So you must be going to see somebody fairly important.' Jack hung his scissors back up and took a small hand mirror down from the same place, showing Bob his handiwork.

'Tha's scalped me, but I suppose it'll grow back.' Bob rubbed his hand over his head. 'How much do I owe you?'

'Just a crown, that'll do it,' Jack replied.

'You sure your name's not Dick Turpin? He robbed

110

folk and all.' Bob put his hand in his pocket and paid him. 'Do you think you could sell some bacon and pork to the train drivers this autumn? I've taken on some extra pigs, but no questions asked, and money up front. I don't want the War Ag to find out, so keep it to yourself.'

'Aye, I think I can find you interested customers. Every penny will help towards that fresh farm in Garsdale. And you know me – mum's the word.' Jack opened the signal-box door as the bell rang again, warning of an oncoming train.

'Right, I'll sort it. Leave it with me. There'll be more money in pigs than in rabbits, that's for sure.' Bob smiled as he made his way down the steps. The sun was trying to break through the grey skies, showing glimpses of blue above. It would be another good day for repairing the walls between Dent and Garsdale, and while he was doing that, his fields would be getting spread with the manure they needed to make everything grow. All done by his new farm hand that cost nowt.

Chapter 11

Arriving home later on, Bob found his wife and daughter in the kitchen preparing the evening meal.

'How did you get on with the Italian?' he asked. 'I see he's spread the bottom meadow. Now we're getting a bit of rain to make the grass grow, we'll be right.'

'He worked well and caused no problems,' Sally said quietly. 'He'll do the other meadow tomorrow, if the weather's decent.'

'A bit of rain'll not harm him. It'll make him work faster,' Bob grinned. Ivy watched them, expecting Sally to give a tart reply.

'He could patch and mend the shippon door if it's wet again. I noticed it rotting on the bottom,' Sally said. She kept her tone non-committal, trying not to sound as if she cared what the man she'd sworn to hate was given to do.

'I didn't think you'd be bothered what he did, or if he caught pneumonia. You've changed your tune about him since yesterday.' Bob looked with surprise at his daughter.

'I'm not bothered, but there's plenty he could be doing. He could clean the horse tack, I'm forever doing it,' Sally replied distractedly. The kitchen radio was on, and she reached across and turned the volume up as the announcer described the day's events in Normandy.

Ivy paused in her work to listen. 'It must be carnage on those beaches. Those poor lads! At least America and the Commonwealth countries are with us now. They'll show them bloody Jerries this time.'

Operation Overlord had been put into action, with the beaches of Normandy being taken by Allied soldiers from all over the world. The push to overthrow Hitler and Mussolini was under way: France was alive with soldiers, marines, gliders and bombers, all seeking revenge and pressing Hitler back to where he belonged. The liberation of France and the Netherlands was in full flow, despite the loss of many a good soldier.

'It's worse than the last time they were on those beaches. Listen to the broadcaster – you can hear the desperation and fear in his voice. What a waste of life. I wish it was all over.' Sally's voice was trembling.

'It soon will be, hopefully,' Ivy reassured her. 'And about time. We've got off lightly up here – imagine if you were living in London, or on the coast. They've been bombed relentlessly these last few years. And now they have the threat of those flying bombs that they can only hear when they're about to drop on them! Thank heavens we're up here.'

Bob nodded, sitting down at the table. 'And we don't go without half of what Londoners do.'

They all fell silent as they listened, trying to imagine

the scene of a battle bigger than anything the coast of Normandy had yet seen.

'It seems a lifetime ago that I said goodbye to Edward,' Sally said after a few moments. 'Neither of us had any idea what was going to happen. I sometimes wish he'd done the same as Jonathan Birbeck and thought about absconding.'

'Well, the Birbeck lad's not absconding now. I think he's in the thick of it,' Bob said. Sally and Ivy looked at him, puzzled. 'I wasn't going to mention it, lass, but Jack told me that he saw Jonathan leaving Dent on a train yesterday, heading back to his unit. He'd been on a pass to visit his mother, supposedly. He was cutting it pretty fine to get back in time.'

'He must have wanted to see his family badly. It's a wonder they let him,' Ivy said quietly. So much gossip had swirled around Jonathan Birbeck in recent years, and now he was in the midst of all this.

'I know it's been an age since he visited the dale, but do you know if anyone asked him about Edward?' Sally said urgently.

Bob shook his head. 'No, lass, we don't know. But Jonathan told the station master that he was going back to join in "a big push" – he'll be mixed up in this lot, no doubt about it. It's to be hoped he'll keep his head down, along with the other lads by his side.'

Tears welled up in Sally's eyes. Ivy patted her arm. 'Aye, love. It's past time to lay Edward's ghost to rest and get on with your life.'

'I can't, Mam. I still love him – I can't just forget him,' Sally said quietly.

'I know, lass, but he wouldn't want you to waste your life. Start looking to the future, Sally – this war won't be going on so long now. The Jerries are running out of steam. We'll have them on the run soon, now the Yanks and Russians are giving them what for. Time for you to live your life, else you'll end up on the shelf a lonely old maid,' Ivy said gently. She wondered whether to give her daughter a hug, something rarely done in a Dales household.

'I'm listening, Mam. And I'm trying, I really am. Perhaps when this war is over, I'll find somebody. Don't worry about me. I'm feeling a bit brighter than I did.' Sally blew her nose and managed a watery smile. 'As you say, the war can't go on for ever.'

'*Buongiorno*, Sally.' Luca jumped down from the wagon and grinned. He was delighted to be seeing so much of this young woman who, when they first met, hadn't even been willing to look at him, let alone talk to him.

'Morning, Luca,' Sally replied as she signed the usual papers releasing him into the farm's care. 'How are you?'

'I am now, you say, happy! The Germans, they are getting, errr – a hammering? I hear guards talking. I will soon be able to go home.'

'Not for a while yet. They've only just started the invasion. It could go on for years,' Sally replied. But she smiled as she said it.

'I like here, but home better. War finishes soon, I know it will,' Luca said confidently as they entered the farmyard.

He was surprised to see Bob there, standing and looking out over the pasture gate.

'Now then, lad, you can finish spreading the muck later on. I'm not working for Jim this morning, I've some walling of my own needing doing. So I thought, if you could start by turning your hand to it with me . . .' Bob noticed how Luca looked at Sally to help translate.

Sally went to the garden wall and pointed at it, then turned and looked at the limestone walls that made the countryside appear like a patchwork quilt. 'Walls – building?'

'Ah, I understand,' Luca replied.

'Aye, but it's up there on the knot, right up on the fellside. A bit of a walk.' Bob grinned. His POW was in for a full day of graft, but at least the weather was fine. He opened the gate and summoned Luca to follow him up the side of the fell without waiting for Sally to explain any more to his able worker.

Sally watched them make their way through the gate. Luca looked back at her with an expression of doubt and worry, and she smiled. 'I'll bring you both something to eat and drink at dinner time,' she called, but they were already some distance away and neither replied. She saw Bob put his weight on his walking stick as Luca followed after him like a faithful dog.

She turned back towards the house. It hadn't escaped her notice how dejected Luca had seemed as he'd realized that he wouldn't be working around her today, but with Bob. Sally felt a slight pang of something she couldn't quite put her finger on. It was almost disappointing that she wouldn't see much of the farm's newest asset.

'Now, lad, watch!' Bob said. Luca stood next to him as he bent over the drystone wall and rummaged through the stones that had fallen from the gap onto the rough fell land. 'These are called flats – the ones that fit in if you jiggle them about a bit. Little stones are fillers, long ones are called througher, and the big ones are top stones.' Bob held up a sample of each stone and said their names. He listened to Luca repeat them before moving on to show him where each and every stone went, and why.

'We no do this in Italy. No walls,' Luca said as he bent down to help Bob rebuild the wall.

'Aye, I can tell that. No wonder they said Rome wasn't built in a day.' Bob grinned as he glanced at the young man's hands, already starting to look sore and red. His own hands were almost as tough as leather and unaffected by the sharp edges of the rough stones.

'I do not understand; I have never been to Rome. But very beautiful city. But not as beautiful as here.' Luca stood up and looked around him.

'Aye, God's own kingdom, lad. You can keep your Italy for me. Now get a move on and pass me some of those fillers. The middle of the wall needs filling up, and then it needs some througher to tie it all together.'

As the morning wore on, Bob found he was enjoying himself. Here he was with an Italian, teaching him to wall, and they were both doing their best to understand one another. Luca picked up the wrong stone, then swore softly in Italian as he realized his mistake.

'Never mind, lad. Sally will be here before long with some dinner, then you can have a break.'

'Sally. Nice girl,' Luca said, and put the right stone in the right place.

'Aye, she is. But heartbroken for her man,' Bob said.

They worked on in silence for a minute or two while Luca thought about this.

'Sally is sad? She lost her man in war?' Luca asked without looking too interested.

'Aye, we think so. He can't be found.' Bob stacked the stones, making sure they all fit well, and rearranged some that Luca had put in the wrong way.

'I'm sorry. Bloody Jerries,' Luca said, and spat on the ground.

'Aye, bloody Jerries, tha's right there, lad. Hitler wants shooting. They're all mad, fighting over nowt.'

'I hate Jerries,' Luca said.

'I think tha's been fighting for the wrong side, lad. I don't know how you've got mixed up in all this. Just like our lads here in this dale.'

'I not a fighter. I farm,' Luca replied.

Bob shook his head. Perhaps he was a farmer, but not a farmer used to Dales ways. All the same, he was right enough in Bob's eyes.

Sally climbed steadily up the fellside, carrying a basket that contained a flask of tea along with dinner for her father, Luca and herself. The day was warm and the air was filled with the smell of the thyme and peat moss under her feet. Crickets chirped and skylarks sang overhead as if there was nothing wrong with the world. Not a sound of the raging war was on the wind; the dale was at peace, disturbed only by the bleat of a lamb looking for its mother.

She stopped every so often to catch her breath and look around at the dale she loved. Looking upwards, towards the dividing wall that ran around the fell land of Daleside, she spotted her father and Luca. They were bent over, repairing a section of wall that had been brought down by rough weather or by a sheep trying to find better grazing. She smiled as she heard their voices: her father was taking care to explain what went where and how, while Luca did his best to understand Bob's Yorkshire accent.

If only Ben would take as much interest in looking after the family farm, Sally thought. But her brother had never shown any inclination at all to spend long hours tending to the farm's needs. It made no difference to her, but she knew her father would have preferred his son to show more interest in farming, rather than his daughter. Women were homemakers in Bob's eyes, not farmers – although he still expected Sally to do plenty of jobs, including helping to round up the sheep and cattle when needed.

She raised her hand and waved, shouting 'Hello!' as she made the last few yards to the men. Setting her basket down as she reached them, she drew a deep breath and looked around her.

'I'm amazed at the views every time I climb up here. It's so lovely.' Shading her eyes with her hand, she turned a hundred and eighty degrees, gazing out over the peaks of the Lake District and across to the high mountain of Whernside.

'Yes, *bella vista*.' Luca straightened up and stood next to her. Sally could smell the sweat on him from his work that morning, and she noticed that his white shirt was damp under his overalls. It was hot work walling on top of the fell, and refreshment would be more than welcome.

'How are you both doing?' she asked.

Her father straightened up, rubbing his back, and reached for his jacket, delving into the pocket for his packet of Woodbines and a box of Swan Vestas matches. He offered the cigarettes to Luca, who took one gratefully with a huge smile.

'Fags through the day, lad, pipe of a night. Or whenever I can sit back and take my time and think about things,' Bob said as he lit his own cigarette. Luca smiled, only partly understanding, but enjoying every drag on his free cigarette.

'We're doing all right,' Bob went on, addressing Sally. 'He's not a bad learner. We should have this gap and that other little one up by the time he goes back home tonight. Now, what's your mother sent us? No doubt this fella will be hungry, although I know they get three meals a day down at Sedbergh. They'll be better looked after than our lads will be by Jerry.'

'She's sent bacon-and-egg sandwiches, an apple pasty and some bannocks. There's three mugs for us all to have a drink of tea and some extra in a bottle for me to leave. Mam knows you like cold tea.' Sally found a dry patch to sit on below the stone wall, making sure it was free of sheep droppings and the stunted thistles that grew there. Both men watched as she started to unload her basket and lay the dinner out in front of them. They finished their cigarettes, then sat down to join her.

'Very good,' Luca said, taking a mouthful of sandwich. He looked contented as he sat cross-legged, taking in the view.

'He's a fair lad, but not a bad'en. I don't think he understands half I say but he's tried hard this morning.' Bob leaned back against the wall, enjoying his dinner. 'You'll be back in the shop tomorrow, and I'm going to separate the piglets now they've got used to not having their mother with them. I meant to tell you, I've come to an arrangement with Jack Sedgwick in the signal box. He's going to take orders for bacon from us from the train drivers. We can charge better prices if we sell it to them in Leeds.'

Sally nodded, dropping her gaze to the mossy ground. 'I still can't believe he saw Jonathan Birbeck the other day. I wish I'd known he was home – I might hate the lad, but I just keep thinking he might have known something about Edward. I'd give anything for a bit of news.'

'He'll know nowt, lass, else somebody would have told us by now. Anyway, he's a bad lot, best left alone,' Bob said. Then he lifted his head, listening, as they all heard the distant drone of an aeroplane.

'You sad? No need to be sad, *bella*,' Luca said, smiling

at Sally as their eyes met briefly. He reached out and lightly patted her hand.

'Thank you, Luca. I miss my boyfriend,' Sally replied. She looked up as her father got to his feet, only to drop down again quickly.

'Keep down, keep down – there's a bloody Jerry aircraft heading our way! And it looks to be in trouble – it's only just making it over. It's got flames coming from the engines.'

They all scrambled into the shelter of the wall, crouching there as the noise of the enemy aircraft grew louder and louder. The engines were spluttering, struggling to keep the huge, gleaming bomber in the air as the pilot strained to gain height over the surrounding fells. All three looked up as the plane passed just a matter of feet above their heads. For a moment, Sally had a perfect view of the pilot and co-pilot in the cockpit, working desperately to manoeuvre into a clearer landing space. There was a powerful smell of leaking fuel, and the heat from the plane could clearly be felt as it passed over their heads and on in the direction of Whernside.

'He'll not get over there,' Bob shouted over the engine's roar. 'Whernside is three times taller than this fell – there's no way they're going to make it. They're buggered, poor devils, they need to bail out!' He got to his feet, followed by Luca and Sally, all three of them staring after the plane as it swept down the dale, glinting in the sunlight and burning like a phoenix. Then, presumably thanks to the pilot's desperate efforts, it gained a little height, trying in vain to clear the highest point of Whernside.

'He going to crash,' Luca said breathlessly.

Sally watched in disbelief as the mighty German warplane receded into the distance, hopelessly struggling to gain altitude. Its final moments seemed to pass in slow motion. They all winced as it finally, inevitably crashed into the far side of Whernside.

There was a moment's awful silence as a column of smoke rose up from the crash site.

'I wonder if any bailed out,' Sally said anxiously. 'I can't see any parachutes.'

'Nay, I didn't either. Happen some bailed out before we heard and spotted them. I wonder where they'd been? There's nowt worth bombing round here, that's for sure, so they're a bit off track.' Bob felt shocked. A difference of just a few moments would have seen the plane come down right on top of them.

'They all die, I hope,' Luca said. He sat back down, staring blankly at what was left of their dinner.

'God, this war is terrible. I wish it was over and we were all back to like we used to be.' Sally dropped her head into her hands with a sob.

'It will never be the same again, lass. Of that I'm sure,' Bob said quietly. He tore his gaze away from the distant crash site and looked at the two young people. Both of them were going through hell in different ways; there was nothing anybody could do about it. And that night, in Germany, some mothers would be mourning their sons.

Chapter 12

On Friday, Sally stood behind the counter in Middleton's shop and listened to customers discussing the Whernside aeroplane crash.

'I heard it was on its way back from bombing Manchester, so I have no sympathy. They say all four of the crew were found dead, or what was left of them. It was ablaze for hours. Nobody could put the fire out with it being on the top of Whernside. Terrible it was,' Mary Morphet said as she put her shopping in her bag and made sure her ration card was safe.

'Well, they're still somebody's lads. I wonder how the Germans get to know what's happened to them? Because somebody will be awaiting news of them,' Lizzie Capstick said, and then realized what she'd said in front of Sally. 'Sorry, love. I forgot you still don't know what's happened to Edward. Or – I take it there's no news of him?'

'No, there isn't, Mrs Capstick. I wish there was,' Sally sighed.

'I hear your father's taken on an Italian, the one that's been seeing to the vicar's graveyard. I shouldn't say this, but I couldn't take my eyes off him when he stripped down to his waist and showed his muscles while he was mowing. It's a wonder my old fella didn't rise up out of his grave and give me a good talking to. I'm old enough to be his grandmother.' Lizzie and Mary nudged one another and laughed.

Sally looked embarrassed. She too had noticed that Luca was fit and athletic, but she wasn't about to join in as the two elderly ladies joked about what they'd do if they were thirty years younger.

'He might be an Italian, Sally, but he's a fit one. Your father had better keep an eye on him, what with you being such a bonny lass,' Lizzie said with a smile as she gathered her basket under her arm.

Sally blushed. 'There's no danger of anything happening with me, Mrs Capstick.'

'Well, I remember when Flora Mason was engaged to John Bentham and he went to war. He left her vowing that they'd be married as soon as he returned, and then she got a letter saying he was missing in action. Lo and behold, she married another fella from Kendal within six months. But the worst thing is, poor John came back after the war, still very much alive. It broke his heart when he found she'd given up on him. He shot himself and left a letter that said he'd only survived because he knew she was waiting for him! Poor devil.'

The shop bell rang as the door opened and Mary and Lizzie turned to see Hilda Birbeck, sister of Jonathan, coming in. She never took part in Dales gossip, so they both knew she wouldn't want to join their conversation.

'Anyway, pet, don't give up hope. Edward may still return, and then you can have one of the grandest weddings ever seen in these Dales. Give my love to your mam, and remind her that there's a jumble sale on in the Memorial Hall at the end of the month – I hear there's going to be a lot of good stuff. Them at the Gate have been having a sort-out, all proceeds to go to the war funds.' Mary turned back to Lizzie. 'Have you got everything? Come across to mine and have a natter if you like.'

'Aye, that's all I can afford, and I haven't any ration tickets left for this week, so I'll have to be right.' Lizzie picked her basket up from the counter. They both nodded to Hilda and wished her a good morning, but nothing more, as they left the shop.

'Good morning, Hilda. How are you?' Sally asked. She wondered if she dared mention that she'd heard about Jonathan making a visit home.

Hilda passed her a list and ration book and lifted her shopping basket onto the counter. 'I'm all right. Better than some folk, I daresay.' She watched as Sally placed her entitlement into the basket, wondering whether she ought to tell the girl what she'd heard from Jonathan. After a few moments, she said, 'My brother is over in France and Belgium again. He's part of these D-Day landings. We're hoping that the good Lord keeps him safe. No doubt the gossips of Dent will have told you that he was home to visit us a few days ago,' she added

126

stiffly. She knew what most of the local people thought of her wayward brother.

'Yes, my father mentioned he'd been back. I hope he's safe, Hilda.' Sally hesitated for a moment, looking at the plainly dressed woman. Hilda couldn't be far beyond her own age, but she looked a good twenty years older. 'I don't know if I should ask this – I know it's four years since my Edward went missing – but did Jonathan happen to mention him at all?' she asked with a hint of desperation.

'He did, actually. He talked about many of the lads from his regiment, how they were pinned down on the beaches of Calais, and said that he hoped it wouldn't happen again for them to be sat like sitting ducks. He mentioned that he'd seen Edward lying in the sand dunes as they all fought to be rescued. He didn't know whether he was alive or dead, there was so much carnage that day. So I can't give you any hope,' Hilda said. She paused as Sally brushed away a tear and drew a shaky breath. 'I'm sorry. I don't know what I can say to make it better. All I can say is that this war has changed my brother. He's found humility at last, and realized that he has to change his ways. He would have saved Edward if he'd had the chance, despite the bad feeling between them. He's not such a bad lad, you know, Sally. I just pray that he'll return to us.'

'Thank you, Hilda. I'm sorry – I live in hope every day that Edward will walk into our farmyard just as he used to do, but I know that after so long, I'm probably lying to myself. I hope Jonathan keeps safe,' Sally said between silent sobs. There was a silence as they both looked at the newspapers laid out on a side counter, their headlines shouting news of the 'big push'. Both women knew that Edward and Jonathan were very likely dead, but they each still carried a small sliver of hope in their hearts.

'Aye, well, we're not on our own in grief or worry. But I'll say to you, don't let your life stand still. If you can find love, you find it. Otherwise you'll end up an old maid, like me and my sisters.' Hilda picked up her ration book and basket and handed Sally payment to place in the till. 'I hope you find peace,' she said quietly.

'And I'll pray that Jonathan returns home to you safe and sound,' Sally replied.

Hilda gave a wry smile. 'The devil looks after his own, they say. If that's true, he'll be back.'

She left the shop, leaving Sally fighting back tears. Her legs felt like jelly. It was no good – she really had to accept that Edward was dead, left on the sand dunes of Calais. He would not be coming back.

'Aye, Sally, we all knew it really but didn't want to think it.' Ivy put her arm around her daughter. 'I hope that the Birbecks tell his mother and father. It's only right, else they'll still be up in the air thinking their lad could be alive.'

'He might still be. Jonathan only said he'd seen Edward lying in the sand dunes – he couldn't tell whether he was dead or alive. I don't think anybody should say anything to them,' Sally retorted. Despite her grief after talking with Hilda in the shop earlier, a little of her stubborn resistance to the inevitable was creeping back.

'Well, we'll leave it, then. You never know, and I wouldn't want to be the messenger of bad news. But

Sally – now that you know what's most probably happened – don't waste your life, love. Your father and Ben are going down to Sedbergh to the picture house. Go with them and enjoy yourself. They're both getting fish and chips and bringing some back for me. It'll be grand not to have to make any supper tonight.' Ivy smiled. 'All three of you would fit on the back of his bike – none of you weigh a lot.'

'I'll see, Mam. I don't know that I feel like doing anything tonight. I just want to be on my own,' Sally replied quietly.

'All the more reason for you to get on out with them. They're off to see *In Which We Serve*. It's got Noël Coward in it, and it's all about a ship going down and the crew having to survive – hardly any mention of the army. Getting lost in a film will do you good. I'll tell your father to fit you all on his bike and get your fish and chips. I'll not take no for an answer,' Ivy said firmly. 'You need to get out more, Sally. The world is still turning, and folk are allowed to have fun despite this war. Sulking around home and feeling sorry for yourself won't bring Edward back.'

'Oh, Mam, just shush! You have no idea how I feel. But yes, I'll go along with them. I don't fancy the film but I'll go just to make you happy, all right?' Sally snapped back at her mother.

She had been hoping for a bit of sympathy, not a lecture. Tears were falling as she made her way upstairs and flung herself onto her bed. She knew there was some truth in her mother's words, but it wasn't easy to accept.

Ivy stood for a moment, lost in thought, then went to

the kitchen door and looked out across the farmyard. It was a warm summer's day and the hens were scratching about in the yard, clucking softly among themselves; beyond them, the meadows were a mass of yellow butter-cups, daisies and penny rattle. Soon it would be haytime, when everyone had to lend a hand. At least Ben would have left school by then and they would have Luca to help. However, this year there would be no Stanley for hay-time or clipping time, and it would feel strange without him.

Poor Stan, Bob's brother, had been living on borrowed time ever since he'd come back from fighting on the front in the Great War. Bob had found him dead in his bed in early spring. At least he'd gone peacefully in his sleep, Ivy thought sadly.

Sally's words had cut right through her. Ivy knew all about loss. It was Stanley she'd first fallen in love with, until he'd gone missing and she had grown close to Bob. Then she'd lost two dear brothers of her own in the 'war to end all wars', as they were calling it at the time. So much for that, she thought now, as she saw Ben emerge from his bike workshop with oil streaked on his face and hands. At least her son was safe for now.

She decided to clear her head of dark thoughts by walking down the farm track to see if any scraps had been left in the bucket at the end of the lane. A stroll would do her good, she thought as she wandered down the mossy-banked lane filled with primroses and violets.

Turning the corner, she saw one of their neighbours at the foot of the lane. He waved and called out, 'Just left some scraps for the pigs. I hope they're doing well!' before walking on in the direction of Dent.

Behind him, a black Ford motor car was approaching, driven by a man in a suit. He looked official, Ivy thought. She held back from collecting the scraps, lingering as the car slowed down and the driver glanced up the lane. Then she recognized him: he was the Ministry man from the War Ag. He'd paid a visit to the farm before to speak with Bob.

Ivy held her breath, hoping he hadn't heard their neighbour mention the pigs. The last thing they wanted was to be investigated by the Ministry – it could mean jail for Bob. She walked casually past the bucket of scraps and approached the car, smiling.

'Lovely day – I just thought I'd stretch my legs. Sorry if you heard my neighbour call our POW help "pigs". He really does hate the Germans and Italians with a passion.' Ivy looked ruefully at the driver as he glared at her.

'Don't we all? Terrible state of affairs we're in because of them. Worse than pigs, all of them.' He gave her a firm nod and then drove off.

Ivy watched as he overtook her neighbour, honking his horn, and then disappeared further up the dale. It had been a close call. Her knees felt shaky as she picked up the scrap bucket and hurried home with her heart racing.

Stepping into the house, she smiled at Ben, not wanting him to know anything was amiss. There was so much to worry about these days, with a big invasion in place – although with Jerry hopefully on the run at last,

131

there was a good chance Ben wouldn't be enlisted. That was something to be thankful about, at least. She scuffed him over the head and told him to wash his hands before touching anything.

'Hey, Mam, I'm too old for that now,' Ben said indignantly.

'You'll never be too old for a scuffing, Ben Fothergill. Now get those hands washed, and change out of that ragged old jumper if you're going to the pictures with your father. Once he's milked the cows he'll want to be going. Sally's coming with you, and I'll have no nonsense about it.'

'Oh, Mam. All she'll do is moan about the picture. And then there'll be the Pathé newsreel, and she's bound to start blubbing when she sees all the soldiers,' Ben complained as he scrubbed his hands at the sink.

'Well, she's going. It will do you all good to have a night out together, and it'll do me good to have an hour or two to myself and supper made for me.' Ivy put the bucket of scraps down and caught her breath. She was looking forward to having nobody else to worry about for a few hours.

'All right, but she'll not like it. And there's nothing else on, so she'll have to lump it,' Ben muttered. He was thinking about how ungainly he was going to look, squashed up on the back of his father's bike between him and Sally. Hopefully none of his friends would see them.

'Give us a bit more room. And don't forget to lean into the bends, both of you, or else we'll be off and on the road,' Bob warned as he shuffled backwards, aware that if he pushed any further, Sally would be hanging off the back of the bike. She was already complaining that she'd burned her leg on the hot exhaust, and they were only at the bottom of the farm lane. It was another three miles to Sedbergh and the picture house.

Sally clung to Ben and Ben clung to their father as the three of them made their way past the Elizabethan house called the Gate and up the twisting road to Sedbergh. They passed Loftus Hill workhouse and Sally thought about Luca, who would be inside with his fellow POWs. She could see a group of them sitting outside on a bench, smoking and enjoying the mild evening. When Monday came he would be back with them on the farm, and she had to admit she was looking forward to seeing him again. Everyone in the Fothergill family was beginning to warm to Luca, especially her father, who enjoyed teaching him what he could when he could. Despite all their original doubts and hostility, the young Italian was causing no bother at all and was even starting to feel like part of the farm's day-to-day life.

Bob drove down the main street of Sedbergh and pulled into the layby next to Martin's Bank, sitting on his bike until his two passengers had dismounted. He turned the engine off and put it on its stand. Midges had got caught on his face during the ride, and he brushed them off with his rough hands. 'Right, to the pictures – and then we'll get fish and chips and take some back for your mother. I've not done this for years. I'm looking forward to watching a good film, especially a naval one with that Noël Coward. Grand actor.'

Bob tapped Sally's arm as they walked down the narrow cobbled street towards the picture house, which stood on the outskirts of the town. 'Mother says the Birbeck lass gave you some upsetting news – it'll do you good to watch a decent film, I'm sure. But will you be all right with the newsreel?'

She smiled at his concern. 'Yes, I had a talk with Hilda; but she said Jonathan wasn't really sure what had become of Edward. So I've been thinking – I'll still hold out a little hope, and I'm not that delicate. Our lads in the forces need to be supported, don't they, Father? We should be proud that they're fighting and dying for our country, although it breaks many a heart – not just mine.'

'That's my lass. You make the best of your life,' Bob said. Then he noticed Ben's expression, and followed his gaze to the film poster on display outside the picture house.

'It's bloody well not *In Which We Serve*. It's a blinking soppy romance. We've missed the navy one last week,' Ben growled.

'Oh, well – one for Sally, then. She'll enjoy it even if you don't.' Bob chuckled at the disgust on his son's face. 'It's still a treat, Ben, no matter what we watch. Besides, in another few weeks you'll be earning enough to come by yourself or with your mates. You can watch any film you want then.'

'Ah, ah, now who's sulking?' Sally teased her brother as they queued up at the ticket window. They followed the usherette in her black-and-white uniform down into the darkness and silence of the cinema.

134

'Here, we'll sit halfway down. The trailers have already started, look – there's Popeye in a trailer for you both to watch, seeing as neither of you have grown up,' Bob said wryly as they squabbled in whispers about where to sit. 'Now be quiet, and let's enjoy the film. Although I've sat in many a more comfortable chair than these,' he added, as he discovered there was no space to stretch out his long legs.

Sally smiled at the exploits of Popeye and Olive Oyl, and they saw a trailer for a new film, *Brief Encounter* – she laughed as her father kept nudging her arm and whispering things like, '*That's Carnforth railway station. Pratt's used to send milk there for transport to Liverpool.*' Then the Pathé News propaganda film started, showing the English and Allied troops fighting for their cause. She could have done without seeing it even though she knew it was supposed to raise morale and persuade them all that the war would soon be won, with Hitler and Germany paying the price of defeat. She was thankful when the main film started, and soon lost herself in the love affair on screen.

'Well, that was a lot of rubbish. I'm ready for my fish and chips,' Ben said, walking out of the picture house as quickly as he could. 'I'll not be going to see that again.'

'It was a good film, lad. It'll become a classic, I think, but perhaps it's one for the ladies. I can't get over that trailer too – filmed on Carnforth station! I recognized the clock straight away. I'll look forward to that one,' Bob said for at least the third time. He put his hand in his pocket to find some money for the fish and chips to give to Ben. 'Here, you run ahead of this queue of folk, because they will all be going to the chippy. Fish and chips four times with salt and vinegar, and one wrapped up well to take back to your mother.' Bob passed a ten-shilling note into his son's hand and watched him race past the folk making their way out of the cinema for a late supper at the only fish and chip shop in Sedbergh. 'We'll eat them on the bench outside the bank and then get home.'

'That'll be a real treat, Father; we don't hardly get them, do we? And I really enjoyed the film. I was glad it wasn't a war film. It was bad enough watching the newsreel.' Sally hung her head.

'Aye, but now's not the time to be giving in. We sound as if we're kicking Jerry's arse now that we have a footing in Normandy and Belgium. Hitler will be quaking in his boots, him and Mussolini; they know that things are on the turn. It might take a while, but we'll soon be seeing what's what, and then there will come a day of reckoning. Just like last time around.' Bob sounded upbeat. He put his arm around his lass and kissed her on her forehead. 'Now, my belly is rumbling. Let's get these fish and chips eaten and then go home. It looks like we've company waiting for us on the bench with Ben. I didn't think they would let POWs out this late at night, but isn't that Luca with him?'

Sally lifted her head and managed a smile. 'It is Luca – he's pinching a chip from off Ben. He's brave. Ben never shares with anyone.'

'Aye, well, that lad has got a way with him. He can charm the birds out of the trees. Your mother was even asking him where she could buy spaghetti and garlic. She never lets garlic in the house – it's just because she feels sorry for him, being away from home. I'll give him his due, he's a hard worker.' Bob shook his head and smiled at Luca as they approached.

'Sally, Mr Fothergill. I pinching chips. They are good!' Luca said with a huge grin on his face.

'Shouldn't you be in your barracks, under lock and key?' Bob said as he took his wrapped-up fish and chips from Ben. He watched as Sally squashed in between Ben and Luca and started to unwrap hers.

'Friday night, pub night! We allowed. An *uno* pint at Golden Lion and then home.' Luca watched as Sally unwrapped her supper and offered him a chip. '*Grazie*. I like chips.' Sally watched as he took about six out of her supper and ate them fast.

'Aye, I can tell tha does. You'd better have a few of mine.' Bob offered his portion over and watched as Luca ate another handful. 'Don't they feed you at that spot, then?' he said, grabbing his portion back.

'*Si*, but not good. Not like Mrs Fothergill. I like her bannocks.'

Bob grinned. Up to a few days ago the lad had never heard of a bannock, let alone tasted one. 'Sally usually makes them, so it's her you've to thank. Although it's a Scottish recipe.'

'Sally, you make? You make one for me, *per favore*? I share at Loftus Hill.' Luca looked at Sally seriously.

'Yes, I'll do that. One for you on Tuesday,' Sally said, and smiled. To her astonishment, he bent forward and kissed her openly on her cheek, as if it was a perfectly ordinary thing to do.

'*Grazie, bella*. I see you Tuesday,' Luca said and got up, leaving the Fothergill family open-mouthed – none more so than Sally. '*Ciao*,' he called back as he made his way down the street.

'He kissed you, the cheeky bugger! Right in front of your father.' Bob turned to the blushing Sally in amazement.

'I don't think he meant anything by it. It's their way – they kiss everybody,' she said, flustered. But she had to admit she'd enjoyed it. How her feelings had altered since first meeting Luca.

'He'd better not blinking kiss me,' Ben said. 'I still haven't asked him if he's any relation to Bugatti the car company. All he ever talks about is the farm, and you, Sally. I think he fancies you.' He looked down at his supper. 'And he's pinched half my chips.'

'He'd better not be doing any more kissing of anyone, else I'll have to report him,' Bob said. 'You try not to encourage him, our Sally. With a bit of luck he'll be with us until after haytime and clipping, and then he can get his Italian arse home.' Whatever Sally might say, he could have sworn the lass had enjoyed the spontaneous kiss she'd been given.

Chapter 13

'Where do you think you're going, Ben Fothergill?' Ivy asked as her son pulled his boots on. It was early on a Saturday morning, and she and Ben were the only ones up in the Fothergill family home.

'Me and George Mason are going to climb up Whernside and have a look at the aeroplane that crashed there, if they haven't taken it away. We've been thinking about doing it since it came down the other week. I bet there's all sorts up there that's come out of it, and besides, I've never seen one close up. It's a Heinkel, so we've heard. I wouldn't mind one of its guns.' Ben tied his boots tightly and hoped his mother wasn't going to play hell with him. He'd been planning to sneak out of the house before she got up.

'I think you'll be lucky, Ben. There might be the fuselage left, but all the guns and everything else will have been stripped out long ago. I hope the men have been given a decent burial and their families told. I wouldn't want to go looking through a crash site. You'd be better off staying at home and helping your father or doing your bikes up,' Ivy said.

'I leave school next week, Mam. This will be the last Saturday I can do what I want because I'll be starting work at Morphet's, and that includes Saturday mornings. Please let me be,' Ben pleaded. 'For George and me, it'll be our last day together. He's going to work at the joinery and then we'll both have to enlist when we're old enough.' All the family had hoped that the war would end before Ben was seventeen, but with it dragging on as it was, nothing was certain.

'Oh, Lord, don't say that. I don't want you taking part in this war, there's enough been lost already. You have a few years before they'll take you – I pray it'll all be over before then.' Ivy shook her head; Ben wasn't even fifteen yet, but even he was thinking that the army or one of the forces would need him eventually. 'Go on, get yourself gone. You'll be wanted in the next few days; it's clipping time coming up and then haytime. You'll pay your way as well as working at Morphet's. Now, have you got something to eat? It's a long walk up Whernside and it could be better weather for you. The cloud is low up on the tops, summer or no summer.'

'Yes, Mam. I've got some cheese and bread – that'll do us, we won't be long. I'll be back just after dinner time, so I can help Father then.' Ben pulled his knapsack over his shoulder. It held his dinner, a trowel, a screw-driver and various other items he thought he might need if there were any trophies to be taken from the

140

wrecked Heinkel bomber. 'I'll not be late, I promise, Mam.'

'What about a coat? The weather looks like it's going to change,' Ivy called after him as he rushed out of the kitchen.

'I'm all right, Mam, stop fussing. It's not cold and it won't come to much.' Ben couldn't get to his bike fast enough. He had promised to meet George at Lea Gate, further up the dale, at eight o'clock, and it was already seven-thirty.

'It might be summer but it feels more like December, it's so cold. Have you not brought a coat? It'll be freezing up on those tops.' George looked Ben up and down, thinking his mate seemed underdressed for the heights of Whernside. He himself had been in two minds about coming at all as he'd left the house. His father had belted him to within an inch of his life after the ill-fated fishing trip with Ben in May, and George didn't want to be on the wrong end of his fists again.

'It'll be right. We aren't going to be up there long. Are we going over the top of Blea Moor tunnel and up the slope, or to Ribblehead on our bikes and walk straight up it? I've never been up the top before. They say there's a tarn – I hope the plane isn't in the middle of that.' Ben couldn't wait to set off.

'It's one hell of a trek whichever way we go, and it's going to be wet. Perhaps we shouldn't bother today. We can go when the weather is better,' George suggested. Ben was often quick to throw caution to the wind.

'No, come on, let's get going. I promised my mam I'd be back in time to help my father later on. I'll be in bother if I'm not.' Ben pushed off on his bike, onto the bridge over the river Dee, and shouted back, 'Let's go up beside the railway line and over the tunnel. It'll cut all that road down by Gaily Becks.' He'd decided he would have to take the lead, and if George didn't want to follow it was his lookout.

'I still think we should go in better weather. Look, the fog's coming down,' George called as they followed the twisting road past the Sportsman's Inn and under the two mighty viaducts that carried trains over Arten Gill and Dent Head. Whernside wouldn't be visible until they climbed out of the valley. They had to follow the same line as the trains, walking over the Blea Moor tunnel top until they came to the sweeping fell of Dandry Moss and the twenty-four-arched viaduct of Ribblehead, Whernside rising behind it like a huge sleeping lion. Both boys put their heads down and pedalled hard up and through Dent Head viaduct, then pushed their bikes behind a wall that followed the busy railway line and started walking up the steep side of the tunnel.

Ben didn't like to admit that both his mother and George were right; he needed a coat. He bent double with his hands on his knees to catch his breath as they reached the top of the tunnel, and then they began walking along the fell in the direction of Whernside. Their surroundings were half shrouded in fog and cloud. As they made their way along, rain started to fall.

'I'll be in for another belting if my father finds out

about this. I've only just got over the last one,' George said anxiously. 'It's too wet, Ben. Let's turn back. You're half sodden already, and look at Whernside. Nobody in their right mind would go up there today. I'm not that bothered about a piece of a German aeroplane. There's probably nowt left anyway.'

Ben was still determined to see what he could salvage, but he knew George didn't share his deep interest in anything mechanical. George was set to start working on the Masons' family farm after finishing school, and doing a day or two at the joinery next door to supplement the household income.

They stopped to listen as a steam train passed through the tunnel beneath their feet. Steam escaped through the four shafts that plunged down to the track from the fell top, mixing with the wisps of low cloud and mist that were gathering around them.

'Stop your moaning,' Ben said when the train had gone by. 'Look, we're nearly out of Dent. I'm not stopping now.' He jerked his head to encourage George along but his mate hung back, clearly reluctant to follow.

'I'm going home. It's too wet. We're both soaked already. Come on, don't be daft, let's go up on a better day.' George waved an arm to indicate the wider scene around them. The valley was still clear of clouds, but the fog and rain would only get worse as they climbed the nearly two and half thousand feet of Whernside that was above sea level.

Ben shook his head. 'No. I start work at Morphet's in another week, I'll not get the chance again. You go back and I'll go on my own. I know the way, I'll be all right. You're nothing but chicken – cluck, cluck, cluck.' He bent his elbows and flapped his arms like chicken wings.

'I might be chicken but I'm not bloody daft. Come back with me – a bit of German plane's not worth risking your life for up that fell. You know folk have died when they've got lost in weather like this.' Seeing Ben's dismissive expression, George shook his head and started to turn away.

'That's folk who don't know what it's like up here,' Ben said. 'They aren't used to the weather. I'll be right, but you get yourself back home. I'll bring you a bit of treasure back anyway.'

He watched as his best friend made his way over the bog moss and disappeared into the mist, dipping back down to the valley. He, unlike George, would not be deterred. His mind was set: he would climb Whernside and reach the plane that fascinated him.

Ben put his head down and headed onwards. As the fog became thicker it started to cling to him, making his shirt even wetter, but he was sweating as he started to climb one of the steep tracks up the side. Now and then, the mountain breeze blew a hole in the prevailing mists and he could see for a moment up towards the summit, where the wreckage of the Heinkel bomber lay. He could also make out the curve of the mighty Ribblehead viaduct and the Station Inn far below. Then the fog would descend again, trapping Ben within its layers and making him feel almost claustrophobic as he peered ahead for the sight of the downed aircraft.

He finally reached the summit, passing two small tarns on the approach. He stood still until a sudden breeze moved the white curtain of fog again, allowing him a glimpse of the wreckage he'd been searching for.

The bomber's fuselage and tail parts lay tangled and torn, with scorch marks all around them on the fellside. There was a smashed-up cockpit but the plane's instruments had already been raided by locals or salvaged by officials, so there wasn't much left to see. Slowly, Ben walked around the crash site. He kicked at various pieces of rubbish that lay on the ground and lifted what was left of the engine covering, looking for anything he could take as a memento. The guns had been taken; the joystick was gone. Anything that was worth anything had already been removed. He had wasted his morning for nothing, apart from the chance to stand back and see how big a German bomber actually was when you were so close to it.

The only thing he spotted that looked worth taking home was a silver-coloured ring that he picked up from below the plane's nose. It weighed quite a lot, and as he held it while examining other bits of metal, he realized that it was drawn to them – it was magnetic. Ben smiled. 'Magneto,' he whispered.

Lifting his head after putting the object into his knapsack, he looked around. Everything was white. The fog had come down even lower while he'd been exploring, and the wind had dropped. He could no longer make out the way home. He had no idea which way he'd come; he couldn't even be sure which part of the site had been nearest when he had first approached.

Panic began to set in. Now that he'd found and examined the bomber, the urge that had driven him up here was gone, and he recognized the sheer stupidity of his quest. How many times had his father told him not to go climbing the fells when the fog was down, that it was dangerous? He was alone with a crashed Nazi aeroplane. What if the ghosts of the pilots haunted it? What if one of them was still alive and was up here with him? Cold came over him, and he shuddered and looked up towards where the sun ought to have been, but there was no sign of it.

He stood still and felt his heart pounding as he tried to work out what to do next. He strained to recall his father's advice, regretting the many times he'd only half listened to him. He could almost hear his voice now: *No matter what you do, make your way downhill and follow a stream or a wall. That will always get you down a fell or mountain, and once you're down, you can soon get help or work out where you are.*

Starting from the part of the crash site where he thought he'd first arrived, Ben set off through the thick mist across the rough fellside. It occurred to him that he hadn't passed the two small tarns he remembered from his ascent, but he pressed on, feeling the mountain starting to tell on the muscles of his legs as he made his way downwards. Eventually there was a brief parting of the clouds and he spotted a drystone wall a few yards ahead. He felt a surge of relief as he hurried towards it and touched the rough limestone. Keeping it to the right of him, he stumbled on, cold, wet and shivering, his eyes

146

constantly seeking gaps in the fog that clung to him and smothered everything. His heart leaped every time he caught a quick glimpse of the valley, then sank as whiteness closed over it again. His legs were turning to jelly but he kept on steadily putting one foot in front of the other, trying not to panic about the dressing-down he was going to get at home. He might still be back for dinner time – that was, if he ever got home at all. Other warnings his father had given him were suddenly clear in his memory. *One false move on that shingle and scree up Whernside, and you could break a leg and never be found again.*

Ben picked his way along slowly, following the wall down to what he thought was a valley. Gradually the mist and fog started to thin, and he could see down to Ingleton and beyond. Below him was Brunt Scar, a farm he had visited a few times with his father. He was at the opposite end of the dale to where he should be. He scrambled down, his legs weighing heavy and his clothes sodden and cold.

Once he got to the bottom of the fell and out of the enveloping mist, he stood and wondered what to do. He was wet, exhausted and tired – too tired to walk back home, either along the road to Dent Head or back over the top from where he'd come. He knew the latter was definitely not an option as he climbed over the stone wall that separated the fellside from the Brunt Scar pastureland. He could see the farmyard behind the long, low house – and there was Frank Brennan, his father's friend, going about his business. It looked like he'd penned in some sheep earlier, probably hoping it would be a good day for shearing, but then thought better of it as the weather set in.

Ben raised his hand and waved as Frank spotted him and waved back. He couldn't ignore him now. He had no option but to go and say hello, he thought, as he walked across the soft pastureland and into the farmyard.

'Bloody hell, lad, you look like a drowned rat. You've not been up Whernside, have you, on a day like today? You must be off your head.' Frank looked in amazement at the young lad. He'd had many a nosy parker traipsing through his fields lately to look at the downed Heinkel, but none had been daft enough to go up Whernside in thick fog.

'It wasn't so bad when I started out, but then I got caught in the fog, and I didn't know which direction to turn. I only went up to see the crashed plane. I wish I'd never have gone,' Ben said. He felt like crying, but knew better than to do that at his age. He stood and shivered in front of Frank, feeling exhaustion and relief wash over him.

'You'd better come in and get warmed up. My lass will give you a hot drink and a change of clothes, and I can run you home in the horse and trap – I can't do much else today. It isn't much like flaming June, that is a certainty.' Frank nodded towards the small flock of sheep inside his ancient, stone-walled holding pen. 'I can't start to clip these ladies in weather like this, and it will have to warm up a bit before we start haytime. It'll be another month at least, the way the grass is growing. I'll

148

take you back once you've got warmed up. I'll be glad to have a catch-up with your father.'

'Are you sure? I don't want to put you out. I can walk back home,' Ben said. He knew his father would play hell at him for having to come back with Frank, as well as not helping him out like he had promised.

'Aye, it's no bother. Come on, get yourself into the kitchen. The Rayburn is lit and the kettle will be on. Let's get you dry, fed and watered,' Frank said. He was concerned about the lad, who looked frozen to the bone and white as a sheet.

'Thank you, but really, I can walk home,' Ben said again as he followed Frank into the warmth of the homely kitchen and saw Mrs Brennan look at him in surprise.

'He's been lost up Whernside looking for that blinking plane that came down. I'm going to take him home once he's got warmed through,' Frank said, and pulled the filled kettle onto the top of the Rayburn.

'You're Bob and Ivy's lad, aren't you, from Dent? How are they both? I haven't seen them for a while.' Annie Brennan shook her head and tutted over the young lad as she saw how he was shivering. 'Eh, you can't stop in those clothes, they're sodden. I'll go and find you a change. They'll be Frank's, a bit too big, but at least they will be dry.' She hurried upstairs to find something suitable for Ben to change into, not bothering to listen to his reply.

Frank stirred a strong cup of tea with sugar in it and passed it over to Ben.

'There you are, lad, drink that. Your folk will be

worrying about you. It's not right pleasant out there, even if it's the middle of summer. Although you don't get many good days up on those tops any time of year.' Frank sat down across from Ben and watched him closely as he sipped the welcome brew.

Annie reappeared with a pile of clothing. 'Pop into the front room and pull these on. They're an old pair of Frank's trousers and a shirt and jumper. He never wears them – the jumper has more holes in than I care to mention, but it will keep you warm. And we don't want any of it back. The breeches are too small for him now.' She smiled and directed Ben towards the empty front room. He went through and changed into the dry clothes, returning with his wet ones under his arm.

'There now, sit on that stool for a while next to the Rayburn and get warm while Frank goes and harnesses the horse and cart up. He hadn't a lot to do today, what with the weather being like it is.' Annie and Frank exchanged a look as he left the kitchen. It was best that they get Ben home as soon as possible, by the look of him. He was still shivering and looked as pale as the mist itself.

'Thank you. I should have been home at least two hours ago. My mother will be worrying.' Ben looked at the ticking grandfather clock that told him it was a quarter past three. Where had all the time gone, when he was out on the top of Whernside? He must have been wandering up there for hours. He tried to control his shivering as he virtually hugged the warm sides of the Rayburn.

'If we had a telephone in the house, I'd ring her, but we haven't. And I don't suppose you have one at home anyway? Not many folk have in these parts,' Annie said. She put an oilcloth coat around Ben's shoulders in preparation for the journey home.

'No, we haven't. Mam keeps asking Father for an electric washer but she never gets one, let alone a telephone.' Ben tried to smile, but his teeth wouldn't stop chattering.

'Aye, I keep asking Frank for one, but these farmers are tight. Now if it was a fresh cow or sheep, it would be a different matter.' Annie was thankful to see Frank reappear in the doorway.

'Come on then, lad, let's get you home. There's a tarpaulin you can cover yourself in to keep warm and dry. It's absolutely pissing it down out there. Sooner we get you home and I get back, the better.'

'Thank you. I'm so grateful,' Ben said to both of them. All he wanted was to get home and to his bed.

The drive was made in silence. Ben was dreading confronting his father; he knew that there would be words exchanged once Frank Brennan had gone home. He pulled the tarpaulin around him and shivered, feeling sick, as Frank turned his horse and trap up the farm lane and pulled it to a halt just outside the open kitchen door. His mother came to the doorway, wiping her hands on her pinny and looking surprised to see anyone out on such a day.

Ivy gasped as she saw Ben climbing down from the trap with his bundle of clothes under his arm. 'We were all wondering what had become of you! Aye, Frank – I hope he hasn't put you to any bother,' she said, recognizing her lifelong friend inside the trap. Ben shot past her into the kitchen.

'He's frozen and wet through. He had lost his way up on Whernside and he came down just by us. I wasn't doing much, so I've brought him home.' Frank smiled at Ivy. 'Are you and Bob all right? We'll have to have supper together when the clipping and haytime are over.'

'Oh, thank you, Frank, a supper together would be lovely. I told Ben not to go when he set off this morning, but he wouldn't listen. Are you coming in for a brew? And how's Annie?' Ivy stood next to the horse as she looked up at Frank.

'Annie is grand, thanks. And thanks for the offer of a brew, but I'll get myself back. It'll be milking time before you know it. That lad of yours couldn't stop shivering. He's in some old clothes that Annie found, but we don't need them back. I hope he's all right – he looked terrible pale and worried.' Frank pulled on the reins and turned his trap towards the road. 'Give my best to Bob.'

Ivy watched him make his way down the track. Then she went into the kitchen, where she found Ben sitting shivering with a rueful expression.

'I told you not to go – now look at you!' she exclaimed, looking her son up and down. 'Here, have a cup of tea and I'll fill you a hot-water bottle, and you go and get warmed up in bed. You're best out of your father's way, else he'll have plenty to say to you.' She filled the bottle and handed it over, then put her hand to Ben's brow.

'You might look frozen but you feel as if you're starting a temperature – you'll have caught a chill. Go on, get up those stairs. I'll bring something for you to eat later on.' She watched as he stood up, balancing the hot-water bottle and his cup of tea.

'Sorry, Mam,' Ben said. He felt like crying again. He was exhausted.

'Aye, well. Least said, soonest mended. Go and get warm.' Ivy shook her head. Bob would have plenty to say when he returned, of that she was sure.

Chapter 14

'He's nothing but a bloody idiot,' Bob said as he looked out at the rain pouring down. 'It was good of Frank to fetch him back. He should never have gone – you could tell what the weather was going to do before he even started off. This weather has buggered everything up.'

'Aye, Father, but hold your whisht. You'll have done daft things yourself when you were young, I'm sure. At least he's back safe. He could have broken his leg and died out there on Whernside and not been found for days. I'm just glad he's home, although I think he's caught a right chill. He says he's freezing but his brow feels warm to the touch. His last week at school, and he might end up in bed all week. I hope he's not going to be too ill to start at Morphet's a week on Monday.' Ivy sighed. She was blaming herself for not making Ben stop and put a coat on when he'd left home that morning.

'Well, I thought he could take a day off from school and help gather the fell with everybody else, so I hope he's fit enough to do that this coming week. I'll walk across to Brian Harper in the morning, see if he' agrees that Wednesday is a good enough day if the weather is right. At least if we get the fell gathered and the sheep clipped, it's one less job, and then it's all out to get the hay in.'

'I'll help with the gather. I always do,' Sally chirped up after finishing washing the supper plates. 'I look forward to it every year, and if you're gathering on Wednesday, I'm not at work.'

'We'll see. Brian has two POWs and I have Luca, not that he knows one end of a sheep from another or how to clip it. He knows pigs, horses and hens, but sheep he has no idea about. It must be a funny sort of farm that he comes from – he says he grows olives and wheat and makes a living doing that. I know one thing: he hates the Nazis just as much as us. He said that when Italy first decided to join us, before Mussolini added his four-penneth, their troops raided all the sympathetic Italian homes and stole just about everything they could get their hands on. Sods, they are.' Bob shook his head.

'Yes, I bothered about him coming to work for us, but he couldn't be a grander lad. There's a lot worse, anyway,' Ivy replied. She noticed a slight smile on Sally's face. 'You get on with him as well. At one time you were quite adamant that you were going to hate him.'

'That's because I didn't know him and thought him a cocky devil. Now I know it's just his way,' Sally replied, trying not to sound too interested in Luca.

'Well, if Ben's not well by Wednesday, you and Luca can gather the fell together, because he'll be no good at clipping. I'm just hoping Brian's two Jerries are. That would be a godsend.'

Ivy stood still for a second at the bottom of the stairs and listened to Ben coughing. 'Aye, that lad has caught his death of a cold. I'll have to keep my eye on him. He didn't eat any supper and he felt so hot, even though he says he's cold.'

'That'll serve him right; he should have listened to you.' Bob pulled his boots off, calling it a day. He turned the radio on and lit his pipe.

'Father, mind what you say. I'm a bit worried about him,' Ivy said, frowning.

'He'll be right. Stop fussing, woman,' Bob replied. He sat back, drew on his pipe of Kendal Twist, and tried to ignore his son coughing upstairs.

The following morning, Ivy sat at Ben's bedside as he tossed and turned. He was soaked to the skin with sweat, and between breaths he was gasping for air.

'He's really ill, Father. I'm trying to keep his temperature down with this wet cloth but he's burning up. He needs a doctor – I know they cost, and that it's Sunday, but he needs one.' Ivy looked with pleading eyes at her husband.

'He's young, Mother. See how he is by this afternoon and if he's no better by then, I'll go for Dr Batty. You know how children are, one minute they're ill and the next nothing's wrong.' Bob knew Ivy was worried, but a doctor was an expense, and Ben was young and fit enough to fight off an infection himself.

'He's hardly a child any more, he's nearly fifteen. You'll promise to go for Dr Batty if he's no better by dinner time? Promise!' Ivy urged him.

'Aye, I'll go. But first I've got to see if Brian can gather the fell on Wednesday. He'll be in this morning, it being Sunday.' Bob looked down at his son as he lay in bed, moaning. The lad did seem ill. If he was no better by the time Bob returned, he'd fetch the doctor straight away.

'That's it – put your sheep and the farm first,' Ivy shouted bitterly after him, but it fell on deaf ears. Bob walked on down the stairs and out of the house.

He followed the stone wall that separated his top pastures from the rough ground where his sheep were contentedly grazing. The air was full of insects buzzing, and the chirp of a cricket could be heard as he climbed the narrow stile to his next-door neighbour's farm. He was worried about his lad, but the business with Brian and the clipping had to be settled, he thought, as Ivy's words stung his conscience.

Walking down the thyme-covered pasture, he opened the gate that led into Beck Sides farmyard and noticed Arthur Metcalfe's old Ford car parked there. He swore under his breath. What was Arthur doing at Brian Harper's on a Sunday morning? He hoped his neighbour wasn't showing an interest in buying Deep Well. Bob would stand no chance of trying to outbid Brian, he thought as he knocked on the brown-varnished, peeling door of the farmhouse. The smell of pipe smoke drifted out to him.

'Anybody in? It's nobbut me. I've come to set a day

for shearing and clipping,' Bob called as he caught sight of the sheep shears, ruddle and twine that cluttered the hallway of the farmhouse. Ivy would never let him do that, he thought, as a voice shouted through from the back kitchen.

'Aye, get yourself in here, we're just putting the world to rights,' Brian called. Bob made his way up the cluttered hallway into what had once been a spotless kitchen, but was now piled high with old newspapers, unwashed dishes and dying plants on the windowsills. Since Brian's wife had left, his housekeeping had been non-existent. He might have bought struggling farms up the dale but he had abandoned all the houses that went with the land, just as he'd abandoned his own home.

'Now then, Arthur, I didn't expect to see you here this morning.' Bob nodded to the elderly farmer.

Arthur smiled up at him. 'Brian wants to buy two heifers from me, so we're just doing a bit of business, even though it's supposed to bring you bad luck doing a deal on a Sunday.'

'Aye, an old wives' tale. I think the devil has more to keep him busy than the sale of two heifers on a Sunday. He's got his hands full with what's happening over in Europe. Although it sounds as if we're getting somewhere with these Jerries at the moment. Pull up a chair – I suppose you've come to set a day for clipping, seeing the weather's been against us lately.' Brian leaned back in his chair and looked expectantly at Bob.

'Aye, I thought Wednesday. Would that be all right for you?' Bob remained standing; he wasn't going to sit with the two men, he was going to do as Ivy had asked and go for the doctor. 'If your Germans can help clip, we should soon get through them. We'll be missing my brother this year. It'll be different without him.' He bowed his head for a moment, remembering his brother, who had died earlier that year and had been sadly missed by everyone in the family.

'Aye, he was a good help. Not like your son. I don't know how you went wrong there, Bob, but there's not a bit of farmer in him.' Brian grinned as he taunted his next-door neighbour.

'It makes no difference, does it, Bob? I hear he's good with his hands and can fix almost anything mechanical. There's probably more money to be made doing that nowadays than farming.' Arthur winked at Bob and drew on his pipe.

'Aye, well, he's not up to much today,' Bob said. 'The silly devil went up Whernside to look at the crash site and he got absolutely soaked, and lost. He's in bed with a chill. Ivy's right worried about him. That's why I'm not stopping – I'll have to get back to see how he is. He might need the doctor, but we could do without his bill.' He shook his head.

'Get yourself home, Bob. Your lad's more precious than setting a date for clipping. If he needs a doctor, put your hand in your pocket. Family is everything,' Arthur said. He leaned forward towards Brian Harper, who just sniggered. *Family* was a dirty word as far as he was concerned, ever since his wife had left him and Marjorie had disgraced herself.

159

'Aye, I will – Ivy knows when somebody is ill. I'd better get myself back home.' Bob turned to go. 'Wednesday, six o'clock?'

'Aye, that's right with me.' Brian re-lit his pipe.

'Look after that lad. A son is precious,' Arthur said, and added, 'I haven't forgotten our business either, by the way. I'll be over shortly. I'm just waiting for a few things.'

'Right you are, Arthur. I'll look forward to seeing you.' Bob was grateful that Arthur hadn't mentioned his business in front of Brian. The more he thought about it, the more certain he became that he would never have the money for Deep Well, and Brian Harper would just make him feel a fool.

Dr Batty followed Ivy up the stairs. 'Don't worry, Ivy, I know you only send for me when it's urgent. Bob was apologetic about calling me away from Sunday dinner, but I knew that you needed me.'

They reached the top of the stairs and entered Ben's small, sparse bedroom.

'Open the window and let in some fresh air while I take a look at him, please, Ivy.' The doctor bent over Ben, who lay sweating and listless in bed, his lips parched and his breathing laboured.

Bob came into the room and watched as the doctor took Ben's temperature and listened to his chest with his stethoscope.

'You've sent for me just in time,' Dr Batty said after a minute. 'This lad has got pneumonia. He's quite ill. The next twenty-four hours will tell us just how bad things really are.' He stepped back from the bed and looked at Ivy and Bob, both of whom he had known from birth. 'He's in a bad way.'

Ivy took hold of Bob's arm as a sob escaped her. 'I should have stopped him from going. I knew what it would be like on the top of Whernside yesterday, but he was that determined to go.'

'Whisht, now, lass. He'd have gone no matter what you said. He's got a stubborn head on him, has that one, just like his old man.' Bob put his arm round Ivy, a thing he would never normally do, as he looked at Dr Batty. 'Is there anything you can do for him?'

Dr Batty drew a deep breath. 'Well, when you described what was wrong, I happened to pick up a phial of something that's on trial with a few of us doctors. It's called penicillin, and it has been used on our troops for a while to help combat infectious wounds or chest infections similar to the one Ben has. With good results, I might add.' He paused and looked consideringly at Ben. 'If you are in agreement, I'll give him an injection now and then come back later this evening to give him another. It will take twenty-four hours for the penicillin to start fighting the infection, but it should give him a better chance of recovery than any other methods we know of.'

Bob looked at Ivy and saw the heartache and worry etched on her face. Ben was their son, loved by both, more precious than any money – just as Arthur Metcalfe had said. 'Aye, go on. If you think it will work, you give him a shot. If it's good enough for our fighting lads, then it's good enough for our Ben.'

161

Ivy managed a smile, and they watched as Dr Batty took a syringe and a phial out of his bag.

'He'll not feel a thing,' the doctor said as he took Ben's arm and injected him. Ben looked up at him, half delirious. 'There you are, young man. It will take more than one of these, but I'm sure it will work for you.' He pulled up the small bedroom chair and sat down on it. 'I'll sit with him for the next hour to make sure he doesn't suffer any side effects, but by tomorrow morning I expect his temperature to be getting back to normal. He's young, he should be able to shake it off quickly with the aid of penicillin.'

Bob looked awkwardly at Dr Batty. 'I don't know how to thank you.'

'It's all right, Bob, it's the least I can do for you. And don't worry about payment. The drug is on trial. I'll get paid for giving a report to *The Lancet*, with your permission.' Dr Batty smiled.

'Nay, that won't cover your time here with us,' Bob said, shaking his head.

'Then a cup of tea and one of your scones, Ivy, would not go amiss. I left my pudding on the dining table to come here, although I'm not complaining.'

'Right you are, Doctor, and I'll fill it with jam and cream. Anything is yours if you can save our lad.' Ivy turned and went downstairs with tears in her eyes and a prayer on her tongue.

'I'll see you right, Doctor. There'll be a salmon out of the beck this autumn, and the best turkey on your Christmas table,' Bob promised. 'It's the least we can do.'

Chapter 15

'What time is it, Mam? There's a lot of noise in the yard.' Ben rubbed his eyes and blinked as his mother put a breakfast tray down on the chair next to his bed. She opened the curtains, letting the sun flood into his bedroom.

'It's only early yet, pet, just six-thirty. They're putting the pens up for the sheep – they're going to be busy clipping today. Seeing the weather is being kind to us.' Ivy sat on the bed edge and put her hand on her son's head to feel his temperature. 'That's more like it. A lot cooler, although you're looking a bit pasty now.'

'I've never been in bed this long. Father will be playing heck with me. Won't he be wanting me to help with the sheep?' Ben lay back on his pillows, frowning.

'He's just glad that you're still with us. He's been worried sick about you. Now, you try and eat a few spoonfuls of porridge.' Ivy ran her fingers through his hair and kissed his clammy brow. 'Look, Sally has even walked into Dent for you and got a bottle of Lucozade to help you recover. It'll do you good, so they say.' She held up the bobbly glass bottle to show him and then took off its orange cellophane wrapper, twisting the cap open. 'Here, I'll pour you some in your glass.'

'Can you ask our Sal to pick my bike up for me? I left it behind a gate just after Dent Head viaduct. I don't want it pinching,' Ben said as he took a tentative sip of the glucose-filled drink before tackling his breakfast.

'Oh, now I know you're on the mend, asking about your bike. Yes, I'll ask her. She's at work tomorrow. She can walk up the dale for it and bring it back. Now, you can stay in your bed for another day or two. You might as well not go back to school now; it finishes on Friday, but you need to be fit to start work at Morphet's, so we'll see how you feel.' Ivy rose and headed for the door before turning back to look at her son, whom she and Bob had been afraid they were going to lose. Thank the heavens for penicillin, she thought – it was going to save many a life, no doubt. With a last smile at Ben, she went downstairs to prepare for one of the busiest days of the year.

Ben lay back in his bed after eating his breakfast. He was exhausted and feeble, but he was alive, and that was more than he deserved after acting like such a selfish idiot. He'd not do that again in a hurry, he thought as he curled up beneath the blankets and looked at the aircraft's magneto lying on the floor beside his bed. Retrieving it had nearly cost him his life. He had learned a valuable lesson – that life was more precious than any possession.

Sally walked over to Luca and the two POWs who had come with Brian Harper. She was carrying a tray laden with bread, jam and glasses of ginger beer: an early-morning drink and a bite to eat before the real work started.

The two German POWs looked at her and then nudged one another, grinning. They said something to Luca that Sally couldn't understand, but she could see and hear his anger when he replied.

'What did they say, Luca?' she asked as she passed them their drinks and encouraged them to take some bread.

'They say, now they know why I come to work with a smile on my face,' Luca replied. He glared at his two German colleagues.

'Do they, now? And why is that?' Sally smiled.

'Because you feed him well,' replied the taller of the two German POWs. 'I am Fritz, and this is my friend Hans. We both speak good English, *ja*?'

'You do indeed. I didn't know that, else I would have asked you if you wanted the drink.' Sally watched as they ate the bread and quickly drained their glasses.

'We both learn English at school, but him over there – he doesn't know. He doesn't deserve our respect.' Fritz nodded his head at Brian. 'He treats us like slaves, even though we are farmers just like him. He's not a good man.' He glowered at Brian. 'Luca is lucky he comes here. This is a good home, I can tell.'

'We know you didn't want to fight, just like half of our own men in the war. It has hurt so many homes and families,' Sally said. She looked across at Brian and her father leaning against the kitchen doorway, deep in conversation about the day of work ahead. 'Not everyone understands.'

'They just think we are Nazis. We hate Hitler as much as you do,' Hans said, spitting into the dust of the farm-yard.

'Well, you'll be treated right and fed while you are here, as long as you do what is needed of you.' Sally looked at Luca and found him watching her. She felt herself blushing as she met his dark eyes.

'Don't you get too friendly with those two bastards,' Brian Harper shouted at her from the doorway.

'Brian, hold your tongue. They're welcome here, just as Luca is. They are here because they're not radical, and you should know that,' Bob said. Then he shouted across to Sally, 'You and Luca are to gather the fell for any strays the dogs leave behind. You can both start climbing up there as soon as you're ready.'

'Right, Father, we'll go now. Luca can walk up the far side and I'll walk up this side.' Sally quickly picked up the glasses and glanced at Luca. 'You know what you have to do?'

'*Si*, any sheep, I send down here,' he replied, glaring at his fellow POWs as they both sniggered.

'That's right. I'll just take these in to Mam and then we'll go. Father will walk halfway up the fell with the dogs, and then it'll be up to us that none are left behind.'

Brian Harper shouted at his two men, 'Move, you idle buggers. Let's get everything ready for the gather. It's going to be a long day, and a hot'en.'

Sally and Luca made their way through the bottom fell gate, leaving it open for the flock to run straight into the holding pens. Sally followed the wall side up the fell; she could see Luca doing the same, sometimes disappearing from sight as he followed the rough fell. It was only just seven o'clock but the sun was already hot, and she kept taking time to catch her breath and look around. Far in the distance she could see the high peaks of the Lake District, and down below she could see Brian and her father with the two sheepdogs. Once sent, the dogs would soon run up the fellside and gather what sheep her father and Brian could see, with the aid of whistles and shouts. Her job and Luca's was to make sure all strays were accounted for, the ones that the dogs might miss in the hollows or wall sides of the fell.

She stood for a moment with her hands on her hips and drew breath. The air was filled with the chirping of crickets and the heather on the very top of the fell was just about to come into bloom. She picked a harebell and placed it behind her ear, then waved at Luca as he came into sight. Between them, the dogs ran up the centre of the fell, rounding up sheep and snapping at the heels of a particularly stubborn ewe. It stamped its foot before following the rest of the herd down the fellside.

Sally scanned the fell and spotted another ewe on the opposite side by the wall. She headed towards it, breathing quickly as she navigated the uneven, boggy surface of sphagnum moss and deep, dark peat. She made it to the far wall and stirred the old ewe that had been overlooked by the dogs. As Luca came walking up towards her, she stumbled over a tufted patch of ground and fell, landing on her hands.

'You all right, Sally?' Luca held his hands out, helping her back onto her feet with a smile.

'Yes, just stumbled.' She held onto his arms and looked into his eyes. Her heart missed a beat; he was so handsome, with his dark hair and eyes. And now he had his arms around her, and she could smell the soap he had washed with that morning. They stood for a moment, looking at one another, with the slight breeze of the fell blowing over them.

Then, suddenly, what they had both been thinking about was actually happening. Luca pulled Sally close and kissed her, calling her *bella* as she returned his kisses.

'We shouldn't – it's wrong,' she said after a minute, stepping back and putting her hand to her mouth.

'It no wrong, Sally – it feels good, *si*?' He smiled and reached for her hand. 'It makes you feel better?'

She smiled and blushed. 'Yes, it did . . . but we still shouldn't.'

'No one know. We keep it secret. Just me and you.' Luca leaned forward and kissed her again.

'Yes, secret, Luca,' Sally murmured as she took his hand. They walked together towards the fellside skyline. Both were afraid they might be seen by prying eyes from the farmyard below as the flock of sheep made their way down, following one another under the guidance of the sheepdogs.

'We do it again – *si*? Soon,' Luca said as he let go of Sally's hand and moved away from her.

'Yes, we will, but no one must find out,' she replied. She tried to compose herself as they exchanged a knowing look before walking down to the farmyard, into the noise and activity of bleating sheep and lambs being penned and sorted by her father and his helpers.

'You've fetched them all down? I've not been counting,' Bob said, looking at their flushed faces.

'Aye, the fell's clear, unless there's one hiding and we've missed it,' Sally replied. She watched as Luca made his way towards the sheep pens.

'Well, now that's done, you can teach Luca how to fold the fleeces. With no Ben, we'll need somebody for that. Both of Brian's Jerries know how to clip, so they can do that.' Bob swung his leg over the wooden railings that penned the sheep in and walked over to where the three men were busy holding the older sheep, handling them deftly as they started to shear the winter coats from off their backs. He picked his shears up, nodding to Sally to join Luca and show him what to do as the others started throwing their fleeces at him.

Sally followed her father across towards Luca, who stood feeling useless.

'Watch.' She grabbed one of the shorn fleeces and shook it out to its full length. 'Pick off any big clumps of dirt or muck, fold the leg pieces in, then fold the fleece into three, leaving the tail hanging out . . . then roll it and tie it with the tailpiece. Easy!' She held up the folded fleece to show him before placing it into a large canvas sack that lay ready beside the fence, stencilled with the words *British Wool Board Bradford*.

Luca picked up the next one and tried to replicate what Sally had shown him. It took him twice the time, but he succeeded eventually.

'That's it. But a bit faster.' Sally smiled at him. She couldn't stop thinking of their kiss and the feel of his arms around her. It had been a long time since she'd felt so happy. She picked up another fleece, folded and bagged it, then watched as he did the same. Standing up, she looked at her father and the other three men in their shirtsleeves, surrounded by bleating sheep and the sounds of summer. This was a clipping day she wouldn't soon forget, she thought, as Luca smiled up at her and whispered, *'Secret.'*

Chapter 16

'It sounds as if our troops are making their way into France,' Sarah Middleton said as she folded and bundled the unsold papers ready for tomorrow's exchange for that day's news. The shop was running down for the evening; everything fresh had been put away in the pantry, the money out of the brass till had been banked and the shelves had been restocked for the following day's trade.

'Yes, things are starting to look a bit more hopeful,' Sally replied as she took off her apron and hung it up on the hook behind the counter. It was the end of her day in the shop, but now she was going to walk all the way up Cowgill dale to collect Ben's bike from next to the viaduct.

'Still no news of your Edward, though? What are you going to be doing this evening? I'll have to stop in, I suppose, there's nothing else to do.' Sarah leaned on the counter as Sally made for the shop doorway and turned the 'Closed' sign around.

'No. It's as if my life is on hold. But lately I've started to accept that he's not coming back. He's been gone too long, and without a word from anywhere or anybody. I have to get on with my life.' Even as Sally said the words, she still didn't quite believe them. Somewhere, somehow, Edward could still be alive, and he could still return to her. The guilt she had felt after kissing Luca and experiencing the butterflies in her stomach had kept her awake all night. Their attraction to one another was wrong in so many ways, not only because he was a POW – but she had enjoyed his advances so much. She wondered whether to say something to Sarah about it, but thought better of it.

'I'd get on with your life. None of us wants to be left an old maid. I've got my eye on John Woof, and he keeps coming in and looking at me, but he's shy. I don't know what to say to him.' Sarah cupped her face in her hands.

'Faint heart never won fair maiden. You'll just have to talk to him and put him at his ease.' Sally smiled at her friend, thinking how good it would be to see her find happiness with her young man. 'Right, I'm going. I'll see you in the morning. Remember, you make the first move. Men are sometimes a bit slow at coming forward.'

'Thanks, Sally. I'll take your advice.' Sarah beamed as Sally left the shop, its bell ringing behind her, and passed by the window on her way up the dale.

Sally hummed a song and smiled to herself, running her hands through the hedgerow plants. She was thinking about Luca, about the look he had given her and the kisses they had exchanged. She hadn't felt the way she did now for so long, and was trying hard not to feel guilty about their friendship. She knew what was happening between them was wrong; but if it made them both feel good, where was the harm?

As she passed the small church of St John, she stopped on the church bridge and looked down into the stream that ran under it. Across the next two fields stood Rayside, where Edward's parents lived. Perhaps she should call in and see if they'd heard any news of their son? If there was even the slightest glimmer of hope, she would behave herself and not encourage Luca. She couldn't bear to think of breaking Edward's heart if he were ever to return.

Sally sighed. She wanted her life back just as much as she wanted Edward to come home, but couldn't move on until she knew what had become of him.

Soon she was standing at the bottom of the lane to Rayside. From there she could see that the front door was open. She walked up the dusty path and looked at the hay meadow on either side; it was like her father's, another few weeks and it would be ready for mowing, providing the weather was good. She opened the garden gate and made her way towards the open door, admiring the pansies and geraniums that Maggie Riley had within her plot.

'Hello! Is anybody in?' Sally lifted the brass knocker, which was shaped like a fox, and knocked gently on the well-painted door. She looked in and saw a low-ceilinged room with a table set ready for the evening meal.

'Hello? Just a minute and I'll be with you,' Maggie called from the pantry, and came out carrying some cooked ham to go with the salad already on the table. 'Oh, now it's Sally, isn't it? I haven't seen you for a while,' she said as she placed the ham down and draped it with a mesh covering to keep the summer flies off.

'Yes, I'm on my way to pick up my brother's bike from further up the dale, and I thought I'd pop my head in to say hello.' Looking at Edward's mother, Sally sensed that perhaps Maggie wasn't very pleased to see her.

'Oh, I see. Burt is just up at the top barn milking. He'll be wanting his supper when he comes back in.' Maggie didn't ask Sally to sit down or have a drink, but stood and looked at her, crossing her arms.

'I just thought I'd come and ask if you had heard anything about Edward. I still live in hope,' Sally said quietly, and held her breath.

'We have heard nothing, lass. We won't now; it's been too long. Burt says we have to live with it and try to move on. There isn't a day I don't think of Edward, and Burt blames himself for not keeping him on the farm.' Maggie looked hard at Sally. 'Perhaps it's best if you're gone before he comes back. His nerves are not good at the moment.'

'I'm sorry. Perhaps I shouldn't have called in, but I still think of him as well. I don't think I'll ever forget him.' Sally bowed her head. If even Edward's family had decided it was time to move on, perhaps she shouldn't feel so guilty for enjoying Luca's company.

'Well, it breaks my heart to say it, but forget him, Sally. Live your life. He's obviously dead on some battlefield in France. I only hope someday someone might be able to

174

tell us what happened to him. Now, as I say, it's supper time, and you have your brother's bike to pick up.' Maggie hesitated. 'Couldn't he pick his own bike up?'

Sally shook her head slightly, her heart aching. 'He's been ill with pneumonia. We nearly lost him,' she said quietly.

'Oh, I didn't know. Thank the Lord you didn't – your mother would have been broken-hearted, just like me. Take care, Sally. You enjoy your life. You can put Edward in the past where he belongs, no matter how much it hurts.' Maggie turned away, fighting back tears, and grabbed some knives and forks from a kitchen drawer. Edward was never coming back to her or to Sally, and it was time they both realized it.

Sally walked down the path and closed the farm gate behind her. She didn't know how she felt. One minute she was trying to be true to Edward, and the next she was feeling the rush of happiness as she thought about Luca and his arms holding her so tightly.

She set out towards the small hamlet of Lea Gate, stepping aside after a few minutes as she heard a wagon coming along the narrow country road. Turning back to look at it, she realized it was the open-backed wagon that picked up the POWs to go back to Loftus Hill. They would all be sitting in the back. She felt her heart miss a beat and felt like a silly schoolgirl as she wondered if Luca was there, and if she should wave as it passed by.

The wagon driver pipped his horn as he recognized Sally from his morning drop-offs and the men in the back, sitting on either side of the wagon, cheered as they went past. Sally blushed as she looked up at them, searching for Luca's face. She could see Fritz and Hans, the two Germans who had helped shear the sheep, but there was no sign of Luca as the wagon went over the humpbacked bridge to travel further up the dale. Perhaps he was being picked up on the way down the dale, she thought as she carried on her way.

Passing the local pub, The Cow Dubb, Sally looked up to the second viaduct that crossed the dale carrying the Settle–Carlisle railway. The dale had been completely cut off until the coming of the railway, which now ran high on the fellside. Its main station was a good two miles from the village of Dent, confusing some passengers as they alighted too soon only to realize they had quite a walk before reaching their destination.

After a few minutes, Sally had to step aside once more as she heard the POW wagon coming back down the road. It must have picked up a worker from Stone House Farm, she thought. This time, as it passed, cheers went up and Fritz and Hans yelled something to her at the top of their voices, but she couldn't make out what they were saying. She made her way up the steep road that passed underneath the huge piers of Dent Head viaduct.

'Hello, my *bella*.'

Sally nearly jumped out of her skin as Luca appeared from behind one of the viaduct piers.

'I jump out of the wagon. They no miss me.' He grinned and put his hands around her waist as she caught her breath. 'I hear you father say you be here, so I come.'

'Heavens, Luca, you scared me! They will miss you –

you'll be in bother.' Sally put her hands on his shoulders as he pulled her towards him and kissed her. 'Stop it, somebody might see us,' she said half-heartedly as he stepped back, looking intently at her and pulling on her hand. He was leading her towards the old original pack-horse bridge that still stood under the viaduct's large arches. The two bridges, built in different centuries, looked quite at home together as the warm breeze of the fell passed over them and rustled the leaves on the trees.

'No one sees us here.' Luca indicated to her to sit down next to him and embraced her. 'There, we happy now.'

'Oh, Luca, we shouldn't. It's so wrong.' Sally felt her heart beating quickly as she looked into his eyes and remembered Maggie Riley's words.

'We do no wrong. We both no married.' Luca ran his hands through Sally's hair, pulled her close and kissed her, running his hands down her body. He held her tightly and whispered words in Italian that she didn't understand.

'No, Luca, not yet – it's wrong. We shouldn't.' Sally grabbed his hand from around her breast and looked at him. 'No. Just kiss, nothing more.' She moved away from him – she would have liked more, but her conscience was warning her against it. 'You could get into terrible trouble, and we don't want that,' she said. She was also questioning her wisdom in being alone, quite a way from the nearest house, with an Italian POW that she hardly knew. He could do anything to her, and nobody would know.

'I wait. *Mi scusi* – I sorry.' Luca stood up and took Sally's hand. 'I rush you.'

'Yes, you do. Let me get used to the idea. There are

so many things against us.' Sally smiled. 'You being Italian and me English, and us both at war.'

'*Si* – and you think of Edward. I know you do,' Luca whispered as they walked back towards the road.

'I do. I can't help it.' Sally drew a deep breath and took Luca's hand. 'Good friends that kiss?' she said, and squeezed his hand as they walked under the large arch and towards the gate where Ben said he had hidden his bike.

'*Si*, kiss and friends. I understand.' Luca watched as Sally found Ben's bike behind the wall, wheeled it onto the road and started pushing it back. 'I show you a fast way.' He got her to balance on the seat as he stood on the pedals and pushed with his feet to get the bike rolling down the hill, back down the dale. 'We soon get home.'

Sally held tight to his waist and just hoped that nobody would see them as they flew down the road, laughing and enjoying each other's company.

'Go around Dent on the back road – it's more private, we don't want people to see us,' Sally said into his ear as they approached the bridge into Dent.

'*Si*. Home soon.' Luca turned with a grin on his face and Sally nearly lost her balance. She was holding onto both the saddle and Luca's jacket as he pedalled the last mile to the bottom of Daleside's lane and finally stopped. He stood and waited until Sally climbed down from the saddle and then took his leg from one side of the bike and passed her it back. 'We were quick!'

'Yes, we were quick.' Sally's legs were shaking as she stood next to him and looked at him. She could love this man, she thought, if only things were easier for them both. 'You get home now; you will be missed.'

'They no miss me. We don't eat until seven.' Luca stepped forward, took Sally's hand and kissed her gently on the lips. '*Buonasera*, my *bella*.' He gazed into her eyes and lingered for a moment, his hand in hers, before turning to go.

'Good night, Luca. Sweet dreams,' Sally called softly as she watched him heading down the road towards Sedbergh. Yes, she could quite easily give her heart to him if things were different.

'You look flushed, have you rushed getting home?' Ivy asked as she saw Sally prop the bike up next to Ben's shed and come into the kitchen.

'No, it's just a warm evening. And it's quite a way up to Dent Head.' Sally took a drink of water from the kitchen tap and looked out across the yard. Her mother and father must never know what she and Luca had been up to.

'Well, it is for a girl. I'd have freewheeled it and stood on the pedals for most of the way back home, but you wouldn't dare,' came a voice from out of the chair next to the fireplace.

'Oh, Ben, you're dressed and up!' Sally turned with a smile, wishing she could tell him that that was exactly what she and Luca had done.

'Yes, I'm up. A bit wobbly on the pins, but I can't lie in bed all the time. I have a job to go to now.' Ben grinned. 'I was only poorly so I could miss the last week of school.'

'You were more than poorly, mister. And work can wait another week, your father's seen to that. He called in and had a word with Bill Morphet this morning. Another week at home and then you can start work,' Ivy said as she put Sally's warmed-up supper in front of her and listened to Ben complain.

'Thanks, Mam, I'm ready for this.' Sally pulled her chair up to the table. Ben was getting better, and she had a new love in her life, she thought. She just hoped that Edward would forgive her.

Chapter 17

Ivy put on her best hat, adjusted her imitation pearls and checked herself in the mirror before glancing back at her family sitting round the kitchen table. She never went anywhere on her own, so they would have to lump it, she thought as she turned with her handbag on her arm.

'I'll be back for supper time, so you'll not go hungry. If you do, there's plenty of stuff to eat in the pantry.' She suppressed a pang of guilt as Bob scowled at her. 'It's a fundraiser for our lads that are fighting. We have to be seen to be doing something. And anyway, there might be one or two good bits that I can buy and bring home with me.' Ivy tried to rationalize her attendance at the bring-and-buy sale held at the Memorial Hall by using bribery with the promise of new clothes or something useful.

'It's an excuse for a good gossip and to put the world to rights, that's what it is. You'll come back with all sorts of rubbish to tell me,' Bob said, leaning back in his chair.

'Go and enjoy yourself, Mam. And if you're late back don't worry, I'll make supper.' Sally smiled and started to tidy the dinner table.

'Mam, can I go down to Sedbergh on my bike? I'm feeling a lot stronger now,' Ben said.

'No, you bloody well can't, Ben. I've told Morphet's that you need another week before you start work with them, so you stop around home,' Bob said firmly. 'If you want something to do, you can come and mend the hay rakes with new teeth. You should be able to manage that without any bother. It'll be haytime before we know it, the grass is growing nicely now.'

'Do as your father says, and just for once, behave yourself. If Madge Sedgwick has made any of that toffee you like, I'll bring you some back. But I doubt it, with sugar rationing being as tight as it is.' Ivy headed for the door. 'Right, I'm going – it will take me twenty minutes to walk into Dent in this heat.'

Her unspoken hopes for a lift on the back of Bob's motorbike were dashed as her husband reached for his newspaper before starting on the jobs he had planned for the rest of the day.

'Take care, Mam. Enjoy yourself,' Sally said as she clattered the dirty dishes in the sink. With luck, her mother would bring her something back from the sale.

'Aye, see you all later.' Ivy stepped outside and breathed in deeply. An afternoon to herself – what a luxury. Even though she would be running a stall with Sissie Bain, it would be a chance to have a catch-up and a natter. Or gossip, as Bob had called it.

When she walked into the hall – the central hub of Dent, along with the church – things were already in full swing. Trestle tables had been arranged around the space and patriotic bunting hung from the walls and beams. In the kitchen, the women of Dent were busy setting out cups and saucers along with whatever biscuits they could spare from their meagre rations; at the back of the hall, others were sorting through boxes of donated gifts, discussing prices and placing the items out for sale.

'Ah, Ivy! Glad you could make it. I thought perhaps I was going to be on my own when I heard how ill your Ben has been.' Sissie Bain came towards Ivy and guided her to their table. 'We have drawn the short straw – second-hand clothes,' she said, with a look of disgust on her face.

'Ben is a lot better, thank you. We're hoping he'll be able to start work next week.' Ivy looked at the bags of clothes that needed sorting and folding. It didn't seem such a bad job to her; she was thankful she wasn't serving the teas. 'I don't mind looking after the clothes stall. I'm always amazed at what people decide to give away.'

'I don't like looking through it all. Some things just belong in the recycled rags. It's a waste of our time, but never mind; we will make use of them.' Sissie stood with her hands on her hips. 'I see that Hilda Birbeck is helping in the kitchen. Her face would curdle milk, but she's doing well to be here, seeing that her brother is still over there fighting. Her parents are that ashamed of him, you hardly see them in public any more.'

'Hilda seems to be the normal one in the family, so

183

I have more time for her,' Ivy replied as she began emptying bags of clothing onto the table. 'She must be worried about Jonathan, no matter what he's done. He's stuck to fighting for his country and we should still support him.'

'Try telling that to the poor lasses he made in the family way. I still have no time for him,' Sissie said. She helped Ivy fold the clothes and sort the tatty items from the saleable goods before picking up another full bag. 'Eh, Ivy, this is a good lot! Just look at what's in here. It must have come from the Gate; their lass has just moved away from home. Have a rummage – I daresay everything in the bag would fit your Sally. There are even some women's breeches. Although I still don't think women should wear trousers; it's not right,' Sissie added as she passed the bag to Ivy. First pick of the donations was one of the perks of helping.

Ivy looked into the bag, pulling out the contents. 'My Bob would go mad if our Sally wore these. He doesn't think lasses should wear trousers either, but I could see Sally in them, and she's always saying she wants some. I'll take them. They're quite smart, that navy blue with the white trim. And there's a jumper to match. They will suit her to bits, no matter what Bob thinks. There's all sorts in here for her – I'll have a rummage through and donate a good price. It will make her day.'

'Well, only give what you can afford. Sally's already donated her fella to the war,' Sissie said. 'He was far too young to be lost. The poor lass. Although – I was just happening to look out of my kitchen window the other evening when I saw her flying past on the back of a bike with what looked like one of them from Loftus Hill pedalling. She doesn't want to be getting too close to them. We know nowt about them.'

'No, that couldn't have been our Sally. She'd not bother with any of them. Although we do have Luca working for us, and she does talk to him,' Ivy added, and went quiet. Sally on the bike with, presumably, Luca? She was going to have to talk to her. If Bob found out, there would be hell to pay.

'I could have been wrong. They passed in a flash.' Sissie kept folding the clothes and seemed about to say something else, but then Hilda Birbeck approached the table with a cup of tea for each of them.

'A drink for you before the doors open. There's a queue already outside. Mrs Dinsdale's pickles and jams will go down well, everyone is saying.' Hilda looked at Ivy. 'You and your family all right? Hopefully there will be good news from our boys shortly.'

Sissie gave Ivy a sly look and said nothing.

'Yes, we're all fine. You'll be glad to have Jonathan back once this war is over,' Ivy said as Hilda leaned against the table.

'He's over in France. They're making a push to Paris, we think, from reading between the lines. But he doesn't say a lot – he can't. I hope Sally finds peace and a good man when this war is over. She deserves it,' Hilda said quietly. With a nod to them both, she returned to the kitchen as the main doors were opened at the other end of the hall. Villagers started to stream in.

'That's the most I've ever heard her say. You are privileged!' Sissie remarked sarcastically, and then smiled as their first customer approached.

'Oh, my legs ache! That's the busiest I've seen one of these sales. We made three pound two and six on our stall alone.' Ivy sank into a kitchen chair and rubbed her aching feet. 'I hope you're not expecting a lot for supper, because I'm shattered.'

'It's all right, Mam, I made a bacon-and-egg pie while you were out. I thought you'd probably come back tired. And there's a rice pudding in the side oven, so you have a sit. Supper is sorted. Ben is in his bike shed and father is just tidying the forks up that they repaired earlier today.' Sally passed her mother a cup of tea and sat down beside her.

'Hilda Birbeck was asking after you today. And Sissie said something strange. She swears she saw you on the bike with a POW – Ben's bike, I suppose. Is that right?' Ivy saw colour come into her daughter's cheeks.

'No, why would I do that? Besides, Luca would have been here or back at Sedbergh when I picked the bike up,' Sally pointed out. But she couldn't quite meet Ivy's eyes.

'Well, I never mentioned Luca, just a POW. Make sure you behave yourself with that one – like Sissie says, we know nothing about them. Keep your distance, young lady,' Ivy said sternly. She bent down and rooted in her bag. 'Look at what I've brought back for you. They came from the Gate, so they're a good make, but your father

186

will play heck with me.' She pulled out the well-cut navy blue trousers and held them up to show Sally, followed by the knitted navy-and-white jumper. 'Now, isn't that smart? But your father won't be keen on them trousers, the old-fashioned devil. I can see why you young women like them.' She handed the outfit to Sally, who smiled as she held them up against herself.

'Oh, Mam. They are lovely – they must have cost a fortune when new. I'll keep them for best, they look just my size. How could they throw stuff like this out? It's far too good.' Sally felt the quality of the material and thought just how smart she would look in both.

'Well, some folk still have more money than sense. Perhaps it was just your lucky day that I ended up on the second-hand clothes stall with Sissie. I only paid a few pence for them. Although I nearly thought of putting them back when I heard what she had to say.' Ivy hesitated. 'You behave yourself with that lad. Anybody but him, Sally. Else you'll have your heart broken again, and I don't want that for you.'

'I hear you, Mam; you don't have to say any more,' Sally replied, looking at her new outfit. She was thinking that she and Luca would have to be more careful. It had been foolish to imagine they could travel the length of the dale without being noticed. Somebody always knew what you were up to, and if they didn't, they made it up.

Chapter 18

'Now, you are sure you're up to starting work? It's a big step at any time, and you've been so ill.' Ivy worriedly straightened her son's shirt collar. 'You tell Bill Morphet if you don't feel well. And don't take any bullying from off Dennis Slater – you can't believe a word he says, he takes after his father. I never liked him.'

'For heaven's sake, Mother, stop fussing over him. He's only working half a day today with it being Saturday. Besides, he's well now. He can't be at home for ever, you know,' Bob said as he put on his jacket. 'He's got a lift into Sedbergh, anyway, because I've to go there for Jim before I start work on Monday. He wants some whetstones to sharpen his scythes with – I'll get us one and all. Brian Harper might be mowing the main of the meadows, but he'll not get into every corner with that big War Ag tractor.' Bob took a last sip of his tea and patted Ben on the back. 'Come on, then. Let's get going, else you're going to make both of us late.' He put on his cap and picked up his keys for the motorbike.

Ben followed his father out of the house. He had been waiting for the past week to start his new job in the garage. Now that the time had finally come, his stomach was churning, even though he knew both Bill and Dennis well. Today he would have to show them that his work was worth paying for. He would need to prove himself. Instead of being one of the oldest at school, he would be at the bottom of the pile in the garage, and he was just a tad frightened.

'Right, lad, off you get. I'll pick you up at one when I've done my bit of business.' Bob stood astride his bike as Ben climbed off the back. Morphet's garage consisted of two large sheds at the side of the main road through Sedbergh. Outside, there were two pumps, one that gave you petrol and the other red derv for the running of tractors, which were still new to the Dales. 'You'll be all right. They'll look after you,' Bob added as Ben headed towards the shabby-looking building.

Ben turned back and waved before disappearing into the garage depths, where a car was parked over its motor pit and Dennis Slater had his head under the bonnet. Bob watched as Bill came to the garage doorway and waved to him – a silent way of saying he would look after his son while he worked for him.

'Now then, lad, your father says you've been ill and that they nearly lost you, so I'll not be asking a lot of you this week. I know you're good at mechanics anyway – you've never been away from this place since you were about ten. You know it inside out. But now you're here to learn, and to make me money.' Bill Morphet patted Ben on the shoulder. 'Dennis here is looking at Mr Taylor's old banger. It's not firing properly, so he's just checking the spark plugs – he thinks they might just be damp. I'll leave you with him to lend a hand. You know where we keep the tools – you might have to be his runner this morning and fetch him various things.' Dennis lifted his head out from the car's bonnet, and Bill winked at him.

'Aye – in fact, you can help me right now,' he said to Ben. 'It's like Bill says, I think the plugs are damp. A good covering of elbow grease will do the trick. It's on the top shelf in the hut next door, in a blue-and-yellow can, if you fancy going to fetch it for me.' Dennis rubbed his hands on an oily cloth and leaned against the car as Ben put down his packed-lunch tin and looked at Bill.

'Aye, go on, lad, that's just what it wants. Dennis knows his job.' Bill nodded encouragingly to Ben, and the two men watched as he nearly ran towards the hut where he knew the tools were kept.

Ben looked up at all the tools arranged in their places and the countless tins of oil, paint, grease and anything else that a garage needed. There was no sign of elbow grease. He stood on tiptoe on the little old wooden step-ladder and peered up towards the top shelf. His heart beat fast – his first job, and he couldn't even do that right! He hung his head and returned to the two men. 'I can't find it,' he said. 'I've looked everywhere.'

'Never mind – I can manage without it. But if you can

go back and get me a left-handed screwdriver, these screws are really rusty. It'll be hanging up on the wall,' Dennis said. He pretended to be busy again under the bonnet.

Ben ran off again with a curious glance at Bill Morphet, who looked as if he was suffering from a bad case of wind – he was nearly bent double.

It was only when he was back in the hut, looking up at the immaculately set out wall covered in tools, that he realized they had been playing him for a fool. There was no such thing as tinned elbow grease or a left-handed screwdriver. He'd play them at their own game, thought Ben, as he walked back into the garage cool and sober-faced.

'I couldn't find a left-handed screwdriver; I think they are hard to find, just like glass hammers. And the same with your elbow grease. I know you're having me on!' grinned Ben. 'I was just so nervous, I didn't think.'

'Aye, we thought we would welcome you properly. We always have the apprentice on and give him the most important job of all, making the morning's brew. At least you have a sense of humour, lad.' Bill tousled Ben's short hair. 'You know where everything is in the back, don't you – you've sat in there long enough when you've been here in the past. I've gone to the expense of buying you a new enamel mug, so you'd better be stopping with us. Mine's a strong tea and this one likes it weak, just like his head.'

'Aye, watch what you're saying there. You'd be lost without me!' Dennis retorted. He looked at Ben. 'When we've had our brew, you can take a look under this old banger. Its brakes are failing. You can tell me how you'd fix it, and then we'll see if we both agree. But first, let's have a brew like Bill says. I'm fair parched.'

Ben was more at ease now. He'd be all right with Bill and Dennis, he thought as he waited for the kettle to boil and looked at their oil-smeared enamel mugs lined up with his nice clean one. It was good to be a part of the garage banter.

'Well, you make a good brew,' Bill said after they'd all drained the mugs. He nodded towards the garage front as a local farmer pulled up in his van. 'Now, how about you serve Tom Price? He'll want his jerry can filled up with red derv. He's got an account with the garage that he pays every month, so you tell me how much he takes and then I'll do the rest.'

Ben went to the derv pump, picked up the spout and waited until Tom passed him the can.

'You working here now? You'll be better than that gobby Dennis,' Tom said. He watched the dial on the pump as Ben filled up his can, making sure not to spill any, and put the lid back on tightly.

'Yes, first day today,' Ben replied, and passed Tom his can.

'Well, make sure you don't fiddle me, else you'll lose my custom. Now put it down in the book and make sure it's the right amount,' Tom said shortly. He put the can into the back of his van before driving off without another word.

'One of our more charming customers,' Dennis said with a grin as Ben went inside and reported to Bill that two gallons had been taken. 'Speaking of which, look who's coming down the road – the Italian Stallion, regular as clockwork.' He nodded across to the other side of the road, and Ben turned to see Luca walking along the pavement.

'That's Luca. He works for us when he comes on the POW wagon.' Ben waved, but Luca did not see him as he concentrated on where he was going.

'He'll not have time to look at you this morning, lad. He's on a mission to see Lottie Oversby. Goes every Saturday morning, regular as clockwork, stops for two hours and then goes back for his dinner. Then later on he'll be sitting on the steps of Metcalfe's shop looking at our women, the dirty devil. I hear he's married as well. Dirty Italians,' Dennis said, and spat a tea leaf out of his mouth in disgust.

'He always seems all right when he's at our house. He gets on with our Sally,' Ben said. He couldn't see what the fuss was about if Luca did visit Lottie Oversby.

'I bet he does, lad. You tell her that he's married and got a bit of stuff up Guldrey Terrace. I bet she won't be so interested in talking to him then.' Dennis pulled a face. 'Come on, drink up. Let's take a look at these brakes. Some of us have to work for a living, even on a Saturday.'

Chapter 19

Sally and Ben leaned over the meadow gate and looked out at the sea of clover, buttercups and blue bugle. There was a heated discussion going on in the kitchen between their parents about whether or not to get some turkeys to rear for Christmas. As usual, Ivy was not in favour, while Bob thought only of the brass he could make.

'It's blinking months off Christmas yet. And besides, the way Father is talking, we might not be living here anyway,' Ben said, and turned his face to the setting sun.

'They always argue over turkeys. They've done it for the past four years, so what's new? If it isn't turkeys, it's the pigs we're raising without the War Ag knowing. Mam worries, and Father tries to make as much money as possible from everything.' Sally sighed. 'How did you go on at the garage?'

'I really enjoyed it, Sal. We mended some brakes on Mr Taylor's black Ford, they needed new liners. Dennis is good at his job and I get on with him.' Ben hesitated.

'The only thing we didn't agree on was Luca. He passed by the garage. Dennis hates him.'

'Why? He won't even know him,' Sally said, puzzled.

'He says that Luca goes and sees a bit of stuff up Guldrey Terrace, and that all he does is sit on Metcalfe's shop steps and watch the women go by, even though he's married with a wife back in Italy. What's a bit of stuff? Whatever it is, he spends two hours with it every Saturday, and Dennis doesn't like that he does.'

Sally's face reddened with anger and hurt. 'It means he has a lady friend that lives up Guldrey Terrace. He's never said he's married, although I can believe that he would sit on the steps. He likes watching people, not just the women.' She felt a surge of anger towards her new love – had he been lying to her? 'But that Dennis Slater doesn't know everything. He's always talking, and what he doesn't know he makes up. He'll be jealous, that's all.'

'Why should he be jealous? Luca's just a POW. Dennis has a home in Sedbergh, and a job,' Ben replied defensively.

'Because he's a spotty, ginger-haired idiot who can't keep his mouth shut,' Sally snapped. 'Even though you do get on with him. Now come on, let's go in and see if peace has been restored. The midges are biting and I'm ready for my bed.'

Sally lay in her bed. It was still light outside, and she really wasn't very tired; she'd just needed to get away from everybody and think about what Ben had said. Her mother's words – *We don't know anything about him* – went around in her head. Had that been Ivy's way of telling her

195

that Luca was married, even though she shouldn't be setting her cap at him regardless? If he was married, she would never look at him again. She should have been true to Edward's memory. It just served her right, she thought, as she curled up and cried into her pillow.

The sun had been shining for two full days. Bob tapped the barometer that hung on the wall next to the back door and the needle shot around to show that there was high pressure on the way. It would bring just the right weather for the start of haytime.

'Good job Brian's coming to mow both meadows in the morning. He'll soon get them done. He did all his yesterday and on Sunday. Mowing hay fields on a Sunday – his father would have had something to say about that, strict Methodist that he was.'

'He would indeed, and that wouldn't be the only thing his father would have had something to say about. I forgot to tell you when I came back from the bring-and-buy – somebody told me that Brian's started courting Jean Handley. She only lost her husband a few weeks ago! They were saying he'll be after her land, not Jean.' Ivy crossed her arms and pulled a face.

Bob turned on the wireless to hear the week's weather forecast after the hourly news.

'You should apply for a job on the wireless,' he told Ivy. 'You could talk about everybody's business, you and that Sissie. It would right entertain folk. Leave the poor bugger alone – if he's chasing Jean and her land, he's not looking at buying Deep Well. Be thankful for that.' Bob

196

sat down in his chair and listened to the news of the Allies' latest progress across Europe before the weather report began.

'Aye, let's hope he can come and mow our meadows tomorrow, it's going to be a good week,' he said once it had ended, standing up to switch it off. 'Our lads sound as if they are winning. They're nearly on the outskirts of Paris. That'll sort out those half-Nazis in Vichy and help the free French. Hitler must be quaking in his boots.'

'He's not doing that much quaking. They're saying he's started bombing London with some newfangled rockets he's sending over the channel from Belgium,' Ivy replied as she washed up. 'He'll not be happy until we are all dead.'

'Then he'll never be happy, lass, because there's no way he's going to win over our lads, rockets or not. Now, I know where Ben is, but where's our Sally? I haven't seen hide nor hair, and I need her to hold me a board of wood in place while I mend the barn door. I'm doing all the odd jobs while I have the time, just in case we do move.'

'She went out over an hour ago. She'd a face like thunder and said she had a bad head, but I'd say she's in a mood over something. Probably something I said to her; it usually is,' Ivy commented. She was thinking of her conversation with Sally a few days earlier, but she didn't enlighten Bob about that.

'Well, it doesn't take a lot. I'll find her, wherever she is. Once we get that door done, I'll get myself to Jim's – I need to make sure I can have this week off to start

197

haymaking, although he said it would be right. He's plenty of folk to help without me.' Bob strode out into the yard and made for the barn, where he could see Luca mucking out the pig hulls.

'You haven't come in for a brew, lad. I didn't know you were already here,' Bob said in surprise.

'Sally say I have to clean pigs and then the cowshed,' Luca explained as he continued to load the wheelbarrow with muck. 'She not in a good mood today.'

'No; her mother said she wasn't. Just ignore her, lad. Something has upset her, and soon enough we will all know what – she usually goes quiet and then explodes. It'll be me, probably. It usually is.' Bob clapped Luca on the back. 'The pigs did need cleaning out, but they could have waited until after we'd got the hay in. Do you know where she is?'

'Up there, under the tree, on that big stone.' Luca pointed towards Sally's place of peace.

'Oh, I'll leave her there for a while, let her calm down. She can help me after dinner.' Bob shook his head as he looked up the fell towards where Sally sat. 'I bet she's sulking over me wanting turkeys again this year, even though we might be moving. She hates turkeys!'

A little later, when Bob had gone out on his motorbike, Luca glanced up from his work to see Sally making her way down the hillside. He knew it was more than turkeys upsetting her. She had been cold and heartless towards him.

'Sally, what I do? You no talk to me, you make me clean the pigs – what I do?' he asked as she drew near.

198

Sally stood and looked at him over the pig hull's door.

'You've lied to me, that's what you've done. You said you weren't married, but you are. And if that's not enough, you're seeing a woman down by the garage.' Sally felt tears threatening, but her anger helped her to force them back.

'I not married – who says this? They are wrong.' Luca shook his head and said firmly, 'They lie. I live with my family, but no wife.'

'How can I tell who to believe? You could tell me anything. What about the woman near the garage on Guldrey Terrace?'

'*Si*, I go to her, every Saturday,' Luca replied. Seeing the anger on Sally's face as she turned away, he added, 'Sally, I explain! Listen!'

'Cowshed needs cleaning! Get on with it!' Sally shouted back, still trying to hold back her tears.

So Dennis Slater was right. Luca could at least have made some effort to lie to her about it, she thought as she began walking around the boundary of the meadows. She was making sure there were no stones where the tractor and mower would need to go, so as not to break the cutting bar on the mower. 'Bloody Italians,' she whispered furiously, and didn't allow herself to look back or listen to Luca calling after her.

The following day was sweltering: ideal haymaking weather. Brian Harper entered the yard bright and early with the Fordson tractor, which had a new cutting bar on the back of it.

'Now then, Bob, we'll soon get you mown and then I'm off to see Jean Handley, mow her meadows for her too,' he called down from his seat high up on the tractor. 'Poor devil – what a time for her husband to drop down dead and leave her with all that land to look after.'

'Aye, I'm sure you'll help her out as much as you can, Brian. You're a good man,' Bob grinned at his neighbour. The cunning devil; he knew exactly what he was doing and why he was doing it. 'I'll leave you to it,' he went on. 'Sally and me are just patching up the barn door, doing a few jobs while the sun is shining. Before you know it, it'll be autumn, and then winter, and we both know nowt gets done then.'

'Aye, you're all right. Have you heard Arthur Metcalfe has put Deep Well up for sale at last? The board was just going up when I came down to Garsdale yesterday morning. For sale by auction by Richard Turner. I thought he already had a done deal, the way he was talking,' Brian said. Bob tried not to look surprised.

'Nay, never! I thought he might already have lined up a sale, privately. It'll be worth a bob or two. Maybe the grandbairns have arrived and now they're suddenly in a hurry,' Bob replied, and cursed under his breath. Why hadn't Arthur been to see him yet? He'd promised.

'Aye, probably. Right, I'll get a move on. I was thinking I might make him an offer. I called to see Richard Turner, but he said Arthur had asked him to just put names down of anyone who's interested, as he hadn't quite made his mind up. Funny old bugger, is Arthur.'

'Aye, he's a one-off, but I reckon he's a good'en,' replied Bob with a smile, as Brian revved his tractor up and left the yard. Perhaps he still was in with a chance of Deep Well.

After putting up with Sally's sniping at Luca all morning, Bob decided enough was enough.

'I don't know what's going on between you two, but if you're going to work together, you had better get whatever's annoying you off your chest, Sally. I can't be doing with this bad feeling between you both. Perhaps, Luca, your time with us had better come to an end after haytime.' Bob looked sternly at Sally and Luca as they sat with their backs to one another, eating their lunch from out of the basket that Ivy had brought into the hayfield.

'I need to go home,' Luca replied. 'No longer welcome here,' he added quietly, sneaking a look at Sally.

'Nothing's wrong with me. I'm just getting on with scaling the hay and minding my own business,' Sally replied. She stood up, took hold of her rake, and walked towards the drying grass that was slowly turning into hay in the heat of the summer sun.

'By heck, Luca, you really are in her bad books. I don't know what you've done, but she's sulking. You'll not get any sense out of her until she's sorted herself out. I shouldn't say it, but sometimes she's a bit like me in her ways,' Bob commented. He shook his head and drank the last drops of ginger beer from the bottle that Ivy had left for them, then got to his feet.

'I do nothing. She thinks bad of me and I do nothing,' Luca answered, standing up next to Bob.

'Whisht! Lad, what's that coming? Sounds like an aeroplane. We'd better stay here under the wall – you never know if it's one of ours or one of theirs nowadays. Sally, get yourself back here, there's an aircraft coming. And it's low, by the sound of it,' Bob yelled. They watched as Sally ran back towards them, dropping the hay rake when she saw the aeroplane flying low, the length of the dale. It was clearly marked as German and its bomb doors were open. She crouched down next to her father and looked across at Luca. 'Bloody Germans and Italians! I wish they were all dead, instead of killing us off.'

Bob glared at his daughter. He knew she didn't mean that, especially when it came to Luca.

All three watched as, a few seconds later, a Spitfire followed the bomber's trail. Both disappeared over the horizon.

'He's heading home, but he'll not make it with a Spitfire on his tail.' Bob stood up and looked at Sally and Luca. 'He must have been bombing somewhere up north – the Jerries are starting to become desperate. Now, our Sally, you need to apologize to Luca. He might be a POW but you know as well as I do that he's not a soldier by choice, like a lot of the Italians and even the Germans in some cases. You stay here until you sort yourselves out, because it's like working with two bloody growling dogs.' Bob picked up the basket containing what remained of the hayfield dinner. 'I'll take your mother this back and have a smoke, and by the time I return, I want you to be civil

202

with one another if nothing else. Otherwise I'll tell the van driver not to bother dropping Luca off in the morning.'

'I do nothing, Mr Fothergill,' Luca said. He looked across at Sally as she stared up the hillside.

'Tha's done something, and sulky-drawers here is going to get a tongue-lashing if she can't be civil. Now sort yourselves out!' Bob said sharply, and left them both to argue.

'Sally, I no married, believe me. I tell the truth. I go to woman on Guldrey Lane for help. She teaches me English. I need to speak better to show you how I feel. Believe me, please, Sally.' Luca put a hand on Sally's arm. 'I need to tell you things. She helps me.'

'You're going to her for *English lessons*?' This startled Sally out of her silence. She turned to him in amazement. 'And you're honestly not married? You're not making me out to be a fool, are you, Luca?' Searching his face, she realized that he was telling her the truth.

'*Si*, I not married. I have no woman. I just me.' Luca sighed. 'They tell lies, they no like us. The men are jealous.' He took Sally's hand and looked steadily into her eyes. 'We can stay friends. I go home soon. The war is nearly over.'

'Oh, Luca. I've had it all wrong – I truly am sorry. But yes, let's just be friends. Anything else is asking too much of us both.' Sally held his hand, squeezed it, and smiled. 'I should have believed you. I was so upset at the idea that you had lied to me.'

'I never lie to you, Sally, but now I know that we can only ever be friends.'

'Friends it is, then, Luca. I should never have looked for anything more. My heart is still Edward's and I know it is.'

'*Si*, I know. I never replace Edward; I know that when I kiss you.' Luca smiled. 'Your father, he returns; I get back to my work.' He stood up and helped Sally to her feet.

'Thank you, Luca. Things will be all right now.' Sally turned as her father strode across the rows of dying hay. 'We had fallen out over one thing or another, but we're all right now,' she said, hoping that would be enough to satisfy her father.

'That's all right, then. I thought your mother said something about you two being on a bike, but I were only half listening. Now, let's get this hay scaled and dried, and then we'll be able to lead it in come Friday. It should be good stuff, as well. The weather's been kind to us, as long as it holds.' Bob was more concerned about getting the hay in than whatever his daughter and the POW had fallen out over, especially now that they were both working together in harmony.

Chapter 20

The hay was in; the sheep were clipped, dosed and happily grazing upon the fellside. All was well in Bob's life, except that Arthur Metcalfe had not yet paid him a visit.

'I don't think he's ever going to come and see us about Deep Well,' Ivy said, as she sat and knitted a new pair of socks to put into Ben's Christmas box.

'He's a man of his word. He'll come. Just give him time,' Bob said, leaning against the kitchen doorway. 'In fact, you had better hold your whisht, because he's just this minute appearing up our lane. He's heard you talking about him.' He grinned. 'Put the kettle on, lass, and have you some of those scones left that you made this morning? Let's look after him properly.'

Bob watched as Arthur Metcalfe's battered old car drew up in front of him. It sounded so rough that you could hear it coming for miles, and one of the headlights was tied on with string. However, it served Arthur well as family car and hay-bale carrier, and it had even been known to transport calves to the auction. It looked a bit like its owner – long in the tooth, but with a lot of life still under the bonnet.

'Now then, Bob, I bet you thought I was never going to come, especially since you've heard the For Sale board has gone up.' Arthur, dressed in his usual mackintosh and trilby hat, got out of the car and walked over to Bob with papers under his arm. He patted him on the back as he greeted him.

'Nay, I knew you'd come. I was just bothered that you were taking your time,' Bob said, shaking his hand.

'Aye, well, I had to sort a few things out before coming to you. Sorry I've taken a while – I just wanted things to be right,' Arthur said. He gave Bob a look that was hard to read as they turned to go into the farmhouse.

'Hello, Arthur – we were just saying we hadn't heard from you, weren't we, Bob? I've put the kettle on.' Ivy pulled out a chair from the kitchen table and urged Arthur to sit down.

'Nay, Ivy, I think Arthur and me had better go into the front room if we're to discuss business. Fetch the tea and scones in when it's ready, would you?' Bob noticed Ivy's expression change. It was her business and all – but in his eyes, it was best left to the fellas.

'Yes, I will. I'll leave you to it, then.' Ivy knew her place. She'd have time to say what she thought after Arthur had gone.

It was cool in the front room as Arthur sat down in one of the two armchairs with a small table dividing them. The sun had dipped down behind the fell, and what strength was left in it only warmed the bedrooms of the house. Arthur held up the paperwork he had brought along, put together by Richard Turner.

'Now, Bob, I don't want you to look at these and think, bloody hell – I can't afford any of this. I already know that you can't. No disrespect to you and Ivy, but I know you're not the richest folk in the dale. However, I believe everybody should have a chance to better themselves. And you, my lad, are a lot like me – you work hard for what you get and are honest with it. There are not many of us left.' Arthur leafed through the papers, separating them out, then passed one set across to Bob while he kept hold of an identical set.

Bob picked the papers up and looked at them.

Lot 1. Four-bedroom farmhouse with yard, outbuildings and barn: £850.00

Lot 2. Twenty acres of best meadow land: £1,300

Lot 3. Eight acres of pasture, with adjoining barns: £900

Lot 4. Seventy acres of open fell with grazing rights: £1,200

Lot 5. Twenty sheep gates giving right to grazing for three sheep and followers per gate on Garsdale Common: Open to best offers.

Bob felt the blood drain from his face. His hand shook as he turned over the pages and read the details of each lot. 'I think I'm wasting your time, Arthur. I could just about afford the house and half the meadow land, but the rest is way out of my reach.' He sat back and looked at the older man, who had a wry smile on his face.

'Aye, I know – I'm worth a bob or two. Never thought I would be. Although Deep Well was passed down from my father and grandfather; I never bought that farm. I've set my daughter up on three hundred acres near Lanarkshire and bought a farm for me and Mary, so I've not done so badly.' Arthur smiled. 'Now, let's talk about what I can do for you and see if I can meet you halfway. The main thing is to keep that bloody Brian Harper from buying it. He's ruining half the Dales with not renting the farmhouses out and leaving them empty. I'll not have that happening to Deep Well.'

'Aye, I can't understand why he's doing that. Since his wife and lass have left him, all he thinks about is making money, not friends,' Bob said. He sensed a small bit of hope.

'He's going to be a lonely man one day. Unless he marries the widow Handley – but I think she already knows what game he's playing. Now, give your Ivy a shout. If you're anything like Mary and me, you work as a team, like any good marriage does. And then I'll tell you what I have in mind.' Arthur looked around the small best room. It was full of pictures in frames, set on old but well-polished furniture. On top of the sideboard were photographs of either side of the family. 'Aye, there's your mother, Beth. She was a grand woman. You're a lot like her,' Arthur said with a smile, taking out his handkerchief to blow his nose. Bob, getting to his feet to fetch Ivy, paused in surprise as he realized the other man was near to tears.

'She's been dead nearly fifteen years now. She was a good mother to me.' He looked at his mother's face for the first time in a long while, remembering her smile and the lily-of-the-valley perfume she used to wear. 'I'll get Ivy with the tea to join us,' he said. His legs felt wobbly as he went to the door, afraid he was about to make a fool of himself in front of both Ivy and Arthur.

Ivy was just putting the tea cosy over the pot when Bob entered the kitchen. In a low voice, she whispered, 'Well, do you think we can buy it?'

'Not a cat in hell's chance. We can only afford the main house and an acre or two. But he wants to talk to you as well as me. He says he has something in mind.' Bob opened the door back into the front room. He let Ivy go through first with her tray of tea and scones, and she gave him an encouraging little smile as she passed by.

'There we go, Arthur, a cup of tea and some home-made scones. Gone are the cake days, I'm afraid – there's never enough sugar to do a decent bake.' Ivy poured the tea out into their best china cups and handed one to Arthur. 'Scone, treat yourself.'

'Aye, that will be grand, although don't let my Mary know. She's trying to get me to lose a bit of weight.' Arthur sipped his tea and took a bite of his scone. 'Now, I'll tell you what this is all about, and why I'm giving you first chance.'

Bob and Ivy exchanged a glance, wondering what Arthur was going to say.

'I've known you since you were a baby, Bob. I held you on my knee and I've watched you grow into a grand fella who works every minute of the day and is right with most folk. Now, Deep Well has always been in my family. I need it to be in the right hands – I don't want it going to somebody who doesn't feel for these Dales. Besides, I'd like to still come back and visit from time to time.' Arthur hesitated and looked across at them.

'If you can afford the farmhouse and buildings, and perhaps the pastureland, I would be willing to let you rent the rest of the land at whatever rate you can manage with a view to buying it as and when you can. It's better being in your hands and still partly in mine, instead of with somebody who just makes as much money out of the land as they can, without any proper care towards it.' Arthur relaxed and sat back, watching as his friends looked at one another. He'd made his proposal; now they would have to think it through and let him know how they felt.

'You can't do that, Arthur – you'll need your money. I appreciate the offer, but it doesn't seem right to me.' Bob glanced at Ivy as she placed her hand on his knee to stop him from saying any more before she had her say.

'Money's not a problem, lad. I've enough for me to see my days out, so the rent will be minimal, and it will be an agreement just between me and thee and my solicitor. Ivy, you can see it makes sense, I know you can. That house is made for you, and you've got a lad and lass that can farm it after your days. Although I hear Ben is more of a mechanic than a farmer – but he might change.'

'You really can afford to do that? It would work out perfectly for us. As it stands now, as Bob has said, we couldn't afford hardly any of the land.' Ivy bowed her head and said quietly, 'I have always thought Deep Well is such a bonny house.'

'Aye, Mary does and all. She doesn't want to leave, but she needs to be near our lass and the babies. At the same time, she loves her house. She needs for nothing in it, either, I've seen to that. But the new home also has everything she wants, so she should be happy.'

'We'd have to see the bank manager. I can afford the house and outbuildings, but I'll borrow some money for the pastureland.' Bob glanced at Ivy and saw her face relaxing as he said it. She had set her heart on moving, and in her eyes Arthur was offering a good deal.

'Don't bother, lad, just rent it like the rest. I'll put some figures together for you and we will take it from there. Now, how about you and Ivy come over for a bite of supper? Ivy can have a good look around the house, and you can walk the farm's boundary so that you know what you're taking on if you are still interested?' Arthur stood up and looked at Ivy. 'You two women can talk about what Mary's taking with her and what she's leaving. I know that she's not taking the washing machine, and I only bought it last year. Could have saved myself a bit of brass there, but I didn't know we were going to be moving.'

Ivy's eyes lit up and she squeezed Bob's hand. A washing machine! She had always wanted a washing machine.

'Let's say supper on Friday night? Mary will make something or other and we can sit around the table and talk. Friday gives you time to see your bank manager and all. Will that be right for you both?' Arthur asked as they stood in the kitchen. He spotted Sally sitting on the stairs. 'Are you coming with them and all, young lady? You are more than welcome. I hear you're a bit of a farmer – Deep Well will really give you something to farm.'

'Thank you, Mr Metcalfe, but it sounds like my parents' business, so I'll stay at home,' Sally replied, coming to stand beside her mother.

'You'll be finding a fella soon, especially with those bonny looks. You've a look of your grandmother about you,' Arthur said with a smile. 'Right, I'll be away.'

Bob shook his hand. 'Well, you've certainly given us something to think about, Arthur. And aye, supper Friday night will just be grand. We'll look forward to it.'

'I'm hoping you'll take me up on my offer, Bob. It would mean a lot to me to know that the old homestead is being looked after properly. Mary made me put it on the market and get it valued, else I might have been here sooner.' The two men stepped outside and Arthur opened the door of his old car. 'She's made me buy a fresh car and all, so this one will be needing a home or to be scrapped, although it still gets me from A to B. I'll leave you it as a settling-in present.' He got into the driver's seat and turned the ignition. 'She sometimes needs crank starting, especially in cold weather, but she's served me well.'

Bob watched as Arthur backed the car around and trundled off down the lane. He rubbed his head, wondering if he had really understood Arthur correctly. Could he truly have meant it?

Ivy came out and stood beside him, linking her arm into his.

'Has that really happened?' she said, echoing his own thoughts. 'Has Arthur Metcalfe just about begged us to buy and rent Deep Well?' She turned her head to gaze up at Bob.

'It would seem he has. And he says we can have his old banger of a car. He must have lost leave of his senses. I mean, I've always known him; he's always been there in my life, but I never thought I meant that much to him.' Bob stared down the lane, wondering what to make of it all.

'Well, don't you look a gift horse in the mouth, Bob Fothergill. We'd better go and see that bank manager as soon as we can. And we'll go and have dinner with them before they change their minds.' Ivy sighed. 'A car and a washing machine! I can't believe it.'

Bob and Ivy stood outside Martin's Bank on the high street in Sedbergh, feeling as if they had just won a hundred thousand pounds.

'I can't believe it, Bob – they are quite happy for us to buy Deep Well farmhouse, and they even offered to give you a loan for stock. It never used to be like that! We had to bow and scrape nearly every time we went in there when the children were young.' Ivy could hardly contain her excitement.

'Aye, well, I'm not borrowing a penny off them – if I can't afford it, we don't buy it. That's how you get into bother. I'd like to know how much Brian Harper

213

owes. He can't have all the money he's been spending of late; I bet he's in hock to the bank.' Bob crossed the cobbled road and looked through the window of a small tearoom, realizing it was dinner time. 'Come on – I'll treat you to a pot of tea and one of those pork pies before we go home.'

'By heck, you know how to celebrate! Go on, then; and we'll have two of those custard slices to top it off.' Ivy grinned as they went inside and Bob ordered their lunch.

'Now, don't push your luck, Ivy. Money doesn't grow on trees.' He put on a serious face, then grinned. 'Aye, and two custard slices, please. They'll be a real treat for the pair of us.'

Chapter 21

'Do I look all right, Bob? Mary is always dressed just so.' Ivy assessed herself in the kitchen mirror and straightened the imitation pearls around her neck.

'Of course you do. We're only going for supper, and it's not the King we're dining with. Besides, you've often seen them in your pinny, so stop flapping.' Bob didn't even glance at his wife as he went out into the yard and mounted the small trap that stood waiting, along with the tethered horse, for Ivy to get ready. 'Are you right now, woman? Let's get going, else it'll be midnight before we get there. I'd have gone on the motorbike if I'd had my say.' He watched as Ivy climbed up next to him and settled herself with her handbag on her knee.

'I know you would, and I'd have arrived looking like a scarecrow. Now stop complaining, and let's go. Oh, I hope we're doing right,' Ivy said anxiously. 'All that money we've saved, going at the drop of a hat – and to make things worse, we'll still be renting the land.'

'It'll be right, lass. We couldn't wish for a better deal. We'll get the land paid for, and then it will be all ours.' Bob urged the horse on and glanced at her. 'It will all be right – stop bothering.'

'Have they gone? I thought they'd never leave. I want to go fishing – I think I saw a salmon making its way up to spawn this morning. But Mam wouldn't let me anywhere near the beck, she says it's too damp and it'll make me ill again.' Ben pulled his fishing rod from under the stairs and looked at Sally, who was washing the pots up in the sink. 'You'll not tell them, will you? I'll not be long.'

'You shouldn't be going,' his sister said. 'Mam's right, the night air is damp down by the beck. It won't be good for you. I'll pretend I know nothing about it, so go on, get yourself gone, but don't stay long. Anyway, how are you going to explain if you catch anything?' She dried her hands. She was just glad that Ben seemed to be back to his usual self.

'I'll wangle it somehow. Thanks, Sal, you're a good'en.' Ben put his rod over his shoulder and headed down the lane towards the river Dee.

In honesty, Sally was glad to be left on her own. She had a bit of business to do while the house was empty – business that she wanted to keep to herself for now. She made her way into the front room and turned the key to the oak desk that held all the important family documents. She was never usually allowed in it, and her heart beat fast as she opened the metal document box that lay within.

On the very top was Luca's employment agreement, along with his personal details. She quickly looked at it and read that he was indeed a single man. Not that it mattered any more, she thought as she folded it and placed it aside. Certificates for births, deaths and marriages were within the tin, along with the document she was looking for – the rental agreement for Daleside.

She held her breath as she read through it, taking in every word, before folding it back up and closing the tin in exactly the same way as she had found it. Now she knew what she was going to do, and she hoped that no one would stop her.

'Just look at this garden! The dahlias are beautiful. I wonder if Mary's taking them with her,' Ivy commented as they made their way through the front gate of Deep Well and stood at the white-painted door. Bob lifted the brass knocker and tapped it down hard.

'You'll have to ask her; she will probably tell you anyway.' For the first time in a long while, Bob felt frightened of what he was about to agree to. It was a backward step when it came to renting land again. But with hard work, he'd own it in a few years – and it would mean that he was working for himself, instead of days with Jim Mattinson or wherever he could find work. He tried to calm his nerves as he heard Arthur open the door, welcoming them into his home.

'Now then, you two, you couldn't have come on a better evening. So come in – Mary's made an easy supper so that you and me, Bob, can have a walk around the fields when we've eaten, and you and Mary can talk about the house and things.' Arthur opened the front door wide and showed them the way down the stone-paved corridor to the front room. 'That's it, go in there, and I'll tell Mary that you're here. She's just whisking the cream for the trifle. I tell you what, it's been a grand day. And I've just heard on the radio that the Allies are liberating Paris. They'll soon have those Jerries on the run.' He smiled. 'Now, make yourselves comfortable, and I'll get Mary.'

Ivy looked around the front room. 'I've never been in here before; she usually just keeps me in the kitchen. It's carpeted, Bob, and look at the curtains,' Ivy whispered. 'We will need more furniture.' She sat down on the leather sofa and held her breath. It might not be the King they were dining with, but compared to their own humble home, Deep Well felt like Buckingham Palace.

Bob just smiled. It might be a lot posher than their house, but it was just as old – a Dales longhouse, with the barn attached at the other end. Mary had obviously put her heart and soul into making it homely and she had managed that hands down, he thought as he watched Ivy take in every piece of furniture and ornament.

'Bob, Mary, how grand to see you. And what a lovely evening! I'm so glad you are here. When Arthur told me of his plans, I couldn't be happier for you both.' Mary came into the front room, smiling brightly at the couple who would soon be Deep Well's new owners, if Arthur had his way. 'I hope you're in agreement – or perhaps I'm jumping the gun?' Seeing the expression on their faces, she glanced at Arthur as he came in behind her.

'We've got a lot to talk about yet, Mary – but aye, I'm hoping they will be moving in. Now, let's go through and have some supper, and then Bob and I can look around the land and you and Ivy can sort out the house. Does that sound about right?' Arthur asked his two visitors. He hoped Mary wouldn't speak out of turn after what he had confessed to her earlier in the day.

'You've a lovely house, Mary. I didn't realize how big it is,' Ivy said as Mary led them through to a room that came off the back kitchen. It was laid out with a dresser, dining table and six chairs.

'Yes, it's larger than it looks from the outside. This used to be the old shippon, but Arthur made it into a dining room for me. He built a new cowshed out in the yard. We only use this for special occasions,' Mary said quietly as they took their seats. Their supper was already laid out, with willow-pattern plates and ham, salad and a plate of bread-and-butter in the centre of the table.

'This looks lovely, Mary, thank you ever so much,' Bob said as he sat down. He could imagine Christmas with his family around this table. At this point, he wanted the house for Ivy's sake almost as much as he wanted the land. 'Before we start eating, I'd like to say that we are not going to waste your time. We will be taking you up on your generous offer, Arthur and Mary. We can hardly believe how kind you're being to us.' Bob looked at Ivy. He hadn't planned to come out with it so early in the evening, but he knew the house was meant for them – and he already had a good idea of what the land

219

was like, having helped with walling and clipping many a year previously.

Ivy looked at him with wide eyes. His speech had come completely out of the blue.

'Well, I'm right glad of that, lad. I was hoping that you'd know it was the place for yourselves. It's always been a family house, and I'll be sad to leave it – and the land,' Arthur said. His wife said nothing, but put a fork through a pickled onion with force as it nearly escaped her plate. 'Now, let's enjoy our meal, and then we'll both show you around and discuss the financial side of it. That's a weight off my mind, I can tell you.' He sighed and gave a glance across the table to Mary, who didn't reply.

After the meal, Ivy offered to help Mary with the washing up. Mary had been quiet all evening, and it seemed to Ivy that she might not be entirely happy with her husband's decision to sell to them. She folded the tea-towel she was holding and leaned against the sink. 'That was a lovely meal, Mary – it is a treat to have someone else cook for you.'

'It was nothing, really, just a salad and a trifle. You've to make the most of what you have in the pantry and the garden nowadays, haven't you?' Mary smiled. 'Now, you'll be wanting a look around now the men have gone out. Well, as you know, this is the kitchen – I'll be leaving the washer and the cooker, I think Arthur has already told you. You've seen the hallway and dining room, the front room; and we have this other room that we very rarely use, through this door.'

Mary opened another side door and showed Ivy a large room with an oak desk and a leather three-piece suite set on an Axminster rug. 'Arthur keeps this as his sort of office, where he does most of his business. Sometimes I use it for sewing.' She pointed to her treadle sewing machine, then went to the window with its view down the dale. 'I don't suppose Arthur has explained why he wants you and Bob to have this farm so much, has he?' she asked, turning to fix Ivy with a sharp gaze.

'No,' Ivy replied hesitantly. Mary's manner was making her feel a little uneasy. 'He just said he didn't want it to go to somebody who didn't value it, as it's his family home.'

'Then I'm going to tell you why, so at least you know. Then perhaps you'll feel more at ease, rather than wondering why he's bending over backwards to see that Bob has it. It's up to you if you want to tell Bob. Sometimes it is easier to let sleeping dogs lie.' Mary drew a deep breath. She hoped that she was doing right. If it had been up to her, Deep Well would have been sold to the highest bidder, not virtually given away to Bob and Ivy.

'I don't know what you mean.' Ivy looked bemused.

'This is a family farm, always has been,' Mary said. 'The Metcalfes have been here for centuries. As far as Arthur is concerned, it's still going to be in the hands of a Metcalfe, because he believes Bob is his son.' She paused for a moment. 'Bob's mother and Arthur were lovers, long before I knew him. She used to court both Arthur and Matthew Fothergill. When she found out she was carrying a child, she thought it was Matthew's. But you've only to look at Arthur and Bob standing together to know that she got it wrong.'

Ivy stared at her, unable to respond for a moment. '. . . No! And Bob really doesn't have a clue? He can't do, else he would have said.'

She was deeply shocked. Bob had loved Matthew Fothergill, the man he thought of as his father, and he wouldn't have a word said against his mother. How could she tell him? Should she tell him?

'No; and perhaps it should stay that way, just in case we're mistaken. It would shatter his world and spoil the memory of his mother. Arthur is only trying to right a wrong and not hurt anyone in the process.' Mary took Ivy's hand. 'He's seen our daughter right by buying her a farm; now he wants to be right with Bob.'

'I can't believe it . . . but yes, I can, now that you say. Arthur used to come to our house often when we were first married, and there is a resemblance between them. What a shock!' Ivy put a hand to her heart, feeling it racing. 'I don't think I will tell him – or not now, anyway. Else he might take it the wrong way and have nothing to do with Arthur and the sale.'

'You do whatever you feel is right. But as it stands, Arthur is happy with what he's doing. Bob, I can tell, is over the moon with the idea of owning his farm; and I wish you all the best in my old home. It was made for you and your family. A dark family secret should not spoil happiness.' Mary smiled. 'Now, let me show you the bedrooms – and perhaps this is best kept between the two of us and Arthur?'

'Yes, I think that's what we will do. We will keep it as a secret. It's best that way,' Ivy said as she followed Mary up the stairs. Bob was Arthur's son. He looked like him, worked hard like him. The Metcalfe bloodline was also strong in their daughter and son – especially the stubborn streak. However, she would keep that fact to herself.

'Now then, Bob, did you ever see a finer view than this? Just look at it!' Arthur leaned on his walking stick and looked down at the farmhouse where he had been brought up since birth, and around at his land in the low evening light. 'I'm going to miss this spot so much. If I know it's in good hands, I'll not bother the same. If it were up to me, I'd be staying until they had to take me away in a coffin. However, Mary wants to be next to our lass.'

'Well, if you'll let me, I will look after it as best I can,' Bob said, gazing around him. He couldn't believe that the land, farmhouse and buildings would soon be his.

'Aye, you have it, lad. I'll get the paperwork seen to and take it off the market. I know it's now in the right hands and will be looked after, even after I'm gone. I can rest easy now I'm in the new place up Scotland.' Arthur patted Bob on the back and they shook hands. 'Now, let's go and see what those women are up to.'

Chapter 22

'When are you going to see Gerald Franklin to ask him about the termination of our tenancy?' Mary asked Bob as he ate his breakfast.

'I'll tell him next week. Let's get the pigs butchered first. We'll get them out of the way, and then we'll have to start thinking about what we're taking with us. At least it's coming up to the lamb sales, so that's a good time to sort out what stock I'm taking with me.' Bob leaned back in his chair. 'I'll have to be going; Jim Mattinson will be waiting for me. I'll have to tell him that I'm finishing working for him as well. I won't have time, with the acreage we will have once we move to Deep Well. I've been thinking that we might keep Luca on – that is, until he goes back to Italy. He seems to think that once the war is over, he'll get back straight away. He was even hoping to be home by Christmas, but I doubt he'll be doing that.'

'Don't forget to pick up the salt and saltpetre from

the chemist's for curing the ham. And don't forget that you're picking Ben up from the garage on your way back,' Ivy reminded him as he pulled on his oilcloth coat. It was raining hard, and it would be no pleasure riding down the dale on the back of his motorbike.

'I know, woman. I've got that much on my mind, I'm going to meet myself coming back,' Bob growled. He looked across at the downspout of the barn that was gushing over, with water forming a pool under the barn's doorway. 'I'm glad we are leaving. There's getting to be a lot of jobs that need doing, and I can't see Gerald Franklin putting his hand in his pocket to pay. Bloody weather,' Bob added as he walked out into the rain.

'Lord, Sally, your father thinks he's got a lot on, but we have four pigs to see to when Dick Stanley has butchered them. I'm going to put some pearl barley on to cook for the black pudding. Can you grease the baking tins, and then that's a job done before tomorrow? I hate pig-killing day. It's so much work, especially with four to do this year.' Ivy sighed and watched as Sally cleared the breakfast pots. 'It's a miracle the War Ag hasn't come to inspect us and confiscated two. Thank heaven for Luca and the slops from Loftus Hill, else they would have queried the amount of feed we needed to be supplied with.'

'It's all happening, isn't it, Mam – and then it will be Christmas. Do you think we'll have moved into the new place by then?'

'I'm hoping so; it will be a lovely Christmas in a new home. You will have to go with your father when he starts taking furniture and stock, and choose a bedroom. There's four, so we even have a spare; imagine that!' Ivy said with a delighted smile.

'I like it here, Mam. I don't really want to leave,' Sally said wistfully as she reached for the greaseproof paper.

'Don't be daft, you'll love it up Garsdale. That reminds me, you'll have to tell the shop that we're leaving. Give them plenty of time so they're not left in the lurch – you owe them that.' Ivy looked at her daughter and noticed her sad expression.

'I'll see. There's plenty of time yet,' Sally replied, and made herself scarce to go and hunt out the baking tins they only used once a year for making black pudding.

'I hate the sound of the squeals, and the boiler bubbling away filled with hot water. I hate to think we're going to be eating those poor little things that came so pink and cute in spring,' Sally said as Luca came into the house for a bucket of boiling water. It would be poured over the first butchered pig, to shave its bristles off.

'Your father needs you to stir the blood,' Luca said with a glance at Sally as she passed him the bucket.

'Oh, Mam, I hate that job! I knew he'd give me it,' Sally complained as she turned to follow Luca out of the house. It was important to stir the bucket of pigs' blood until it cooled, stopping it from clotting; otherwise it would be no good for making the black pudding.

'Don't think about it,' Ivy said, and watched as Sally walked across the yard towards the pig hulls. It wasn't the most pleasant job, but it had to be done.

Sally looked at her father as he gave her a large stick covered in blood and passed her the bucket. 'You know what to do. Stir it until it cools and stops clotting, and then take it to your mother.' Bob noticed the disgust on his daughter's face. 'You'll not be pulling a face when you're tucking into your mother's black pudding.'

'Oh, Father, I hate this job. I hate being here.' Sally took the stick and did as her father said, looking up at the butchered pigs' carcasses hanging splayed from a beam in each sty ready for Dick Stanley to chop them into manageable cuts.

'Well, it's to be done, and it's a job you can do.' Bob picked up each of the now decapitated pigs' heads and directed Luca to take them into the house to Ivy. 'Pigs' cheeks for supper tonight, and the rest Ivy will put in the boiler and make into brawn. There's only the squeal that's not used in a pig,' Bob said as he watched Luca struggling to carry the pig's heads to the farmhouse. 'Another day or two when you are eating your mother's pudding, pork scratchings and savoury ducks – I know they are your favourites, lovely little bites of pâté covered with the pig's caul – you'll have forgotten all this. And the bacon and ham will keep us all fed over the coming months.'

Sally knew her father was right, but at that moment she felt quite sick as she stirred the deep red blood with its strong smell of iron. Sometimes she wondered how anybody could eat slaughtered animals; but it was the farm's main income, and it was what hill farming was all about. The day would soon be over, and as her father had said, the kitchen would be filled with the smells of Ivy's home-made delights and her father would be out delivering flitches of bacon and whatever else people had ordered on the sly. Money would be put into the savings pot, and this time it would already be spent – on new stock, or even a three-piece suite for the front room at Deep Well, which her mother had decided she couldn't live without. So she kept stirring, at the same time wondering if she dared do what she had planned in her mind. She had to, she thought as she looked around her at the place she loved.

Bob had borrowed Jim Mattinson's van for the day and loaded it up with various cuts of meat and produce made by Ivy. It was now that they saw a reward for keeping the four pigs and just hoped that nobody had said anything to the War Ag – not that any good Dales person would. It was an unwritten code that if you could make a bob or two without hurting anybody, you did. Times were hard for everyone and all were in the same boat, so a few deals on the black market were overlooked.

Bob drove up to Dent station. Another month or two and the steep hill road would be nearly unpassable, covered by ice and snow. Passengers alighting the train would be in for a shock when they realized that Dent itself was over two miles away: a lovely walk in summer, but a different matter in winter.

He made his way to the signal box and called up from the bottom of the steps. 'Hey up, Jack. I hope you got my message that Sally said she'd put through your door when she was at work the other day? Just to say I would be delivering what's been ordered today.'

Jack Sedgwick came to the door to greet him. 'Aye, I got it, and I've got payment from everybody for you. The ten-forty to Carlisle is picking theirs up in the morning, and the three-thirty up to Leeds is picking it up this afternoon. Now, I can't have all this meat in my signal box, but the coal bunker next to the waiting room is empty. Put it all in that. I daren't have it in here with me just in case an inspector visits. Nobody will look in there, and it's handy for the guard to pick it up from.' Jack came halfway down the steps and passed Bob a handful of money. 'It's all there, including mine. Dorothy's fair looking forward to a bit of black pudding, a real luxury.'

'I'll do that, then. It's all packaged up, with names on it. Ivy and I double-checked we had everyone's. I'll put yours right on the top.' Bob stepped back, tucked the money into his inside pocket and retraced his footsteps to the van.

'I hear you're leaving Dent! Going to live in Garsdale – tha must have made some brass to be able to buy Deep Well,' Jack called as Bob picked up the first delivery of meat. He hoped that it would be safe and fairly clean in the heavy-lidded coal bunker.

'Nay, just lucky; and we have been saving ever since we got married. We both wanted our own farm instead of renting.' Bob caught his breath and looked up at Jack.

'Brian Harper isn't so suited that you've bought it, but he says he's going to buy Daleside from off your landlord

Franklin. He's always having to be flash with his brass and trying to lord it over everybody.' Jack shook his head and drew on his pipe of tobacco.

'Aye, I hope he doesn't buy it. I can't see Franklin wanting to part, but you never know. Money talks.' Bob walked back to the van and brought out the last box full of meat.

'Well, I hope you'll be happy in Garsdale. You'll be missed. You let us know if you're able to supply bacon and the like next year; I bet it will still be on ration then, but hopefully the war will be over. You can bring it straight over the coal road from where you live, providing it's good weather,' Jack shouted. Then he returned to his signal box as he heard a ring on the telegraph system letting him know a train was on its way.

Bob smiled. He could bring it over the old coal road, although that was even steeper than the climb out of Dentdale. But the view was spectacular, as the road split both Garsdale and Dent down the middle and was thousands of feet above sea level. He might go home that way, he thought. The road passed Deep Well, and he would like to see the place again and just get that feeling of excitement and happiness as he passed the 'Sold' board that was now up in the farmhouse garden.

He still couldn't quite believe that at long last, he and Ivy were going to own their own home. It felt so good, although he knew their new life was going to be one of hard work.

Chapter 23

'Now, you ask him if we can have three months' rent, as we are leaving in December and the tenancy finishes in April. He will at least owe us that,' Ivy said as she straightened Bob's tie and ran her hand over his for once bristle-free chin. He was on his way to see Gerald Franklin to tell him they were planning to leave Daleside, a meeting Bob was not looking forward to.

'I will, but you know what he's like. I know what he'll say: that we signed the agreement and it's our look-out if we're leaving early.' Bob pulled on his best tweed jacket. 'Is our Sally coming with me, or what is she doing? I don't know why she likes going to see Franklin, but he always makes a fuss of her for some reason.'

'She is, she's just getting ready. I think she's as nervous as you. She's not wanting to leave here; she's been moaning about it ever since we signed up for the new place.' Ivy glanced up as they heard the floorboards creaking above their heads and murmured, 'Just humour her, will you, Bob? She's in a right way with herself.'

'She'll get told what I think if she doesn't stop being so bloody moody,' Bob said in a low voice. He leaned on a kitchen chair as he waited for his daughter to show.

'Shh! She's coming. She just doesn't want to leave here – I can understand,' Ivy said, and went about her business.

'What on earth do you think you are dressed in? Where did you get them from? Lasses should wear frocks and skirts.' Bob straightened up, staring at Sally as she came downstairs dressed in her second-hand trousers and jumper.

'Mam got me it at the second-hand sale. It's from one of the lasses at the Gate, Father, so it's good quality. And everyone is wearing trousers nowadays.' Sally returned her father's glare.

'You look more like a fella than a woman,' Bob grunted.

'Nay, she doesn't, Bob, she looks every inch the perfect woman. It's just you that are set in your ways.' Ivy smiled and winked at her daughter. 'Go on, both of you. Get gone, else it will be dark by the time you get home.'

Bob patted his jacket pocket and made sure he had the tenancy agreement there, then watched as Sally climbed onto the buggy with much more ease than she usually did. Happen she was right – trousers were a whole lot more practical for women, but he still didn't like them. As he urged the horse forward, he admitted to himself that she was too old to be told how to dress. He'd leave it for now, but that didn't mean he liked these new fashions.

'I like going to see Gerald Franklin at the Manse. I'm always fascinated by the big house,' Sally said as they trotted along the quiet country road, past Dent and up the sharp hill to the grand turn-off with trees planted on either side of the drive.

'Money made on the slave trade, that's what that house is. And now he exploits us with the amount of rent he charges everybody,' Bob said as they approached the square-pillared Georgian house that dominated the top end of the dale. The horse's hooves clattered over the cobbled backyard to the stables at the back.

There were various grand houses in Dentdale, telling the story of how the dale had been an important part of society. Whernside Manor stood at the bottom of Deepdale, built by a slave-owning family and believed to be haunted by the poor souls whose lives they had made hell. The Gate, where Sally's new outfit had come from, was a Tudor hall towards the bottom of the dale, and the Manse stood grand and proud over the top end of the dale.

'Franklin's never done a hard day's work in his life, just inherited it all. Can't be a bad thing to be born into a wealthy family.' Bob got down from the trap, walked his horse into the stables and tied it to a metal ring. 'Come on. I'll not take him out of harness, we won't be that long.' He watched as Sally climbed down. She had been quiet for most of the journey. Probably upset by his comments about her trousers, he thought.

Sally felt her stomach churn as he knocked on the back kitchen door. If Father was out of sorts with her just for wearing trousers, he would be furious when he heard what else was on her mind.

'Mr Franklin is expecting you in the study,' said the

butler, leading them into the large, still Victorian kitchen and then up the back stairs to a highly polished hall. Paintings of the Franklin family hung on its walls.

The butler knocked on a door. 'Mr Fothergill and his daughter, sir.' He left the door open as he stepped back to allow Bob and Sally into the handsomely furnished room.

'Ah, Fothergill. Now, let me guess – you have to surrender your tenancy on Daleside. I've heard through the grapevine about you buying that farm up in Garsdale. You must have made some money out of my little farm.' Gerald Franklin rose to greet them, then gestured for them to sit down as he took a seat behind his desk.

'Through hard work, sir. Some days, I've worked the clock round. But aye, that's what I'm here for. We would like to leave at the beginning of December, so as we understand it, there will hopefully be four months' rent to be returned to us.' Bob thought he'd better say what he needed to straight away, although he didn't hold out much hope of receiving a refund.

'Now, Bob, you signed for a year's tenancy. It isn't my fault you are leaving before the year is up. Besides, I suspect that I will have to make some repairs before my next tenant moves in. That is, if I'm not tempted to sell to your neighbour, because he is already showing interest in buying it.' Franklin looked at Sally. 'You are looking suitably ladylike, Sally. Has there been any news of your intended? I suppose not; this war has brought so much heartache to the dale.'

'No, sir, no news of Edward.' Sally's heart was in her mouth as she plucked up the courage to say the words she had spent weeks rehearsing in her mind. 'Mr Franklin, if my father is to leave Daleside in December, would it be possible for me to keep the tenancy on until April? And perhaps continue to rent the following year?' Sally felt her legs go weak. She didn't dare look at her father, but she heard him swear under his breath.

Gerald Franklin raised his eyebrows. He looked at Bob with amusement. 'Didn't you know she was going to ask that, Fothergill? You look surprised. And a little angry.'

'No, I did not.' Bob turned to Sally. 'She must have taken leave of her senses – she can't farm Daleside on her own. It's a man's job. She wouldn't survive winter on her own.' He shook his head. 'You want nowt with doing that, my lass. Don't talk so soft.'

'I could, Father. You could let me give it a go until April – that way, you don't lose anything. I just want to stay at Daleside. I don't want to go to Deep Well, and I can farm as well as any man.' Sally stood her ground despite her fear of upsetting her father. She never challenged his will.

'Well, Bob Fothergill, what am I going to do? It's as Sally says – it makes no difference to you or me until April. However, I think the best thing you can do is go home and sort it out between yourselves.' Gerald Franklin looked consideringly at her. 'I'll give you your due, Sally, you have a mind of your own. A bit like your father, I think.'

'Aye, she's that all right.' Bob stood abruptly and pulled on Sally's arm to get her up from her chair. 'We'll be away now, and I'll come back and let you know as soon as we've talked some sense into her head.'

'But it is sense, Father. I'm as good a farmer as any

fella. And I know every inch of Daleside,' Sally protested, standing her ground.

'Go home with your father, Sally. Talk it through and then let me know what you all decide. It makes no difference to me if the farm is lived in or empty over winter. However, when it comes to spring, I will be looking for a full year's rent.' Gerald rose and watched as Bob nearly pushed his daughter out of the study. He shook his head. He liked Sally Fothergill – he had always admired her spirit. But he had no doubt her father would be furious with her for showing him up.

Sally followed Bob out to the trap and climbed up to sit beside him. 'Can't you see it's a good idea, Father? I've been thinking about it for weeks. I love Daleside, I don't want to leave and as I've no man in my life, I could farm it on my own. I know I could.'

'Just you hold your noise. I have never been so embarrassed in all my life. I looked like an absolute idiot. It was bad enough that you said you wanted to rent it until April so that we wouldn't get any rent back. But to say that you would rent it for the following year was just stupid.' Bob urged the horse on. 'Now shut up. I don't want to hear another word.'

Sally looked down at her feet and held back her tears. She wasn't going to back down. She could afford to farm Daleside – she had kept what she'd been allowed of her wages from Middleton's, and she had some money in a savings account that her grandparents had given her. She could quite easily be self-sufficient. There was no need for a man in her life.

'I can farm, Father. I can do it and I will,' she said quietly.

'Just whisht! I don't even want to talk to you,' Bob growled, flicking the reins over the horse's flanks. The sooner he was home, the better; otherwise he might say something he regretted to his precious daughter.

'Well, how did you get on? What did Gerald Franklin have to say?' Ivy sat up in alarm, setting aside her knitting as she saw her husband march in with a face like thunder.

'You'd better ask your daughter; she seems to think she's the farmer. Never have I felt such a fool!' Bob said. He swore as he strode across and turned off the wireless that had been keeping Ivy company. 'Why is she so bloody headstrong? And she's that secretive – I had no idea what she was coming out with. I looked like an idiot!' He threw himself down in his favourite chair.

'What on earth has she done that's so wrong?' Ivy asked.

'She's said she wants to take on Daleside herself and farm it. And Gerald Franklin is daft enough to let her think she's in with a chance. Not a word she had said to us until she got into that room and talked to him as if she had everything planned out. Bye, I could have clouted her!' Bob put his head in his hands. 'She couldn't farm here on her own – that is stupidity. Especially since she'll be starting out in the worst three months of the year.'

'Just like we did, when we were first married. Remember, it was the best Christmas ever, that December when we moved in here – it seems we always move in December.' Ivy smiled, and couldn't help but stick up for her daughter. 'She loves it here, Bob; I knew she didn't want to leave.

There wouldn't be much harm in letting her see if she could manage on her own for three months. After all, I don't suppose he offered you the three months' rent money back?'

'No, he didn't; but he never got the chance when Sally butted in.' Bob shook his head. 'It's not right, Ivy, a young lass on her own taking on a farm. It's too hard a life. She never will find a fella if she's going to be that pig-headed.'

'She happen doesn't want one, have you ever thought about that? She still thinks of Edward and hopes he will come back.' Ivy reached for Bob's hand and squeezed it. 'There would be no harm in her farming here until April. It would make or break her. Besides, if somebody's going to be here up to Christmas, you could rear and sell some turkeys like you usually do. I'm sure Harold will have a dozen or so spare birds needing a home. He'll have missed your usual order for chicks.'

'She'll not be staying after April, not if she's on her own. She won't stick it,' Bob said. 'But I suppose there's nothing lost if she does stay until then. And as you say, I can rear some turkeys as usual, and she can look after them in the shed where we always have them. I wasn't going to get any this year because of the move, but they do make us good money.' He felt a little calmer as he began to realize that Sally's proposal could be turned to the family's advantage.

'Well, then, that's that sorted. You can both go back in the morning and tell Gerald Franklin that Sally will be farming here until April at the least, and you can pick up what turkeys Harold can spare you. Luca can help you clean and dress them this year, because I'll be busy in our new home. I'm really looking forward to getting everything just right for a grand Christmas.' Ivy smiled, feeling that she had missed her way in life; she should have had a role in the diplomatic corps. That sweetener of turkeys had soon got Bob changing his tune.

'Oh, I can, can I? Bye, you women. It's a wonder I'm not six feet deep in my grave with worry, the amount this family gives me.' Bob lit his pipe.

'I think our Sally could make a go of farming here. You make sure you help her out with a few bits and give her advice. Besides, you wouldn't have it any other way, Bob Fothergill. Sally has been your right-hand man since the day she was born. And in fact, you'll miss her help when we're at the new farm without her!'

'Aye, she's always been keen, happen you are right. I'll back her on one condition, and that is that she gets rid of those trousers.' Bob grinned.

'Bob, they suit her and are practical. Time to change your ideas, my old man.' Ivy picked up her knitting, glad that she had talked him around.

'They might be, but I don't like them. She can wear what she wants when I'm not here.' Bob turned the wireless back on and hummed along to one of the catchy tunes that had come across with the Americans. There was one good thing about the idea of his daughter farming Daleside: it would upset Brian Harper no end. Bob decided it might be worth it after all, just to see his neighbour's face.

Chapter 24

Bob had come away from Gerald Franklin's wondering if he had taken leave of his senses by agreeing that Sally would take the farm on until the start of spring. Franklin himself had seemed unconcerned; as long as he kept the rent money, that was all he cared about. Bob put his leg over his motorbike and went straight on to see if Harold had any young turkeys he could part with. At least they would bring a bit of money in for Christmas, and Sally could keep an eye on them back at Daleside.

'Now, part of the deal with you staying here is that you look after these until Christmas, and then Luca and I will come and kill and dress them. You'll have to feed them, though. Are you listening?' Bob said to Sally now, as they both watched the young turkeys that had arrived. The birds were strutting about on a thin bed of straw in one of the outbuildings.

'I know, Father. I'll look after them when you eventually get moved. Thank you for understanding – I know

I should have said something before I blurted my intention out in front of Gerald Franklin. I just knew you would never agree to it if I asked beforehand.' Sally's tone was gentle. Relations between her and her father had been rather tense over the past few days, but the frosty atmosphere had started to melt with the arrival of the turkeys.

'Aye, well, I still think that you are crackers. I can't understand why you want to stay here when Deep Well is twice the farm this will ever be. I suppose three months will give you time to see if you can hack it or not. I still don't know how you will make it pay, because I'll have to take most of my stock with me. But as you know, it's the lamb sales down at Sedbergh auction next week. I'll have to make my main money with my lambs, else I'm going to struggle.' Bob sighed. He didn't understand how Sally expected to farm with no stock on the acres she would not leave. 'I can leave you a shearling or two, and old Daisy for your milk cow. I don't want the hens – Arthur is leaving me his, some Rhode Island reds, although they look a bit long in the tooth. I'll leave you ours. So at least you will have eggs and milk.'

'It'll be enough until spring, until I know I want to stay. And then I'll use my savings to pay the rent and buy some sheep.' Sally was thankful that her father had come round to her way of thinking as she opened up to him.

'Aye, well, we will see. A bad winter and you might see sense. I hope that you do, but no doubt you'll do what you want.' Bob smiled at his daughter. 'You are a

241

stubborn devil when you want to be, Sally Fothergill. I wonder who you take after?'

'I wonder?' Sally grinned. She had hated falling out with her father.

The sheep were gathered and held in the fold next to the house. Sally and Bob had sorted out that year's lambs from the older ewes, taking up most of the day. It was time to take them to auction and make the farm's main income of the year.

The lambs' bleating filled the air as Bob and Sally walked back into the house, tired and ready for their beds. They were planning to sell forty lambs – they would walk them over to the auction in the morning, droving them along the country road to Sedbergh and the auction mart.

'Are you happy that I'm going to leave you with those shearlings and the six old lasses? They were born here, a bit like yourself, and wouldn't enjoy moving to a new home at their stage of life. They should be in lamb, but it'll be their last year.' Bob was starting to be concerned that he might not be doing enough for his daughter.

'That will be grand, Father. I can manage on a little until spring. I've decided not to give my job up at Middleton's; it's only two days a week, and as you say, I've hardly any stock to look after. Every penny will count, as well you know,' Sally said. 'I'm not bothered about that, as long as I can stay here.'

'I still can't believe that you want to stay. I'll leave you the hay in the barn, that will help you out. Arthur is leaving me his at Deep Well. I've to see him tomorrow at the auction; he's going to give me the keys to the house and give me his old car, so at least we can ride back in style after selling the lambs.' Bob pulled off his boots and watched as a pile of hayseeds fell out onto the mat. He noticed Ivy glare at him.

'That's it, Bob Fothergill, make me more work. As if I haven't enough. Packing this and that and getting rid of what we don't want. Not to mention making sure the hams are curing well and making sure all of you are fed,' Ivy moaned. She had already begun packing things that were not used daily, and she was tired.

'You'll not be moaning when you're settled in at Deep Well,' Bob said. 'We can start taking things over there next week – Arthur and Mary are leaving earlier than they thought, now that all is sorted and he's sold what stock he didn't want.' He turned to Sally. 'In fact, me and you will take a load next week, and then you can see what you're missing. We'll take it in Arthur's car. It'll fit all sorts in it if he's cleaned it out. He had a calf in there last week when I met him going to Scotchergill Farm.'

'I'm not putting my best linens in that car if it smells of calf pee, let alone riding in it,' Ivy objected.

'He'll have cleaned it out. Mary will have made him. I'll talk to Henry Mackreth tomorrow and book him to move both the furniture and the stock. We might as well get settled in a bit earlier too. You'll be all right, won't you, Sally? And Ben is closer to his work up Garsdale. Once I get Arthur's car he can have my motorbike to go to work on, but don't say anything to him yet. He can have it once we're settled.' Bob reached for his pipe. Things were working out just right, he thought as he watched Sally say goodnight. She disappeared up the stairs to her bed, even though it was still fairly light.

Sally lay in bed and listened to the low murmur of her mother and father's voices in the room below her. They were overshadowed by the bleating of the lambs outside in the yard, crying for their mothers. It was a pitiful sound, and Sally's heart went out to them as she hugged her pillow, worried for the first time about what she had actually let herself in for. Farming Daleside on her own! Would she be able to do it? Or would she just look like a fool come April?

Bob and Sally, along with their sheepdog, Spot, walked down the road from Dent to Sedbergh, both with a walking stick in their hands, making sure that the lambs kept to the path and urging them on when the temptation of vegetation in the hedges became too strong.

'I'll not have this to do next year, I'll be taking them to Hawes Auction,' Bob said, and looked at his pocket watch. 'We're only just going to make it in time. Our lots are due for sale at eleven – it's a good job we aren't one of the first ones on.' He whistled for Spot to keep one of the stragglers in line and flapped his arms to stop the lambs turning up a lane to the hamlet of Millthrop.

'I'll have to do it if I'm still at Daleside,' Sally said. She sneaked to the front of the flock to keep them safe as they were herded over the main road, stopping the few cars as the lambs wandered across into the newly built auction mart to be sold. With the help of the auction hands, they penned the lambs up into two lots, ready to be sold along with other bleating lambs that panted their warm breath into the cooling autumn air. Now it was a matter of waiting their turn to be called into the ring; and then hopefully, if sales were good, there would be a quick trip around Sedbergh's shops and a catch-up with fellow farmers.

'There's Arthur over there. I'll just go and have a word with him – you stay here and shout or wave when we're on in the ring.' Bob waved at Arthur, patted Sally on the back and left her standing next to the penned-up sheep.

Sally looked around her. There were various faces and people she knew, and she felt at ease as she balanced herself upon the wooden fence of the pen and waited for their number to be called. Her father seemed to be coming round to the idea of her staying at Daleside, which she was grateful for. She had to admit that her stay might just be for three months, but at least she could say she had tried.

'Right, Fothergill, you're up next, two pens of fat lambs. Numbers thirty-four and thirty-five, first lot into the ring now.' Tommy Raw looked at Sally and checked his sheet as he opened the sheep pen and started to herd the flock into the ring.

'But my father should be selling them. I can't do it!' Sally objected as she followed Tommy into the ring, looking back and waving as she did so to try to get her father's attention. But he had disappeared out of sight, so rather than forgo their lot, she followed the flock. She took her walking stick and stepped forward with the first twenty lambs. All eyes were on her as she kept close behind them, moving them around the ring for the buyers to see. She was aware of some grinning faces and whispering among the farmers as they leaned on their walking sticks and viewed both lambs and young woman, admiring one or the other; but she kept her nerve and decided to prove she could sell stock as well as anybody else.

The auctioneer caught her eye and winked.

'Now then, what are we bid for these twenty fine fat lambs from Daleside, with Miss Sally Fothergill showing them to you this morning? A grand sight, I must say.' The auctioneer looked around at his crowd and saw them all smiling. 'Now, come on, let's get them sold! Two, three, four, five and arrr . . . six-pound bid. Bye heck, Bob will be sending you more often to sell his lambs.' The auctioneer looked around him and shouted, 'There's another lot yet, so you haven't missed your chance yet, gents.' He lifted his gavel and slammed it down. 'Sold to Irvine, Harbourhill.'

Sally glanced around and saw everyone looking at her as she followed the first lot of sheep out of the ring back to the pens, where she found her father waiting. She didn't dare look at him as Tommy Raw fastened the sold lambs in the pen and started to untie the second pen for selling.

'I couldn't see you, Father – I yelled and waved but you weren't about, so I had to go in with them,' Sally quickly said, unsure how her father might react.

'She's got the best price this morning and all. I'd let

her take these in. They're bidding daft, just because Sally is showing them round the ring,' Tommy said. He urged the next twenty bewildered lambs past Bob and Sally without Bob saying anything to him.

'Go on then, get on with it. If you can make the same again, dinner is on me.' Bob nodded at his daughter and rubbed his head with his cap. His lass had some nerve, if nothing else. To walk out and show lambs around the ring with a hundred or more Dales farmers judging her every move took some guts. He listened as he heard the auctioneer shout.

'Who's going to stand on at the last bid? They're just as fit as the last lot. Six, six it is, sold to Hill Top.' He wrote the price down in his book and looked up at the farmer from Hill Top. 'Tha's going to be in bother with the wife tonight when she finds out the price of these, Jim.' After which the auction erupted with laughter, making Sally blush from her hair roots to her toes as she walked out of the ring towards her father.

'They can laugh all they like, it's us with brass in the bank, my lass. Well done.' Bob smiled and tied the pen tight as he looked at his Sally. 'Now, a good dinner, and then we'll both ride home in Arthur's old jalopy. I've got the house keys, and he says that they move out on Friday. I told him Friday flit, short sit, but he assured me that he wasn't going to return, so that's the main thing.' In a rare moment, Bob put his arm round Sally and grinned. 'You'll have to sell our lambs more often, tha did a right good job.'

* * *

247

'No wonder Arthur gave it away. It's just about held together with string.' Ivy looked critically at the old black Ford car.

'It needs a bit of work, that's all. Our lad will be able to spend some time on it, and with a bit of work here and there it'll look good as new.' Bob opened the back passenger door to reveal a floor covered with straw. 'I'll tidy it up and it'll get at least some of our things to Deep Well dry and safe. It's better than the motorbike. Give it a polish and put a new brake light on the back, it will be grand.' He slammed the door – twice, as it struggled to stay closed.

'Well, I can't say anything. He gave it to us, and our Ben will like working on it once we've moved. Although he's that tired when he comes home from work nowadays. A bit like myself, but I think I'm winning. A lot of things are boxed now and can be taken as soon as you want to Deep Well.'

'Aye, well, next week I'll start taking things up there, and then it isn't such a big move. Mackreth is booked for moving the furniture and the stock. It'll ease the move if I keep taking bits as and when I can. We could do with being in there before the really bad weather starts.' Bob glanced round him at Daleside, imagining it in winter once they had gone and left Sally there.

'When you go, take Sally with you to help. I'm proud that she wants to stand on her own two feet and stay here, but I'd be happier if she moved with us – I don't like the thought of her being alone.' Ivy leaned on the car. With so much still to do, it was hard to believe their move to Deep Well was so near. She wondered how they would manage it and whether they should really be leaving their daughter to farm alone.

Bob nudged her. 'You told me she would be all right, woman. Make your mind up.'

'She will; she's old enough. But it's still a worry,' Ivy replied.

'Father, we cannot get another thing in this car.' Sally sat with a bundle of feather pillows on her knee and boxes and household items padded all around her. 'You can't see out of the back window, you know. Your main mirror is blocked by this box.'

'It will be right; we're only going up Garsdale. The bobbies won't stop us. Besides, that's the least of our problems when the back brake lights don't work – and we'll need to get back before it's dark, because there are no headlight hoods on the old lass. Jerry could see us coming down the road from outer space.' Bob turned the ignition and held his breath, hoping he wouldn't have to crank start the car. With a sigh of relief, he felt the engine catch. They made their way, fully loaded, down the road to the new home, with just the one windscreen wiper working as the rain started to fall.

'Bloody rain – it would come on when we have all this to unload.' Bob peered through the windscreen as he made his way slowly through Millthrop and around the back of Sedbergh, so as not to encounter the police. He'd hardly driven before, only a neighbour's car once or twice, but it wasn't so different to the bike really. And, although he'd laughed it off lightly with Sally, he knew the car was hardly fit on the road and that it needed a lot of work doing. 'This damn lorry up our backside is a nuisance. He keeps flashing his lights at me, but he will have to wait.'

'Why don't you pull in and let him pass, Father?' Sally looked through her side window and could see that the driver was impatient to pass them.

'Nay, we're nearly here now; he can wait,' Bob growled as he braked on a tight corner. The lorry had to brake even harder to avoid crashing into him.

Sally had never felt so glad to get out of a car. She shoved the pillows onto the seat and turned to look at the lorry driver, who had pulled over to shout at her father as they parked up in front of Deep Well.

'Bloody hell, you're not fit on the road in that thing! D'you know your brake lights are out? You nearly killed both of us! I'd come out and give you a piece of my mind, but I've to pick someone up from the station who's waited long enough.' The driver looked furious.

'Didn't know, mate, thanks for telling me. I'll have to get it fixed,' Bob shouted back. He passed Sally the key to open the main door and began unloading the death-trap.

'Aye, well – see that you do, else the coppers will be doing you.' The driver revved his engine, wound his window up and drove off at a pace.

'Everybody is always in a hurry. No matter who he's picking up, they will just have to wait.' Bob struggled to control a big armful of bedding as he passed Sally going

250

for the pillows that she had left behind. 'Bloody rain – don't carry any of the heavy boxes, I'll carry them.'

The car was soon unloaded, and while her father went for a look at the empty cattle sheds, Sally wandered through the house. She smiled as she went from room to room; her mother would think she had died and gone to heaven, she thought as she saw the Belling cooker and washing machine in the kitchen and the worn but colourful carpet on the front room floor. Mam had always wanted all that Mary had left behind, plus the house itself was twice the size of Daleside.

Climbing the stairs, she went from bedroom to bedroom, wondering which one her mother would put her in if she came to stay. She hoped it would be the one at the front, which had a view all the way down the dale, even though the road ran right below it. She watched as the army truck that had followed them went past the window, returning from picking up its passenger from the station. At least her father wasn't going to be in front of it on their way back, she thought as she opened the last upstairs door and gasped. A bathroom! Deep Well had a bathroom and an inside toilet – what luxury. No wonder her mother and father couldn't wait to move in. Still, it might have all mod cons, but it wasn't a patch on Daleside, she thought, as her father yelled at her to hurry up before darkness fell.

Chapter 25

'Sorry for the wait, mate. I got held up behind a car on my way up,' the lorry driver said. Looking at the man he had been sent to meet, he saw someone who had been through hell.

'No need to apologize. It might be raining and freezing, but I couldn't be a happier man.' Edward Riley bent down to pick up what few belongings he had. He took another look around at the station houses and the familiar sights of Garsdale, which he'd thought he would never see again. He felt as if he had truly died this time and gone to heaven, not quite believing that after being in the hands of evil for so long, he was still alive.

The driver took his belongings and loaded them into the car. 'You are back home, then, I take it?' he said, as his passenger struggled to get into the cab next to him.

'Aye, that I am. Been away over four years, thanks to the Nazis. I never thought I'd ever come home some days – it was only the thought of these Dales and loved ones that kept me alive.' Edward hoped that the driver wouldn't ask him too many questions. He wanted to forget the horrors he had left behind.

'You must have had it bad,' the driver said, glancing sideways at him. Edward looked like skin and bone, and there was a scar running down the left side of his face from his hairline.

'Aye, you could say that. But now I'm hoping to go forward with my life. My days for king and country are over.' Edward briefly closed his eyes. He was safe in the lorry cab and going back home. He opened his eyes again and looked out of the window as the rain came on heavier. It didn't matter to Edward what the weather was doing. All that mattered was that he could, at long last, sleep without the threat of Nazi guards or the next wave of Jewish prisoners being transported through the camp to their deaths. The next faces he would see, he hoped, would be his mother's and father's – faces he had kept safe in his thoughts, along with that of Sally. He closed his eyes again and hoped that they all would be glad to see him – especially Sally. He had changed, but he hoped they would understand.

By the time he climbed down from the lorry, the rain had stopped. The night was drawing in as he opened the farm gate and gazed up towards his birthplace, Rayside. The lights had just been lit and smoke was rising from the chimney. How many times had he dreamed of this sight? And now he was home.

He walked up the lane and through the garden gate, hesitating at the green-painted door with its brass fox knocker, wondering if he should formally knock or just walk straight into his family home. It would be a shock for his parents. They hadn't been told of his return, or even that he was alive. He decided to knock gently and then enter. He could feel his heart pounding and tears nearly rising in his eyes as the door handle turned and he entered the warmth of the kitchen, and was transported instantly back home.

'Oh, my Lord, it can't be!' Maggie Riley stood frozen for a moment and then burst into tears, trembling so hard that she had to hold onto the table before rushing across the room and holding her arms out to her long-lost son. 'Father, Father, he's home! Edward is home.'

Burt had risen to his feet, and he felt his heart miss a beat as he came face to face with the shadow of the son they had thought lost. 'Aye, lad, tha's back. I never thought I'd see you again,' he said as he came forward and patted his son on his back. He was shocked by the change in Edward, how thin he was. 'Come, come and sit by the fire. Mother, make him a drink of tea and something to eat. Don't drown the lad in tears and hugs.' Burt smiled. For all the years Edward had been away, he'd done nothing but blame himself for his lad having been conscripted.

'I never thought I was ever going to see you again.' Edward broke down and held his head in his hands. 'I never, never, thought I'd ever be in my home again.'

'Well, you are back now, and tha's not going anywhere again. Now come and sit down by the fire and have something to eat. Then, when you are up to it, can you tell us all about what you have been through?' Burt said.

He watched as Maggie took her arm from around her son, took his coat off and sat him down in front of the fire. 'Now, you take your time. You have all the time in the world to tell us where you've been.'

'I've been to hell, Father, that's where I've been. But please, all I want is a drink of tea and my bed. Just a night in my own bed, safe and warm.' Edward held the cup of tea in his shaking hands and looked at his mother and father. 'I'll tell you everything in the morning.'

'You tell us when you want, lad. The main thing is that you're home, and that is a true miracle. We'd come to believe we had lost you,' Maggie said. She reached for the stone pottery water bottle to fill with boiling water and put into her son's old bed.

'Thanks, Mam.' Edward took hold of his mother's hand and kissed it. He had missed her love so much.

'Oh, Burt, what has our lad been through? He's so thin, and he's covered in scars. Did you hear him shouting and talking in the night? I got up and sat downstairs in my nightie and just listened – he broke my heart with his ramblings,' Maggie whispered as she stoked up the fire for the coming day.

'He'll tell us in his own time. Although some who fought in the last war never said owt about it, the memories were too painful. Be patient, our Maggie, and just be there for him. That's all we can do.' Burt put his arm around his wife and kissed her brow. 'Shh, now – the floorboards are creaking. He's wakened. I'm just glad that he's back.'

Edward came downstairs and sat at the kitchen table. His mother put a plate of bacon, egg and fried bread in front of him and he ate as if he had never been fed in his life. At last he sat back and looked at them both.

'I know you want to know what happened to me; I'll tell you what I can remember. Time and shock have made me forget a lot, and I'd rather it stayed forgotten.' Edward paused to gather his thoughts.

'I was left for dead on the beaches of Calais when we first invaded. Everything of value, including my identity papers, had been stolen from me, and it wasn't until a half-decent German soldier came across me still living that I was taken to a German hospital to be patched up. And then, once I was strong enough, they took me to a holding camp on the outskirts of Paris. The Nazis were at least letting me live and feeding me, but I had no memory. The one that gave me this scar across my head also had taken my memory. So that's why you have never been told that I was alive and being held as a POW.'

He stopped and put his head in his hands, his body shaking. Then he looked up at both his parents. 'The camp I was held in was, when I first went there, a POW camp with a mixture of detainees. Some lived, some died and some were transferred into camps in Germany, but I was always left there. I think they hoped that I would eventually die.' He grimaced, and his parents listened silently with tears in their eyes. 'The worst was yet to come, because as I started to gain a little strength and my memory started to come back, the camp started to fill with Jewish prisoners. My POW camp had turned into a holding camp where the poor devils were robbed of their possessions before being placed on trains to their deaths.' He swallowed hard. 'To survive, I had to work for the Nazis, sorting through the valuables that the poor Jews left behind, and all the while keeping to myself the memory of home in my mind. They would have put me on one of their death trains too if I had told them I knew who I was. The secret of their atrocities had to be just that.'

'Oh, lad, you don't have to say any more. It will hurt to remember. Best that it's forgotten.' Burt patted his son's hand. 'You're back now, safe with your family.'

'I can't forget, Father. The faces of the poor innocent Jews haunt me. Children and mothers, treated like animals – I will never forget what I saw. I had to do what I did, or else they would have killed me too.' Edward broke down and wept.

'No more. Don't say a word more until you feel strong enough.' Maggie put her arms around her son. 'The Allies got you out of there – you are safe and sound at home now. That's all that matters. We will get you back fit and strong and show you the love that was always here for you.' She kissed Edward and looked into his eyes. They had seen so much misery; she could tell as she held him close. 'Now, I think you need to build yourself up slowly and try to settle your thoughts. We won't tell anybody you are back until you're ready to face the world, or else they'll want to know all that you have told us, and you are not strong enough for that.' Maggie knew she had to protect her son. His body and mind were both frail.

'Thanks, Mam. All I want to do is sleep. I feel so exhausted. I want to clear my head of these images that I saw every day, day in and day out.' Edward wiped tears from his eyes.

'Then you sleep, and eat, and get your strength back, and we will do all that we can for you.' Burt patted his lad on the knee.

Edward looked at his mother and father. There was one question he had to ask. 'Is Sally all right? Is she still waiting for me, or is she married to another?'

'Sally is still waiting for you. She's been faithful to your name, so you don't have any worries there. Now all you need do is get yourself strong and fit before you go to see her. She will wait another few weeks, I'm sure,' Maggie said softly.

'Then I can't wait to see her. But not yet – she would hardly recognize me. I love her, Mam, and I'm going to marry her,' Edward said as he made his way to the bottom of the stairs.

'Aye, I know, lad. And it will be with our blessing,' Maggie told him as she held back tears.

Chapter 26

'I don't know how we've acquired all this stuff,' Ivy said as she pushed the last box into Henry Mackreth's cattle wagon, which was doubling up as a removal van.

'Nay, you've not that much, Ivy. You look to be leaving a lot for your lass. She'll be grateful for that.' Henry slammed the back gate of the wagon closed as they heard Bob shouting for his wife to get a move on.

'Well, I've had to, bless her. I couldn't leave her with nothing. We'll probably want you again after Christmas to move her stuff, Henry, because I can't see her farming here on her own. She might not want to move now, but give her a month or two with the water frozen and the snow piled high and she will soon realize it's no party. Although I know her heart lies here; it always has.' Ivy sighed. 'Right, listen to Bob blathering. He wants to get ahead of you and open up at Deep Well. If you see us broken down in that death trap of Arthur Metcalfe's, pick me up if nobody else.' Ivy grinned and made her way over to the car, shouting to Bob, 'I'm coming, hold your hosses,' as he revved up the engine.

She hugged Sally, who stood beside the car. 'You'll be all right, won't you? I don't like leaving you on your own.'

'Mam, I will be fine. I'm a grown woman. Besides, I've neighbours, and everybody knows me if I need anything.' Sally didn't feel quite as confident as she sounded. She would be fine, she knew; but it was hard not to wonder if she had done the right thing as she watched most of her home comforts disappearing down the road in Henry Mackreth's wagon.

'Don't forget to feed them turkeys of a night and morning. But I'll be back in the morning; there's a few things I need that I've left here.' Bob leaned across Ivy in the passenger seat to peer up at his daughter. He didn't much like leaving her on her own either, but she had made her bed and she would have to lie in it – for a short while, anyway. 'Bugger me – I told Henry Mackreth to follow us, but he's going. I hope he knows where Deep Well is.'

'No, I'll not forget the turkeys,' Sally assured him. 'Get yourselves gone, I'm fine.' She stood back as her mother slammed the car door shut and her father drove off, the old Ford kicking up dust as it followed in the trail of the wagon.

Sally stood for a moment, her arms folded, and listened to the silence of the farmyard. Apart from the few hens that were scratching about, there was no noise; not of cattle nor sheep. The few that she had kept were content- edly grazing in the pasture behind the house, and the fell

260

was now virtually free of any flock apart from the few that her father had left behind – the ones that were not of much value to him. It was strange; she had often been left at home alone, but this felt different. She was in charge of herself, and she had to feed herself and the animals that were left. At that moment she truly realized what she had done, and that she was now dependent on herself alone.

She walked into the kitchen. Her parents had left her the kitchen table and a chair, a dresser that had belonged to her grandmother, and a few essential pots and pans. At least the pantry had eggs, cheese, flour and bacon in it – she was not going to starve. In the front room there were two comfy chairs and a small table, but no radio to keep her company. Life was going to be quiet, she thought as she sat down in one of the chairs and looked around her with a sinking feeling. She had decided to start her independent life in one of the worst months of the year, dreary November, when the days were cold and wet and night-time came down too early. Another few days and it would be December, and she could probably expect snow, she thought as she sat and gathered her thoughts.

She would be all right. Tomorrow she would be at work at Middleton's shop, which would make her some money. She would buy a few extra treats to cheer herself up, she thought as she looked around her. Next year, come spring, she might change the wallpaper to something cheerier than the dark brown and cream stripes that were on the walls now. Yes, she would be all right. It was just a moment of doubt.

* * *

'Are you going to manage to work your hours here at the shop as well as keep the farm?' Mrs Middleton asked, seeing Sally yawn as she put the newspapers into their rack and tidied the magazines.

'Yes, it should be no problem. In fact, I don't think I'm going to be as busy as I usually am. I've only got the minimum of stock until spring. If I didn't have my father's turkeys to feed and water, there would be very little to do. And they'll be gone once Christmas is here,' Sally replied, staring at the pile of boxes that had just been delivered with Christmas stock in them.

'Oh, Christmas – that terrible word. We are always so busy. That's the next thing I was going to ask you. Can you decorate both windows with Christmas gifts this morning? There's tinsel and a few glass baubles in the usual cupboard, and the gifts are in those boxes over there. You can tell customers that our upstairs showroom will be open next week for them to come and see what we have in stock; not that there will be a lot. I can't get my hands on a lot of things. Still, neither will our rivals, Dinsdale's, so we're both in the same situation. It's a wonder either of us can survive in Dent, what with rationing and lack of goods.'

'I can't believe it's nearly Christmas. I don't know where this year has gone,' Sally said as she began to open the box. It was a job she always relished. She loved to see what they had found to catch children's eyes as they gazed into the shop window in wonder.

'Well, let's hope that this war will be well and truly over by next year. Then we can really celebrate Christmas.'

Mrs Middleton smiled. 'The Birbeck family will be glad that their Jonathan has returned, even though he is injured.'

'Jonathan's back?' Sally exclaimed. 'I didn't know. That will be a relief for them all – but is he badly injured?'

'A bullet through the top of his thigh, from what I can gather. It could be worse, but it has made him lame. He got it when they were liberating Paris. It will be lovely when our lads arrive home again. They should never have gone in the first place,' Mrs Middleton said. She looked sympathetically at Sally, thinking that she would never see her Edward again.

'It will. There's been too many lost,' Sally agreed. She picked up a toy tank and placed it in the shop window along with a box of toy soldiers, wondering as she did so why any child should be given toys that represented war. Christmas should be a time of love and peace, not war, she thought. She smiled as a teddy bear and an American Kewpie doll were lifted from the box; they were more like things to be loved and cherished.

On Saturday morning, her father drove into the yard. The old banger sounded rougher than ever as he pulled up next to the kitchen door.

'Sally, are you in?' Bob yelled as he opened the kitchen door.

'Yes, through here – I'm just setting the fire for tonight. I like to sit in the front room, it's cosier when I'm on my own.' Sally came into the kitchen with coal-covered hands and quickly washed them under the cold-water tap. 'Do you want a brew? I've already fed the turkeys, if you're checking up on me,' she added, noticing her father's expression and wondering if something was wrong.

'No, I'll not bother you for a drink. I just wondered if you'd heard the news that the Birbeck lad is home. I bet that lorry driver we saw was on his way to pick him up from Garsdale station. That would be why he was in a hurry.' Bob knew that Sally would be wishing it was Edward who had come home.

'Yes, they were talking about it in the shop. It's good news for his family, especially at Christmas,' Sally quietly replied. 'Has Mother got everything as she likes it? I bet everything is just so.'

'Oh, don't ask. She's been getting your brother to move furniture all over the place. All we hear is, "Does that look right there? No, happen I'll move it to under the window or onto that wall." She was never this demanding when she lived here. You'd think that house was Buckingham Palace. It's grand to get a minute's peace.' Bob looked around the spartan kitchen. 'Are you sure you're all right? We haven't left you with much.'

'I'm fine, Father. I don't need much. There's only me here, after all.' Sally smiled.

'Well, I've been looking at how much hay Arthur has left me, and there's more than enough for what stock I have. So, like we said, you make use of what we harvested this haytime. You'll need it for your few sheep, from what they've been saying on the wireless. They're warning that we might have a white Christmas. I only hope you'll be all right; I've lagged all the outside pipes before I went, just in case it came bad weather.' Bob looked worried; he wasn't happy that his lass was on her own.

'I'll be grand, Father. There's only one thing I miss, and that's the wireless. Only because the evenings are a bit long now I'm on my own. But Sarah at the shop has given me a good book or two to read, so I'm happy. I can lose myself in those.'

'You are sure you're all right? You know your mother and I both worry about you being on your own.' Bob looked hard at his daughter, knowing that even if she wasn't all right, she wouldn't want to say.

'Father, it's only been a matter of days since you left me. Of course I'm all right. Now stop fretting.' Sally was glad that her parents cared, but she was no longer a child and she knew how to take care of herself. 'Go and see your turkeys, why don't you? They're getting plumper by the day as you left me with a good stock of corn. Poor devils, they'll soon be having their necks wrung – there's one in particular I can't look at, because I know it's going to end up on somebody's table in another few weeks.'

'It's best not to get attached, you should know that. Besides, I thought you didn't like turkeys,' Bob said with a smile.

'I don't; but this one is tamer than the rest and doesn't make as much noise. Poor thing!'

'Aye, well, it will have to go. I've got orders for all of them. So try not to look at it.' Bob made his way to the doorway. 'I'll tell your mother that you're doing fine. She wanted me to tell you something, but I'm damned if I can remember what. It'll no doubt keep.'

265

'As long as it wasn't important. And it can't have been, else you'd remember.' Sally smiled at her father. His head was filled with his new farm, turkeys and the weather; he hadn't time for giving messages. He would probably remember when he got home, and then it would be too late.

'Aye, you're right. Anyway, I'll be back before long, and Luca can come with me and all. I'll need him to help pluck the turkeys. Your mother won't have anything to do with them this year.'

Sally watched him amble across the farmyard to check on his precious fowl. She did miss her family, even Ben. She thought about Luca; she had lost her heart to him for a short while, but thankfully sense had prevailed. Their love could never have been.

Daleside was everything to her. If she had her way, she would be buried there under the big flat stone where she often sat to look down the dale after her day's work. Better than any graveyard, she thought as she closed the kitchen door against the cold winter air.

Chapter 27

23 December 1944

It was the day before Christmas Eve, Sally's last day of work at Middleton's shop. They had been busy all day, and Mrs Middleton had even employed a lad with a bicycle to deliver the essentials to the villagers and outlying farms. The shelves were looking unusually empty as five o'clock came around.

'What are you doing for Christmas, Sally? I bet you're going to your mother and father at Deep Well? It will be strange for you, though,' Sarah said as they leaned on the counter and waited for the clock to strike five.

'I don't know what I'm doing. Mother or father haven't asked me, but they could be assuming that I'll be going.' Sally took one of her shoes off and rubbed her foot. 'Come on, clock, make it five o'clock. I'm ready for home. Although my father and Luca will be there – it's the last batch of turkeys to be slaughtered for local delivery in the morning. I'm not much looking forward to that shed standing empty when it's been filled for weeks with all those trusting turkeys that thought I was their friend.'

'Oh, don't. We have turkey this year, and I'll think of them when my mother's carving it. I didn't mind when we had goose because I hated them. Horrible birds that chase and hiss at you.' Sarah shook her head and cringed.

The clock struck five and Sally reached for her coat, pushing her shoe back on. Turning to Sarah, she gave her a quick hug. 'Have a good Christmas. I hope Father Christmas brings you what you want.' She smiled as Sarah followed her to the door.

'I don't think he will, but you can hope. You have a good one too – make sure you're not on your own. Nobody should be alone on Christmas Day.' Sarah turned the shop sign and stood watching as Sally walked away down the cobbled street in the direction of home. She was thankful that Christmas at her own house would be with family, and with the shop closed over the Christmas period. She could never be Sally Fothergill – the first bump she heard in the night and she'd be petrified, she thought, as she yawned and turned away from the door.

'I thought I might have missed you, but you're both still here.' Sally put her head around the shed door and saw her father tidying the now plucked and dressed turkeys, while Luca swept the feathers from the shed floor into an enormous bag.

'Aye, nearly finished. Another ten minutes and we'll be on our way. I'm dropping Luca off at Loftus Hill and four of the turkeys off in Sedbergh, so you can say I'm killing four birds with one stone.' Bob grinned at his joke, but he was the only one to do so.

'Father, you get worse! I'll put the kettle on. Come in and have a brew before you both go.' Sally turned to go.

'No, I'd better not – I've got to get home for milking. And Luca here has got to be in by six-thirty so they can all go to a Loftus Hill church service. Seemingly the vicar has decided to save their souls this Christmas.'

'I come, Sally – I have present for you.' Luca dropped his brush and bag of feathers and followed her across the yard while Bob yelled at him to come back and finish his job.

'I miss seeing you, Sally. It is not the same at the new farm,' Luca told her as she turned on the light and pushed the kettle on to boil. 'There is so much land, and I not used to so many cows. All I do is clean muck all day.' He moaned.

'There can't be that many, Luca? I didn't think my father had bought more than ten from Arthur Metcalfe.' Sally leaned against the table and smiled at him, amused.

'Well, you'd think there was more. I clean, I brush, I swill. That is all I do. Everything to be clean, for the milk.'

'Never mind; it's Christmas in another day. What are you doing for Christmas dinner? Something special at Loftus Hill?' She handed him a mug of tea.

'No, I'm with your parents. They said Christmas dinner with them. You not coming?' Luca looked puzzled.

'I don't know; nobody has said anything. I don't know what I'm doing.'

'I sure you be there, but I have brought you this. I

give while we are alone. I hope you like it; I make it myself.' Luca pulled from out of his pocket a heart-shaped piece of wood with a red ribbon through it. Sally took it and admired the beautifully carved birds and flowers. 'It is to remind you of me.' Luca leaned forward and kissed her gently on the cheek.

'It's beautiful, Luca. *Grazie* – I will always cherish it.' Sally bowed her head. She had not thought to get anything for him, and yet he had gone to the bother of carving her this beautiful object.

'I wanted you to have something in case I get to go home. War is nearly over; I go home to Italy in a while.' Luca took her hands and kissed them. 'I no forget you, ever, Sally.'

'Nor me you, Luca. We will always be friends.' Sally felt herself near to tears as she heard her father yelling for Luca to hurry up. 'You'd better go, Luca. I will see you soon, if not at Christmas.'

'You got to be there, Sally. Your mother got a tree and decorations. You have nothing.' Luca said, gesturing around the spartan farmhouse with a shrug of his shoulders.

'I've not bothered, as it's only me here,' Sally replied as Luca made for the door. 'Go on, get a move on, else you will be late for the church and my father will be going without you.'

'Merry Christmas, Sally,' Luca shouted as he ran to catch Bob in the car.

'Merry Christmas, Luca,' she shouted after him, and thought that she had never known her parents to be so hard if they had not asked her for Christmas. She knew she had been stubborn, and perhaps they were teaching her a lesson, but it was really going to hurt having no one to share her Christmas with.

She watched as Luca jumped into the car and suddenly regretted deciding that he was not for her. He was a caring, handsome man, even if he was Italian.

Luca sat in the car as they pulled up outside Loftus Hill. 'Mr Fothergill, you no ask Sally for Christmas dinner? She says she not coming?'

Bob turned to him in surprise. 'Don't be daft, lad, course she's coming. What's she saying that for?'

'She says she not know what she doing. Is she not asked?' Luca had a worried expression on his face.

'She should know to come; but aye, happen I forgot to tell her, now I think about it. I've to pick up the last turkey and deliver it to Dent tomorrow morning – I'll tell her then.' Bob saw the relief on Luca's face. 'You go and get a bit of religion, and you'll see Sally on Christmas Day when I pick both you and her up.'

'*Grazie*. I glad Sally be there.'

Bob shook his head. He'd forgotten to tell Sally that a bed was made up and aired for her and she was expected to stay Christmas Day night. Ivy would play hell with him when she found out. He considered not mentioning it at all, but knew he'd have to confess.

'You would forget your head if it was loose, Bob Fothergill!' Ivy said angrily. 'You tell her in the morning, and make sure you don't forget. The poor lass will think

271

we've turned our backs on her. Aye, I'll not sleep tonight for worrying about her.' She scrubbed furiously at the pots she was washing up. 'It's bad enough I haven't got her a present – I haven't had time to shop. I thought I'd just give Ben and her some money each, then they can buy what they want. Did you remember to ask Brian Harper to milk her cow for the night and morning she's staying?'

'And then you're telling me off! I know what Sally would appreciate, because she said the other day how much she was missing it – a wireless. I can go through Sedbergh in the morning and pick one up for her. Rycroft's will be open, they always are on Christmas Eve. It's when they make the most money.' Bob looked guiltily at Ivy. 'I did remember to ask Brian about the cow. But I thought she'd know she was expected, that's why I forgot to ask her!' He frowned as he thought about the problem. 'I'll drop the wireless off and tell her at the same time that she's to come to us on Christmas Day and stop the night. I'll do all that when I collect the turkey that's left to be delivered.'

'That's a good idea,' Ivy nodded. 'She'll be missing the radio, and it'll be company for her now she's on her own. I've been baking all day as well, so you can take her a batch of mince pies, sausage rolls and an apple pasty. Then I'll know that she's something to eat on Christmas Eve. It will seem strange to her, being on her own.' Ivy was missing her lass more than she realized and just hoped that she would be all right alone on Christmas Eve. 'I only hope it doesn't come with a lot

272

of snow – the weather report keeps saying it's headed our way.'

'It'll not be a lot if it does. We should be all right. Stop fretting,' Bob replied.

He hoped he was right, but the sky had looked heavy with snow for a day or two now. As long as he got his last turkey delivered and had the chance to explain his forgetfulness to Sally.

Sally sat in the Daleside kitchen, cupping a mug of tea in her hands. The weather had warmed up slightly this morning after the freezing, biting temperatures of the previous day – a sure sign that snow was on its way. She looked into her mug and felt a wave of sadness sweep over her, realizing that she really would be on her own over Christmas.

She couldn't believe her parents hadn't asked her to stay. Then again, she couldn't go anyway; she had to stay at home, she had the cow to milk of a morning and night. She was tied to the farm – her time was not her own when she had stock to take care of.

Raising her head, she gazed around the kitchen that had always been so busy with comings and goings. Today it was deadly silent – and dark, as the incoming stormy weather gathered overhead. She didn't even have any Christmas decorations, she thought, feeling a pang of doubt and regret.

'This is getting me nowhere,' she muttered to herself. She put her mug down, pulled on her coat from behind the back door and decided she could at least brighten up her home with some sprigs of holly. And then, when she returned, she would make a cake. It was too late to make a Christmas cake but she could make a Victoria sponge – she had plenty of eggs and butter, and her mother had left her some sugar from their ration. A piece of cake made everybody feel better, she thought as she closed the kitchen door behind her, put her hands in her pockets and made her way up the fellside to where she knew a holly tree never failed to produce berries each year.

Sally followed the limestone wall up to a dip where the grey-trunked holly tree had seeded itself many years earlier. It had always been the source of the family's holly for placing in the windows and on the fireplace. Unlike some hollies, this tree's leaves were not particularly prickly, so it was easy to pick. She reached up into the branches and chose sprigs that were well covered. She had always picked holly from the tree with her mother in previous years to put on loved ones' graves, or for making wreaths while sitting together at the kitchen table; but this year she had never even thought of it, life had been so busy.

With a good amount of branches lying on the ground, Sally bound them all together with a piece of string and then lifted the bundle over her shoulder. She made for the stone where she always gathered her thoughts. A lonesome snowflake fluttered down, but the clouds threatened more as she sat and gazed down the dale, which looked as if it was in deep hibernation with just the smoke from farmhouse fires rising into the still winter air. The best place on a day like today was next to a fire, she thought. Her sheep were safe in the paddock next to the farmhouse, the cow was content in the shippon and everything else was bedded down and keeping warm. She would go back inside, make her cake and curl up with a book. What could be more perfect?

As she made her way through the bottom pasture, the snow was beginning to come down more heavily. Closing the pasture gate behind her, she glanced across to the farmyard. Coming up the lane towards the house was a solitary figure – a man. He was dressed in an army coat with his collar turned up against the cold and snow.

At first Sally thought it was Luca, but a second glance told her the figure was too tall and blond. She caught her breath as she looked again and felt her heart beating faster. It was a ghost she was seeing, surely. She whispered under her breath, 'Edward?' – not quite believing that the man about to knock on the Daleside kitchen door was the one she had waited so long to see.

'Edward – Edward!' Sally yelled. She dropped the holly in the yard as she ran forward to the man standing at her door. 'It can't be, it just can't be,' she cried with tears running down her face.

'Sally, my Sally! I thought I was never going to see you again.' Edward held out his arms to embrace her, kissed her and whispered his love into her ear. 'I'm back. I have waited so long to do this. Every day I thought of you – it was you that kept me alive. I just hoped that you would wait for me, my love.'

'Oh, Edward, I knew you'd return; that's why I had

to stay here.' Sally kissed his lips and ran her fingers over his scar. 'You've been hurt.' She brushed her tears away, buried her head into his body and just held him tight.

'It will heal in time, like everything. I love you, Sally Fothergill, and now I'm home I'm not going to ever let you go.'

'I won't let you.' Sally looked up into his face. He was gaunt and pale, but he was still her Edward, she thought as the snow fell heavily around them. 'Come on, let's go in and get warm, and you can tell me everything.'

'There's enough time for that, Sally. I just want to hold you. I love you so much,' Edward whispered.

Sally closed the door on the outside world, thinking it could snow all it liked now that they had one another to keep warm.

Bob looked at the snow-covered holly left in the yard as he pulled up in the car, wondering why it had been left where it was. He got out, picked it up and placed it next to the doorstep, thinking that his daughter might be looking at her sheep. He couldn't stop – he had to deliver the last turkey and get back home before the roads were blocked with snow. But first he had to make things right with Sally.

With the new wireless under his arm, still in its box and unwrapped, and a basket of baking in his other hand, he opened the kitchen door, expecting to see Sally next to the fire. He set the gifts down on the table and was about to shout to see where his daughter was at.

Then he heard laughter and giggling from the bedroom above his head and noticed the army coat and boots at the bottom of the stairs; and finally he saw a Christmas card up on the mantelpiece in pride of place. He picked it up to read it. His heart nearly stopped as he saw the inscription.

Happy Christmas, Sally, my love. How I have missed you. Not any more, though – come spring we will be married.
Edward xx

Bob read it and nearly yelled up the stairs to let them know he was there. Instead, he reached for a pen and a piece of paper from the kitchen drawer.

Happy Christmas, Sally. So glad that Edward is home. I know how happy you will be. Christmas dinner at Deep Well, but somehow I think you will have better things to do. Best Christmas present you could ever have. Look forward to the wedding and knowing that Daleside will be in good hands next spring.
Love, Mam and Dad

Bob smiled as he closed the door quietly behind him. Sally had never given up hope of her Edward returning, and now he was the perfect Christmas present. A wireless was nothing compared to the man she had always loved – and she deserved it. She had always kept faith in him and Daleside.

'Happy Christmas, you two,' Bob whispered as he looked up at the bedroom window. They had a lot of time to make up, he thought as he picked up the last turkey. He couldn't wait to tell everyone the good news. This was going to be a Christmas to remember.

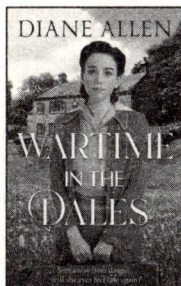

Wartime in the Dales

DIANE ALLEN

September 1939.

Friends Maggie Shaunessy and Lizzie Taylor are heartbroken to be evacuated from their Liverpool homes to rural Yorkshire.

Lizzie is sent to live with a vicar in the village of Gargrave, while Maggie finds herself delivered by chauffeur to Hawith Hall, the home of Lord and Lady Bradley.

Both the hall and the vicarage are far different to what the girls are used to, and both are very homesick – though Maggie finds friendship in the form of Alice, a young servant at the hall who takes her under her wing.

But change is coming to the Dales too, leaving the girls harbouring desperate plans of running away, back to Liverpool . . .

OUT NOW

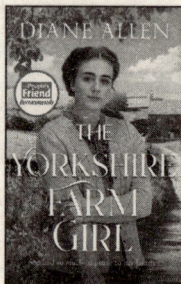

The Yorkshire Farm Girl

DIANE ALLEN

Life is hard for the Fothergill family as they try to make a living on their farm in the Yorkshire Dales. Bob Fothergill has set his sights on buying his own farm instead of renting the one they currently hold. Sally, his teenage daughter, wishes he would see that she could help more with the farm, but he believes that a girl's place is in the home. Ben, the youngest child, has no interest in farming – so is ignored. Bob's wife makes do, knowing her husband wants what's best for them.

But when Bob decides to take a well-paid job collecting milk it causes friction in the family. With Germany shaking its angry fist at other nations, the threat of another war hangs over everything. Will the Fothergills survive the oncoming storm?

OUT NOW

The People's Friend
The Home of Great Reading

If you enjoy quality fiction, you'll love
The People's Friend magazine.
Every weekly issue contains seven original short
stories and two exclusively written serial instalments.

On sale every Wednesday, the *Friend* also includes travel,
puzzles, health advice, knitting and craft projects
and recipes.

It's the magazine for women who love reading!

For great subscription offers, call 0800 318846

𝕏 @ TheFriendMag

f PeoplesFriendMagazine

thepeoplesfriend.co.uk